Some Other Town

Some Other Town

A NOVEL

Elizabeth Collison

HARPER PERENNIAL

NEW YORK • LONDON • TORONTO • SYDNEY • NEW DELHI • AUCKLAND

HARPER PERENNIAL

SOME OTHER TOWN. Copyright © 2015 by Elizabeth Collison. All rights reserved. Printed in the United States of America. No part of this book may be used or reproduced in any manner whatsoever without written permission except in the case of brief quotations embodied in critical articles and reviews. For information address HarperCollins Publishers, 195 Broadway, New York, NY 10007.

HarperCollins books may be purchased for educational, business, or sales promotional use. For information please e-mail the Special Markets Department at SPsales@harpercollins.com.

FIRST EDITION

Designed by Sunil Manchikanti

Library of Congress Cataloging-in-Publication Data has been applied for.

ISBN 978-0-06-234882-1

15 16 17 18 19 OV/RRD 10 9 8 7 6 5 4 3 2 1

For my family

Some Other Town

May 1973

Dawn. I lie breathing hard and stare at the bedroom ceiling. So it has happened again. A white van passes, blasts its horn, disappears just out of sight. And once again I am weightless, midair. That is how always it goes. Although some nights I am driving the truck in the dream, some nights I am driving the van. And sometimes I am in the family's sedan, pale and bawling from the backseat.

Here is how it begins. It is winter, early morning, clear and bitterly cold. There are warnings of windchill, twenty below. Warnings to stay at home.

But I myself am on the way out of town, pushing hard up a hill toward a bridge. Because of the cold, I am the only one out, and it is eerie, alone on that rutty back road. The farmers' fields and the river lie far below, covered in deep new snow. All is stone-still but my truck. So at first, when I spot the white van in my mirror, I am happy that company has arrived.

Then I see the van is coming up fast. It climbs the hill, moves close in, starts to pass. Which is all wrong, I think at the time, that's why they have put yellow lines there. But because whoever it is in the van cannot wait, can't hold on a few yards for the down slope, he passes me just as we reach the bridge, going well over eighty. And he lays on the horn, long and loud.

It takes me by surprise, that combative sound. I turn to look, long enough to see someone large, angry, staring and gesturing at me obscenely. Which is startling and also when my truck hits ice.

Its old tires cannot hold the road. I feel the truck skid, take a sharp turn to the left. And I remember then a car climbing onto the bridge, a blue Volvo from the opposite direction, in the direct path now of where I am spinning.

We come within inches. I grip the wheel. And as my truck slides on by their passenger's side, I look out to see four white faces, turned and pressed to the glass. A family of four, caught in that instant before recognition, captivated, rapt, agog. Until their car goes into a swerve as well, and the four mouths at the glass twist open wide in one blood-chilling family howl.

My truck spins on past, there is no time to look back, to see what becomes of the family. Still skidding, faster, out of control, my truck makes one last sharp arc. And I feel then and hear all at once a loud crack as my truck strikes the bridge side rails. The bridge is old, the rails are wood, they cannot withstand the force. And suddenly my truck is airborne out over the fields below.

I remember then how terribly silent it is. How I can no longer feel the cold or the wind. I look down at the expanse of rolling white snow, I remember a dried stalk of corn jutting through. Then as my truck starts slowly into its dive, and my body grows buoyant and giddy, I see again four floating white faces, eyes open and staring blindly.

But now my truck picks up speed in its great downward arc and I can feel it start to turn over, nose first, then all four wheels to the sky. For a long moment I dangle inverted, gazing into the glint of fresh snow. Then miraculously the truck continues its arc and rotates back to where it has started, several feet closer to ground. We have done a perfect three-sixty midair, well the farmers will never believe this one. And then with a great crash and creaking of ice, the truck slams into the river.

Which is when I begin to cry. Freezing water rushes in all around me. I see it rising, feel the truck going down. Water swirls at my waist, now my chest, my throat. I fight to push open a door, swim free. And gasping for air, I dive under, and awake, and find I can no longer breathe.

This is generally how it goes. Although sometimes no ice appears on the bridge, sometimes my own hand turns the wheel while the family of four in the Volvo sedan watches and cheers from their seats. But always the van shows up then and passes. Always the wind stops, it grows silent. And always I'm suspended in a sky white and endless, and I can see each snowy crystalline star.

But here is the strangest part. Now in the mornings when I wake from the dream, for an instant it's as if there are two of me. The one that will rise and go off to work and come home again to Mrs. Eberline. And the one that awakes from the dream of the van and feels something inside of her rising. Quickening, yearning, keening.

For the life of me, I do not know what it means.

One

On the Bus

Our bus skims along the back way leading into town. It is this route's one bus, the day's last run. We fly over the asphalt.

Our driver is new, young, a student from the university. Reckless boy. We are miles over the limit. But it is Tuesday, the day the sheriff leaves work early. Everyone in town knows this about the sheriff, it is the perfect time to speed.

The driver reads my thoughts, he accelerates. I can see his eyes in the rearview mirror, he is smiling, excited, thrilling to this little joyride into town.

He checks the mirror, catches me staring. "Too fast, ma'am?"

"No," I tell him. And in a voice the others cannot hear, "Faster," I say.

The driver drops his eyes from the mirror.

We are almost to town now, I see. We have reached the last of the farmland. I know these fields, the rolling hills beyond. They are at their best these last few weeks of spring. Narrow green rows of young beans, new corn, ripple over the black earth, wave after wave, relentless. Windbreaks of old oaks stand behind, fogged in the chartreuse of new buds, while along the field fences, wild roses leaf out, wild apples above them.

And oh, some days I do not think I can bear it. I cannot bear all the lushness, this dark fertile soil, hopeful spring. The dogged, futile reawakening. I cannot bear that I know it all so well, that it goes on and on as it does, when in fact nothing now is the same.

I rise. It occurs to me there's a point to be made here. I have something to announce to this bus.

"Ma'am?" the driver says to the mirror. His eyes are stern. There are rules on this bus, we are to keep to our seats. He does not, he thinks, need to remind me.

I sit back down and return to the view. The light has turned soft, the horizon unusually far. I am reminded to give thanks for this window, this second-row-right window seat. I try to be patient and grateful.

Still, to be clear, there is something else now that is bothering me. Although I do not of course say it to the driver, this is not where I prefer to sit, it is not where I normally ride. Generally I sit fourth-row window-seat left. People on the bus understand this by now, they take their places elsewhere.

Except for the bread man, that is, a spindly fellow with a concave chest who carries his lunch in a bread bag. Lately he hurries on ahead of me if he can and eases himself into my exact same spot, four rows back, behind the driver. It is an unremarkable seat, it is not that the view is any better from that row. But it is where I like to ride, and if I do not line up for the bus early now the bread man beats me to my seat.

Elizabeth Collison

"What is wrong with that bread man?" I say to the mirror. The driver does not look up.

I slide down in my seat, feel the vinyl at my back, an uncomfortable fit.

So, it happened again this morning. First thing. Not the bread man, I do not mean the bread man edged me out on the ride into work. The bread man and I do not take the same bus in the mornings. What I mean is it happened this morning and when I awoke there it was, again just out of reach.

A great sneeze from the rear of the bus. I turn, take a quick, wary look back. We are all mindful this spring of the flu.

The others sit facing front and stare blankly. We do not know one another well here, we are not a friendly lot. But we have seen each other around. We all board at the sanatorium. If you ride this bus at all, you get on at the sanatorium. There is nowhere else the bus goes but from the sanatorium back into town.

We are not many today, Tuesdays are always light. Mostly we are just the regulars. The bread man of course. The woman in the blue coat. A nurse I am pretty sure, you can see the white stockings below her coat's hem, although not a cheerful, willing sort of nurse. She spends the ride slumped and muttering. Across from her, the other, louder woman in the light green safari hat. We do not any of us know why she wears that hat on our bus. And at the back, the round and grinning Chinese man, the one extrovert among us. He looks up, spots me, gestures wildly.

I nod, turn back around. The driver twitches once in his seat.

A rise in the road and the bus flies up onto the old Center Street bridge. We are crossing the river that circles our town, that takes a curve not far from here and doubles back on the other side. It is a wide and slow-moving river, with banks always muddy where each spring it always floods. Indians once camped on these banks, canoed the waters, Sioux and Sauk, the Meskwaki after them, descendants of Black Hawk. They called the river the Drowsy, the Big Drowsy.

The bus rushes over the brown water below. Our driver does not slow down.

I look up at the mirror, meet his eyes there. He looks away, concentrates instead on the route. But I know he has been watching, stealing little glances as he drives.

I turn back to the window. We have made good time, we are at the town limits. Reiner's slaughterhouse is nearby, and the municipal park. It is a strange place for a park, for the town's municipal pool. In summers over the shouts of diving children, always there are the sounds from Reiner's, the screams of young calves as bloodied, gloved workers slit open their velvet throats.

Through the closed window, something, a distant cry. I look at the mirror. "My god," I say. "Can you hear them?"

The driver keeps his eyes on the road. His jaw is steel. He shakes his head and slows our speeding flight.

The bread man stands, trudges toward the front of the bus. He is headed for the bus door. The bread man gets off with the rest of us, there is only the one stop at town center, but he likes to stand near the door early so the driver will not forget him. The bread man's face is skeletal, his eyes large and dark, also immensely sad. He carries his lunch in a bread bag tied to his belt. I do not think the driver will forget him.

I watch the bread man in the aisle to my left and pretend I do not. Mostly, although I try not to, I study his bag. The bread man must start out his days with it hopeful, the bag full with a good lunch, a large sandwich and some fresh fruit. But now in the afternoons what shows through the bag, what remains, is only a crust, a sliced pickle, maybe an orange peel. And I think how it is an odd thing all right, to carry one's lunch tied to one's belt. But how odder still to wear one's leftovers home in the afternoon. It makes the bread man look in need of some help, and I should be ashamed, I think, that I fight him over a bus seat.

Our driver shoots him an angry look. The bread man is standing too close, it is annoying, hazardous, unnecessary. The driver has had enough of the bread man. He looks pointedly into the mirror, enough of all of us here. And I know then he will not last.

The fact is, we have a great deal of turnover in our drivers on this bus. They are almost always young, from the university, and I do not think they have their hearts in their work. At night, in the bars of this town, they tell themselves and each other that it is only what they are doing between things, this mindless driving in circles. It is only until they can graduate, they say, and start their lives in earnest.

Vigilance, I want to tell them. You, temporary bus drivers of this town. Youthful hopers and dreamers and soon to be college graduates, take heed.

This, or something close, I want to say to them. Impress on them, urgent and breathing hard. They do not know, they cannot. Still, slouched here low as I am in my second-row seat, I know the day will come when I will find myself standing, wild-eyed and shrieking at whichever of these young drivers it happens to be. Danger ahead! I will bellow. On guard. Beware.

I take a deep breath and hold it.

With more drama than necessary, the driver screeches our bus to a stop. Town center. We have arrived.

The bread man makes little shuffling sounds in the aisle, anxious to be off. I stand, and lowering one shoulder, push out for the door in front of him.

Packing

He pulls the bag from under the bed. He will not need to take much. A few shirts, his old khakis, socks.

Sabbatical, they're calling it. The change of scenery will do him good.

A slow smile. Yes, it is good. It is good to be on his way.

He checks the bag. Socks. Right. He will need socks.

Mott Street

The bus driver offers a small obligatory sort of wave through the windshield. I wave in return and head north up the block.

So this is how it is. My name is Margaret Lydia Benning, and I am twenty-eight years old. I am also tall, single, and on the lanky side. I live in a Midwest university town, and thanks to a bequest of my great-aunt Inez, I own a small house here on Mott Street. Where I live by myself, I should add. As an only child, with parents both dead and now most recently Inez, I am accustomed to living alone.

Regardless, my days are full. Mondays through Fridays I work at the sanatorium outside of town. On weekends I stay home and plant things. And all this spring, in the time in between, I have been on general alert. Something is coming, something is up, closer and louder and higher. Some great locomotive of chance or design fast approaches, most days I am almost certain. And most days I know too that as the others all scatter, I'll be the one still on the tracks. Try as I might to ignore the signs, they leave me not all myself.

The light at Summit turns red. A white van passes close in on my left and honks. I turn to look. No one I know. Always it is no one I know.

I tap my foot for the green.

Just now, I am on my way home. I am also just now in a hurry, as Mrs. Eberline most likely is waiting. Mrs. Eberline visits when she needs to find fault, and I'm pretty sure she'll be at my front step again today.

Green light. I hurry across, continue on Church.

Mrs. Eberline lives next door to the east. Before I left for work this morning, she was already up hurling twigs from the silver maple at my house. It is a sign. Mrs. E has figured out Ben Adams is missing, and she will be wanting to have a talk when I get home.

A right here on Grant.

Ben Adams. Now there is a topic of discussion. He is a good man, Ben Adams, kind, wide-shouldered, wise. It is only for lack of a much better word that I refer to him as my boyfriend. My apparently now former boyfriend, vanished into this soft spring air.

Which can happen with boyfriends at times. Even when things between you are good, that is, they are going OK—well maybe not perfect, not every day, there are problems, you have to admit, but mostly you both are happy—it's then that one day he just does not call. And then another day and another and still no call. So that after the following week or so you've pretty much got the picture. And by then of course so much time has gone by there's no point in calling him yourself, asking, "Anything wrong?" when in fact you know it is over. Has been for a while. And you realize well all right, something has changed his mind about you. Or come to think of it you're now of two minds about him. So you just let it slide, it is better than calling and embarrassing you both, saying anything official about endings.

Besides which, I do not think Ben wants to hear from me now. Not since our misunderstanding this winter. And oh how I wish we could change things. But it's been over three months since I last saw Ben Adams, and I know time for a do-over is over. Still, if I could figure a way back to Ben just now, I would ask for a second chance.

I cross over Court Street, continue. And well here we are, the corner of Grant and Mott, less than a block to home. Enough for now of Ben Adams. First on to Mott Street and home.

I live on Mott in a lopsided limestone cottage, built one half century ago by Mr. Lazarus Mott, namesake and former hog farmer. We are an entire block here of little Mott houses, stone cottages all gone awry, no two in quite the same way. It gives us a certain renown, we are in fact on the National Register, out of flabbergast, we suspect, more than merit. Still, in some architectural circles we are noteworthy. We are the talk of the preservationists in town.

It is an odd street, all right, Mott. It does not in many ways belong here. We are a university town, our streets are mostly old and venerable, also leafy. Mott, however, while old and leafy, is not what could be called venerable. We are instead wide. The town's cable car once ran down this street, we were at the time the end of the line, our width let the grip man stop, turn around. It lends us perspective, this backing up, backing off, this street and its generous expanse. We are of the live and let live, the laissez-faire school of neighborliness here.

Except that is for Mrs. Eberline. Mrs. E is a snoop and a meddler. She is also old, mad, and extraordinarily busy. Always Mrs. Eberline scurries, head down, always on task, on a mission. In winters, she indicts for snow left on walks, then shovels her entire front lawn. In summers she slips into random backyards stalking vermin with a pillowcase and broom. And then, late afternoons whatever the season, she stops by my house just for spite.

Or then again, it is possible there is more to her visits. Lately, I have noticed, something darker and more troubling has crossed Mrs. Eberline's mind. I cannot say what for certain it is. But I am afraid now prophecies are involved.

That is to say, Mrs. Eberline fancies herself a seer, the latter-day sibyl of Mott Street. She has, people say, predicted all manner of disaster on our block, including her own death at the age of forty-two by an ill-fated encounter with a cleaver. But since Mrs. E is well into her sixties, and moreover, as mentioned, mad, we on Mott take her soothsaying lightly. We dismiss her forebodings in general.

Still, they can be distressing, these predictions of hers, when you find she has leveled them at you. She can tell you more than you want to know, more than simply the truth. So I worry about Mrs. E's visit today. I worry what she might have to foresee.

The white van sidles up again and honks. I turn, it speeds on.

Frances at work says I should sell my house and move. Frances has two college degrees and once taught at the university. She is used to telling people what to do. There is no need to live next to a madwoman, she says. There is no need for sticks at your windows. "You have choices here, Margaret," she says, sounding like the old lecturer she is. Other houses, other streets. Places that don't harbor crones.

"Margaret," she tells me, "take charge."

Frances has a point. I could move, I could find another house, another block entirely to live. But I know I will not. The reason is simple, also iron-clad: This is the street where I belong. I know it in every homey fiber.

It is strange, however, about this street. Although I had been searching it for some time, I did not, when the realtor first drove me by, recognize that here it was. Nor did I at first take to the property for sale, my squat stone one-story-and-a-half. Still, the house sat up prettily on a little hill with a silver maple, big and graceful, in front. And when I saw then the other stone houses down the street, old pickups pulled into their driveways, the great tangle of tree limbs arched high overhead, very good, Mr. Abbott, I said. Now we are getting somewhere. And I asked him to drive around the block.

Because, as I explained on our third pass by, what really I'd been looking for all along was not so much house as street. Just one block, without all the rest of the town much attached. Certainly not the university. A block on its own, like some neighborhood geological outcropping, part and yet apart. Respite, refuge, asylum. Mott Street, I told him, was perfect.

It is a wonder of course I did not know about Mott before. I thought I knew this town well, I was what others would call used to it. A university town of desirous people. A town known for its ambition, its culture, its art. A Paris of the Prairie, some people said. And a town where I have just never fit.

But here on Mott, my guess was, things were different. People did not look so aspiring here, they seemed more a no-nonsense crowd. Neighbors who, on the assigned pickup day, rolled their own trash barrels out to the curb. Adults, probably good citizens. Ones at the university once too. Old students who found this town pleasant enough and stayed on as its carpenters and nurses and plumbers.

Yes, I thought, already convinced of the sale. We on Mott are the old students left over, a fact in which we take comfort. We are proud of our levelheaded normalcy here, despite our atypical houses. There's not a romantic or despondent among us.

None of which I said to Mr. Abbott. Who was, our next pass, insisting we pull over and make a house tour. Although already I knew, I obliged Mr. Abbott, I took a quick look inside. It was luckily just right as well, all dark wood and low ceilings and sloping planked floors. And in the front room, a large fireplace of smooth river rock.

So five years ago now, I stood in the front room of the house, my new soon to be home, and I told Mr. Abbott, "Oh I have found it. This is the house, here is the street." I left it at that.

Mr. Abbott just smiled and suggested a bid. And for his part did not bring up Mrs. Eberline.

Looking both ways—no sign of the van—I cross left onto Mott

and check up ahead. Although I live more or less at the center of our block, my little hill makes my house easy to see. And as I suspected, Mrs. Eberline is there at my door. She stands now close up to it hunched inside her red parka, a coat she favors most seasons. She is a small woman, Mrs. Eberline, small and, as I've said, old. The parka is two sizes too large and with its hood pulled in tight engulfing her head, it only makes her look older and smaller. A little red crab of a woman.

I stop to see what Mrs. Eberline is up to. It is a belligerent, strange way she inclines toward my door, hands on both hips, nose pressed to the center wood panel. I wonder how long she has been standing like this, staring so intently at the grain.

Then as I watch, Mrs. Eberline takes a step back and begins pounding—pounding and pounding with both fists at my door. It's impressive how far the sound carries. I must remind Mrs. E to please use the bell, she will upset the whole block with this pounding. But abruptly she stops. Stands still. Then reaching up to one side, she snatches two-handed into the air, turns, slams both palms to the door, and drags, fingers splayed, down the wood.

She is mad all right, Mrs. Eberline. Mad and I'm afraid growing madder. I take my time walking the last half block home.

Socks

He rises, walks to the drawer, looks inside. There, twenty pairs arranged roughly by color. Dark socks on the left, crews on the right, all neatly balled into pairs.

He surveys the drawer. Twenty pairs of socks and not one without holes.

No, not holes. Frays. Not one sock without frays. No new socks at the back to fill in, no Sunday socks saved for good. Now, all at once, all his socks have grown old.

He lifts the drawer from its runners and carries it into the bath. There, in late afternoon light from the window, he chooses the first ball and aims.

Mrs. Eberline

Mrs. Eberline stands facing my front door, her back to me. I pretend not to see her, I slip in by the side door and hope she has not seen me as well. Bending at the waist, I cross the kitchen low, stealthily, below window level. At the dining room, I begin to crawl. I am quiet, I am trying for the stairs. I want only to make it up to my bedroom, where I will shut and possibly lock the door.

But there she is now, knocking and calling out loudly, "Margaret, Margaret. I know you are home, Margaret. I see you in there. Open the door, Margaret."

For all of Mott Street to hear.

Mrs. Eberline, as I have said, is in the habit of stopping by. I am nearly used to it by now, although I never know what to expect. Sometimes Mrs. E does not launch right away into vile accusation and rebuke. Sometimes, to throw me off, she comes by just to use my toilet.

The day I moved in, for instance. I opened the door and there below me she stood and "May I use your toilet?" she said, just like that. It was a strange request. Mrs. Eberline, I knew, lived right next door, she had a toilet, an entire bathroom of her own. Still, "May I use your toilet?" she asked, looking up at me and looking urgent.

Not wanting to appear unneighborly, I stood aside and gestured down the hall. Then keeping the door open, I stepped out to wait for her return, which, I soon realized, was taking longer than it should. And when I looked in to check on her, I found she had already shown herself back up the hall and was pacing off my front room.

"Mrs. Eberline?" I said, and hurried inside. "Mrs. Eberline?" I repeated, my voice rising, and felt then my first spasm of home ownership, the mother-bird rush to fly over and defend.

Mrs. Eberline turned, nodded once, and congratulated me on my new house. That is, she said "you folks'" house. "Nice big house you folks have here," she said.

I smiled in return, still trying for goodwill. But then not wanting to misrepresent, I set Mrs. Eberline straight. I told her I was not folks, I lived here all on my own.

"No children?" she asked, her eyes growing narrow.

"No," I told her. "No children. No family." And then seeing no reason to stop there, "No husband either," I added.

This gave Mrs. Eberline pause. She moved to the foyer, considering.

"Dogs? You got dogs?" She looked at me hard.

"No, no dogs," I told her.

Mrs. Eberline kept her eye on me. She found this suspicious. "Well, it's still a nice big house," she said, as though I might disagree.

"A lot like my mother's," she added, before heading out the door.

I should explain that Mrs. Eberline lives with her mother, a very old woman I have never seen. But Mrs. Krantz across the street, who keeps track of such things, says oh yes, the mother has lived in that house sixty years. Although she too has not seen the old lady for some time, it is possible at some point she succumbed. Still, Mrs. Krantz says, for years now Mrs. Eberline has been the pair's sole support. She cannot say she entirely sees how. "It can't all be from those trash can liners."

I nod. We on Mott all know about Mrs. E's trash can liners, she takes them out with her early each day. They are large and black plastic and they make a lot of noise, as there is almost always something in them that clatters.

Which is to say, Mrs. E is a scavenger, it is loosely her line of work. She is a kind of landed bag lady. And while no one knows for sure all that she hauls in her bags, by the sound we assume it is cans, mostly empty bottles and cans, collected for their nickel deposits. It is a hard way to make a living, cans, and Mrs. Krantz does not think it possible, not even most days on two bags full. She believes it is welfare that supports Mrs. E, welfare and the senior citizen hot lunch that a van delivers each weekday for her mother.

I myself have a different suspicion. It's stolen goods, I think, not hot lunches, that help Mrs. E make ends meet. Mrs. Krantz just refuses to see it.

That is, I have reason to believe Mrs. Eberline is a thief. Almost from the beginning there was evidence. The first summer I moved in, for instance, immediately she began crossing our property line, after which, I then noticed, I kept losing things—the grass clippers, new within the same month, that to this day I know I left in the lilies; a bag of bone meal where I was planting bulbs; a whole new large box of grass seed. Consequently I now garage my possessions, I do not leave them unattended in grass. I keep an eye out for Mrs. Eberline's sticky, long reach.

All that may be, Mrs. Krantz allows. Mr. Krantz has seen her steal too. Still, she says, Mrs. Eberline deserves her due. She grew up on this block, there is that. She has history here, seniority. It naturally allows her rights.

Which apparently in your case, Margaret, she adds, are visiting and using the toilet.

I don't know why Mrs. E prefers the facilities here. I'm not sure why she stops by so often. But over time I have learned to resign to these visits. They are never long and almost always strange, and despite their ominous bent of late, I've come to count on them in a twitchy sort of way. "Well come in, Mrs. E," I say. And while she heads down my hall to the bathroom, I find I'm myself looking for cookies to offer. Then as Mrs. Eberline emerges and proceeds to my front room, I wait for the sport to begin.

Are You All Right?

At the sound of the toilet flushing, she calls. "Is that you?"

She listens, a second flush. "Are you all right?"

A third flush and she is on her feet.

"My god," she says from the door and stares as he stands on the seat of their toilet, dropping what appear to be pairs of his socks between his legs and into the bowl.

"My good god," she says again, but stops when she sees the water rising.

"Aren't you well?" she asks, then quickly backs from the door as a small fountain of navy blue water rushes up over the rim of the toilet bowl and down onto the bathroom tiles.

Ain't Seen Him 'Round

So I open the door now to Mrs. Eberline's pounding. I do in fact catch Mrs. E in the middle of her next attack. She stands below me one step, her fist raised midair for the door. The hood of her red parka is still up, it reaches just past my waistline.

"Well Mrs. Eberline," I say, looking down at the top of her hood. I sound as though this is certainly a lucky surprise. "How nice to see you."

I am always cordial to Mrs. Eberline. She does not buy this of course, she knows well enough that we are not friends. Still, there is no advantage with Mrs. E, I have learned, to incivility. We are stuck with each other, she and I, next door as we perpetually are. There is no need to make things any harder.

Mrs. Eberline steps up into my house and storms past me for the front room. Today it is apparently not my bathroom she is after. I close the door and "Have a seat, Mrs. Eberline," I am going to say. Though when I turn, I see she has already found her place on my couch. Hunched small and withered on the far end cushion, the hood of her parka pulled in tight, she looks up at me. Then glaring, she works her lips back and forth.

"Is something wrong, Mrs. Eberline?" I ask. What little color she has has escaped her face. She does not look the least bit well. "Would you like a glass of water?"

"That Ben feller," Mrs. Eberline says, and looks at me. "Ain't seen him 'round."

Ain't seen him 'round. I consider the diction. And so today, it seems, Mrs. Eberline has gone Appalachian. She is her old hard-scrabble self, just one of her many leading roles. They are part of her madness, these shifting personae, we on this block all expect it. I myself brace for the show.

That is to say, Mrs. Eberline is an actress, or was, of some local renown. She once studied at a famous drama school. She was a starlet in Hollywood in the thirties, it was rumored she was groomed to play Scarlett. But when a dark horse Brit was cast instead, she left film and turned to theater. She played off-Broadway, she played summer stock. She turned to the regional stage. And eventually, though no one in town agrees why, she ended up here with her mother.

Where still there was drama to pursue. For years Mrs. E played character roles in our local community theater or sometimes in university shows. If not great, she was a good actor, reviews said. Certainly she emoted well. Certainly she took theater seriously. Until at some point no longer clear, she took it entirely to heart. So that now, with the madness fully descended, always Mrs. E is in character. Always she is trying out for new parts.

Which means that rarely can we here on Mott in a day predict just who Mrs. E will be. Although sometimes we can guess by wardrobe, by what shows under the ubiquitous red coat. Two personae in particular she favors, and we know both their costumes well. Some days, for example, she dons a silky blue caftan. A sign Mrs. Eberline is having a Belva White day, a role she embraced long ago, a kind of diva à la Vivian Pickles. On Belva White days, Mrs. E throws her arms open wide and lavishes others with Darlings, and But dearest, you-simply-cannot-imagines.

Other days, rolled-up men's trousers appear under Mrs. E's coat and her accent takes a dramatic turn south. She removes her false teeth, drops the endings from words, and believes herself back on Tobacco Road. I check and indeed Mrs. Eberline is in trousers today. I am right. Today Mrs. E is in sharecropper mode.

I take a seat on the other end of the couch. "Ben Adams?" I say to Mrs. E. I smile, I am pleasant. I sound as though I am just making clear which Ben feller she might have in mind.

Mrs. Eberline scowls. "Don't be gittin' smart with me, missy," she says. She sits back in the couch, crosses her arms, holds her line. "I seen him take off. And I ain't seen no truck out here since."

She tucks in her chin, lets out a loud sigh. Mrs. E is disgusted or possibly just pining for Ben. With that parka hood up and hiding her head, it is difficult telling which.

Ben Adams was a favorite of Mrs. Eberline. Ben Adams is good-looking, I should mention, tall with lovely deep-sea green eyes, and whenever he was around, Mrs. E arranged always to be too, out in her yard, available. Ben favored Mrs. Eberline as well. And sometimes when I would call him to the window to watch, to see what now Mrs. E was up to, what new scavenged thing she had dragged onto her lawn, the latest pedestal sink she had managed to upend at her door, he would just smile and look knowing. "She means no harm, Margaret," he would say. "You should not be so hard on the woman."

Mrs. Eberline shifts impatiently on my couch, and I decide to come clean. "You have me there, Mrs. Eberline," I say. "Ben Adams is gone."

Mrs. E looks up. "Gone?"

"Right," I say.

She cocks her little head inside its red hood.

"Well, that is, missing," I say. "Ben Adams has gone missing. Disappeared." And lifting both shoulders, I shrug. For her sake I try to make light of it.

Mrs. Eberline only stares.

I think how to be more clear. "Ben Adams has left, Mrs. Eberline," I say, "and I do not know if he is coming back."

This last part startles me a little. And before I can think what else I can say, a funny thing starts to happen. I feel something inside me beginning to rise just as I do lately when waking. This time it feels like a sob.

I look off, clear my throat, go no further.

Mrs. Eberline still stares, considering. Then suddenly turning piercing, not to mention loud, "I knowed it!" she shouts. "Ben gone, and you's why."

She scowls once more. Then dropping her head and shoulders, she withdraws again inside the red hood. She sits looking down, very still, and does not offer anything more.

I see Mrs. Eberline is onto me. She has been keeping an eye on my house. She knows I'm the reason Ben left. But I have watched Mrs. Eberline with Ben Adams as well. There are things she could answer for too.

Always, as in the rest of her life, Mrs. E overdid it with Ben. When she saw he was here, for instance, if she spotted him lying out back in the grass napping or tossing a baseball over his chest, she would race out of her house and straight back to her garden, from where she would beckon flagrantly to him. Almost always she would be in the slinky silk caftan, it would swish seductively below her red coat. Mrs. Eberline normally wears trousers to garden. It's a wonder she found time to change.

Ben would tell me about Mrs. Eberline's chats, I would not have to watch them to know. When he'd come in at last, generally he'd be quiet and thinking them through.

"Psst," Ben told me. He would just be lying there resting and from out of nowhere he'd hear this loud psst. Psst. Psst. And if he did not sit up right away, give Mrs. Eberline a wave, he knew that when he opened his eyes, there she would be right over-head, throwing her shadow all over him, and peering down into his face.

So always, he said, when he heard that psst he would get up and walk to Mrs. Eberline's side. "Well hello again, Mrs. E," he would say. "Those are some fine-looking asters you have there."

Ben did not know why, but generally Mrs. E would take off then straight into some long-festering grievance. Mostly related to me. "Please darling," she would tell him, and point to my maple, "when you see that young woman next-door, please tell her she really must move her tree. It simply ruins the view and shades my tomatoes and come August I shan't have a single Big Boy."

Mrs. Eberline was not telling Ben the truth here. The reason my tree is shading her garden is that she has planted a good half of it in my grass. Mrs. E is not one for details, not one to worry over property lines. I must remind Ben of this one day.

But that was not the part that concerned Ben. It was what would come next, when Mrs. E would drop back her red hood, shake out her hair, and look again up at him. "I'm an actress you know, dearest," she would say. A sly smile. "They say I'm a star."

Always Ben would tell her he knew. "Yes," he'd say. "They have told me."

And always then Mrs. E would look away. Stare, turn dreamy, look back.

"They say I am beautiful. They say men fall at my feet." She would lift her chin, meet his eyes. Again her sly smile. "They say I'm myself fond of men."

Ben said he would never be sure how to reply. Yes? Yes, they have told me that too.

Ben worried about Mrs. Eberline. She has no one, he would say. There is no one she can tell her stories to. He thought maybe she needed our help.

Help, Ben? I'd say. Ben has not lived next door to Mrs. E as I have, he could not possibly know. But when I said no then, I did not think Mrs. E needed any more help, she was pretty good at helping herself, Ben just gave me a slow, sad smile. "It's a hard thing, Margaret," he said, "to find you've been left all alone."

And now Ben himself is no longer around.

Mrs. Eberline sits in my front room, head down. For a very long time she just sits. And I start to prepare myself then. While I cannot see what it is she is thinking, I can feel in her stillness something brewing.

Calling Before Dawn

Early the day of his flight, he cannot sleep. He rises quietly, slips on a jacket, steps outside. The sun is not up, thick fog has rolled in. He heads east. And at the third block, near a yard he cannot see, he hears a man calling for his dog. The voice sounds distant, it hangs midair.

It is the fog, he thinks. How strange it is walking in fog. You do not hear birdcall or traffic or the sound of your own shoes on pavement. Which is why the man's voice just now is surprising, attached as it is to nothing. "Brownie. Brownie."

It is only the fog. Only a man out calling for his dog. But he thinks he will tell her, he will say how it was, this one voice before dawn. It is how it is with him now, he will say.

There are still things in a day he thinks he will tell her. From habit, from the way it was before. How the peonies in the side yard have all come up, the shoots like chicken feet clawing out of the ground. A funny way to come up, feet first. Or how the wisteria in the cottonwood has buds on it now. The vine thick as a python, has she noticed? It has climbed the cottonwood three stories high. And the buds, he will say, you cannot imagine. Giant grape clusters of new buds, he will say.

Although in the end he does not. He no longer has stories to tell her. They neither of them have the heart for it.

Trouble

Still Mrs. Eberline sits on my couch, and still she does not move. She is beginning to worry me and for the second time today I ask if she would like a glass of water.

It is all I can think to come up with. It is what people generally offer when they don't know what else to do with an unwelcome guest in their house, with someone, say, dormant and downcast hunched in the corner of their couch. Or possibly just silent and seething. Would you like a glass of water, may I get you some water? It's an excuse to head for the kitchen, to spend time there letting the tap run cold. And sometimes it works. When you return with the glass, it is possible your strange guest will be gone.

I do not wait for Mrs. Eberline to reply. I go for the water and when I come back I realize it was a mistake. Mrs. Eberline revived while I was away and she has brought out her tin of cigarillos. Mrs. Eberline is a smoker, lifelong. Her mother will not let her light up at home, so she smokes wherever she can, or even where she cannot, most specifically here on her visits. It is something we have discussed at length. No smoking allowed in my house. It is one of my few hard lines.

But before I can say, "Mrs. Eberline, what is that?" and point dramatically at the open tin, again at the unlit cigarillo now dangling from her fingers, she lifts her head and pulls me urgently back onto the couch. Her eyes narrow, a brow lifts. She takes a long breath, leans in.

"Missy," she says up close to my face, wagging her Swisher Sweet at me. "Missy, we got to go git Ben."

She takes me by surprise. I expected a fight on the no-smoking front. I expected more accusations about Ben. But git him? Has Mrs. E not been listening here? When I say Ben Adams has left, Mrs. E, what I mean is that he has left *me*. I've been dumped, Mrs. E. Do you not understand? We cannot just go off now and git him.

But Mrs. Eberline sees it differently. Or rather, she seems not to see it at all. Or hear anything, for that matter, I've just said. Something has shifted, distracting Mrs. E. She seems now no longer much even in the room. She sits very still, back straight. Her gaze grows distant, her eyes turn to dark flat disks. And I know then it is her sibyl stare, her look when she's feeling prophetic, when she feels a divination coming on.

She turns toward the window, toward the garage beyond. For a moment she only just stares. Then "Ben?" she says slowly, as though trying to make him out in dim light. "Ben," she says again, now watching. She holds her breath, still watching. Then "Ben!" she cries. "Ben!" And eyes opening wide, she howls, "No!"

Flinching, she withdraws back into her hood. And rocking a little, holding herself, "Oh Ben," she says, her voice a deep, frightening whisper, "oh Ben, you in terrible trouble."

For a moment she goes on rocking. But then abruptly she stops, listens, watches. And turning her head to one side, as though tracking now something new, "Or headin' for trouble," she says, and stares trancelike a moment more.

Then shaking herself once, she faces me, eyes clear again and burning, "Missy," she says, "Ben ain't got much time." She takes a quick, anxious breath. "Somethin's 'bout to happen to that man, I seen it. More terrible than I can say."

And in case then I somehow have missed her point, she raises her voice, moves in closer. "I'm sayin', missy, you got to go git Ben. Bring him back. Keep him here where we kin watch him."

I look at Mrs. Eberline. Ben is in trouble? She seen it? And despite her pleas, despite my better self, I cannot help thinking not so fast here.

That is, there are things that need sorting out in all this, in this latest of Mrs. E's visions. And I try to work each one through. First, Mrs. Eberline, prophet though she believes herself to be, in fact is not often on target. That is to say almost never. It is not likely Ben actually is in trouble. Second, her exhortation just now to go save Ben clearly has her own interests at its heart. Third, and this is the deal breaker, I'm not sure I'm the one who should be saving Ben, assuming he actually needs saving, since it is not at all clear he would want me to.

So I tell Mrs. E I am not so sure about Ben. I say I think he is probably doing just fine. And, I add, to tell the truth I don't know it would work, having him back in my house again. I do not go into detail.

Mrs. Eberline looks out again at the garage. "It ain't got to be your house, missy," she says. "You got choices." She nods toward the window. "Ben Adams can stay in that there garage. You ain't even got to know the man's here."

She turns to me, now vehement. "Ben is in danger, I'm tellin' you."

I look back at Mrs. E as though considering. About the endangered Ben Adams.

Mrs. Eberline eyes me sternly, waggles again the Swisher Sweet. "You got a whole garage empty there, missy," she says, and then starts rummaging in her pocket for a match.

I watch Mrs. Eberline, I should stop her. But now I'm thinking about what she's just said, so for her sake, I look out at my empty garage. And on track again now, I have to admit Mrs. Eberline has a point.

Which, to be fair, I am going to acknowledge to her. But I turn and find Mrs. E has gone back into her trance. She stares out the window where just now she's seen Ben. And "No, wait. missy," she says, her eyes dark again, "now I'm seein' you." She stares. "I mean to say I'm seein' Ben, and you is right there too." Then shaking her head, "Looks like the both of you is in trouble."

Pressing and pleading again, she moves closer, Ben Adams still her main concern. "Missy, you gotta save Ben. Bring him back where he be safe."

I think about this. It is generous of Mrs. E to be seeing after Ben, except now I'm as well in the picture. "But Mrs. Eberline," I say, "if I save Ben, who is going to save me?"

Mrs. E stares blankly. She shrugs. "Well I just reckon that's up to you."

Then sitting forward, her voice rising, as though I still have not got the picture, "Missy," she tells me, "you got to go git Ben. Ain't nobody else a'gonna."

Having said her piece, Mrs. Eberline plumps herself back on

my couch. And watching me for my reply, she strikes her match and lifts it blazing, threatening to light up should I delay.

I try to think fast, I try to be fair. I could go find Ben, keep him safe here with me. His demands would be small, there is room, it's all true.

Mrs. Eberline holds the match aloft.

I study her face. The flame reflects in her crazed little eyes, and I know then it's an awful idea.

So "No," I tell Mrs. Eberline. I am sorry, but no. "No, no. Ben will not be moving into my garage."

Mrs. Eberline gives me a long, hostile look. She holds it a beat or two. And then aware of it or not, eyes steady still on me, she loosens her thumb and forefinger, letting the lighted match drop.

We both watch it fall in slow motion, bounce once on my couch, then roll onto the center cushion. And oddly, at first I am calm. The match lies sideways near the cushion's edge and looks like it is going out. Its light goes dim, shrinks in. No need to over-react here, I think. Or give Mrs. E that satisfaction.

But just then I see the match head starts again to grow bright, and beneath where it landed what looks like a large black ink stain spreads out in a menacing halo. The stain grows rapidly larger, the center dissolves to a glowing red rim. And as I watch, now pretty much spellbound, the perimeter suddenly cracks and erupts into a shocking orange flame.

Everything then happens fast. Before Mrs. E or I can move or try to put anything out, the cushion starts sending up thick dark smoke. Great licks of fire leap high.

"Mrs. Eberline!" I cry. "Now look what you've done!" And reaching for her glass of water, I hurl it into the flames.

The water splashes sideways toward Mrs. E. She jerks back out of the way. Then furious and snorting, she jolts to her feet and stomps brusquely off for the front door.

I myself run for more water. But on my return I see Mrs. E has stopped just outside and is glaring back from the top step. Still thinking of Ben, I suppose, not to mention herself, she points a bony finger in my direction. "It just mean of you, missy," she cries. "You just a tall, mean old thing."

Then, with my couch still burning and sending up smoke, she tells me what she always tells me, that I am going to die hard and lonesome.

Two

At the Sanatorium

Wednesday morning and there is more now to attend to than Mrs. E. More to do in a day than wait for her next risky visit. Mrs. Eberline at any rate is away just now, off with her black plastic trash bags, off to the empty bottles and cans and general discards she gathers.

Which actually, I should say, I'm assuming. For all I know, Mrs. Eberline at this moment is somewhere downtown on a corner declaiming my uncharitable heart. I do not know for a fact what Mrs. E is up to because I am not now around to catch her. I am instead myself away, at work at the sanatorium.

Where this morning things are seriously amiss. Joe Trout, for one, appears under a spell and has lost the elusive Trout Route. Sally Ann has herself misplaced Mr. Bones and wanders mute and desperate without him. Then in staff meeting just as the chandelier dimmed, "Look!" Celeste cried, gaping up. "They've returned!" After which, when we hurried back to our suites, we all found crumpled notes on our chairs, illegible and, more importantly, bloodied.

"It's all that Emmaline's fault," Celeste says. "Really the girl knows no limits." She is positively ruining the sanatorium for the rest of us.

Celeste, as usual, dramatizes. All of the above can be explained. But before any further detail, first a few points about context— that is, the sanatorium.

Which, to begin with, is no longer a sanatorium. We just say sanatorium here because that is what it once was, the Elmwood Sanatorium for Sunny Rest and Cure, a fashionable resort for the tubercular. A grand four-story stone building with cross-wings and turrets on one hundred acres of undulating plain. Once an elegant estate of sprawling bent-grass lawns, regal elms, bright meadows of columbine in spring. We had our own farm then, a post office as well, and a station where Silver Streak Pullmans rolled to a stop and stylish pale riders detrained.

But as I said, that is no longer the case. Years ago the sanatorium ceased being a sanatorium when the well-heeled ceased being tubercular. Streptomycin appeared, and soon the main hall here was locked up and abandoned. For years more it stood empty, its lovely green lawns turned fallow. After which, through a series of bank repossessions, the sanatorium was turned over to the state, who renamed it the Elmwood State Institution and moved in all state sorts of things. The medical facility for the nearby state prison, the state lab that tests rodents for rabies, a large wing for the state's crippled children, a whole floor where the state alcoholics detox. And in the basement a state cafeteria too, above a malodorous state steam tunnel.

Then it occurred to the state that the university in our town, being a state sort of university, could also use sanatorium quarters. So we now have a faculty sabbatical lounge. And a wing for university-funded small business, incubator to emerging state jobs. Which is why I, Celeste, and the others are here, or rather, that is, the Project, university-funded and emerging as we all are.

The Project, very like the sanatorium, is not the real name for where we work. To be exact, we work for Steinem Associates, Unified, a publisher of children's early readers. But our director, Dr. H. S. Steinem, prefers that we just say the Project. It makes us sound more academic, he believes, not so pushy and profit-minded.

What we do here is make up stories. Fanciful, structured adventure yarns that teach early readers to read. Tales of thrill-seeking sweet rolls on the loose from their box, whooping field mice in hot pursuit, a large grinning calico at their heels, all bent on a spirited progression throughout of hard consonants and long and short vowels.

It is a project Dr. Steinem, School of Education, proposed over a decade ago. That children must learn to read "oh" sounds before "oo," single vowels before pairs, and so forth. That children learn best through imagination, through goal-oriented flights of fancy. And that fancy can be organized into bound basal readers, in turn grouped into grade-level series.

"Basal readers," Steinem said to anyone who listened. And reiterated in grant proposals. He, Henry Steinem, had seen the future of learning, and the future was basal readers. "Get them early," said Steinem. "Get them basal, and by god, you have got yourself readers."

We consider ourselves lucky at the Project. Although Dr. Steinem's ideas were not new, his proposals were surprisingly well funded. So two years ago, the Project was officially birthed, and I and the series editors were hired. Following which, with the help of our university and state, we all moved here to Elmwood S.I., fourth floor, in a wing of once-private suites.

There are advantages to working in sanatorium suites: the windows are large, we have a fine view. Our offices are all roomy and sunlit, with lovely high carved plaster ceilings. We each have a set of French doors looking out with our own wrought-iron balcony. And each office as well has a full attached bath with a porcelain tub and brass handrail. I have filled my tub with a terrarium of small palms, but Celeste brings bath oils for hers and soaks in lemon verbena on lunch hours.

We have no complaints at our sanatorium, we are happy for all we've been given. That is, we all say, with the possible exception of Earnest. Earnest is our new part-time Tuesday night janitor, recently come out of retirement. He is old and claims to have worked at the sanatorium years ago when it was in its tubercular heyday. Earnest is no longer right in the head. Moreover, he is a big talker, droning on about the old days here. He rambles and says things hard to believe, and if you must work late on a Tuesday, Earnest will most certainly find you. Then he will put down his pail and stand in your light and insist on telling you his stories, about all the long bloody nights that he's seen, how each patient here suffered and died.

On this floor in particular, he'll say. Screamers' wing, that's what they called it. They moved the incurables here, ones whose fever had taken their minds.

"Screamers' wing. You got that?" Earnest says. "Why do you think you're way off on fourth floor?"

That is the kind of thing Earnest says. "Oh the stories," he'll say. "The stories. Things happened here you could not guess."

That balcony there for instance, he will say, when he has come up with his mop to surprise you. "That balcony," he'll say, "that's where the girl in the nightgown jumped." Then he'll leave it at that, and go back to his pail.

It's disconcerting at best, and ever since he arrived, we all try not to listen to Earnest. We just unlock our French doors in the mornings, let in the sun and fresh air. Then we sit down at our desks, pick up our pens, and begin our important days. We have our work after all, our deadlines.

We are busy, engaged people at the Project. Series editors mostly, our offices arranged down one side of the hall, precisely ordered by grade level. Sally Ann for first grade, Lola for second, Frances, in the big suite, for third. Next my suite and next door the verbena-drenched Celeste, editor of the gifted and talented. Then working freelance from home are two illustrators and a nice man named Cliff, editor of reader satisfaction. Only Steinem and Marcie are not editors here, Steinem as he is the director of course, and Marcie as she's his assistant. Actually, what Marcie is is administrative assistant and sometimes acting receptionist, there is no pretending she's anyone's editor.

As for me, I'm the assistant editor of design, a name Dr. Steinem gave me. I am not sure why he calls me all that, in fact what I do here is paste-up. It is not much of a job; generally I just ink lines in tables, wax galleys and burnish them down. At my age I should be doing more. But it is a job I can do, the hours are right, almost never do I have to work weekends. And so for the most part, I've been happy to stay.

That is, until lately. Since Ben Adams, in fact, disappeared. Ever since Ben so abruptly took off, I cannot seem to keep my mind on my work.

The Farm

He has rented a farmhouse outside of town. It is not the same house, but it is big and square and white like the other. So for a while he will live in this farmhouse, and it will be like it was before. He will make it like it was before.

This house, a neighbor has told him, once was a Mennonite church, then for a while a school. It is plain and wood-sided with a cupola on top where sometimes he sits late at night. On the north side, two wood swings hang by chains from a tree. And outside the front door, an American flag flies from a twenty-foot pole.

The house sits on a big rolling farmyard. The grass there is thick and deep green, and white lilacs line a long gravel drive that leads up to the house from the road. He has started a garden to the south of the house. And in the back in a stand of tall pines he keeps a pair of gray geese.

Beyond the yard are his landlord's wide fields, acres of soybeans, seed corn, a barn, and a pen for some black-spotted pigs. The landlord has moved to a house in town, he is almost never around. He only stops by the farm early mornings and leaves again always by dawn.

So for most of his days he, the renter, has this yard and the fields to himself. It is quiet the way it once was. There is time here to think, to remember.

Vision

Now, about this matter of paste-up, something I'd like to get out of the way. Why I hold on to this job as I do, how I came to it in the first place. It is not unlike how I came upon Mott Street, in fact the two are related. The story of which is sometimes tricky to tell, not that I'm often asked to. But when I am, and I have to say something, I say well here is a story about someone I know, a person a little like me. Let me tell you about her instead.

The tale begins a few years ago when this person I know, a young woman, first arrived in the Midwest and this town. She came, as many here do, to study at the university. At the age of twenty-one, she applied as a graduate student of art, specifically painting and drawing, and was accepted on scholarship and waivers. Admissions took a shine to the portfolio she turned in, granting her out-of-state tuition. In return, they said, they expected her work to be worthy, to show talent and most especially vision. They expected a life of beauty and truth. A life spent in pursuit of, well, art.

At first the young woman believed what they said and set out boldly to paint. She believed it a calling, a duty, she believed that eventually art saved. But here is the catch to the story. In fact her life at the school was confounding. Others there did not feel as she did, they had come to do art for other reasons. They had come first of all to be noticed, to attract. They had come for careers, for degrees. And they looked at her oddly when she spoke of art for what she believed was art's sake. Wise up, they all told her. Art can get you somewhere. You have only to name your price. After which, and some thought, the woman in fact did grow wiser. She knew then to never again talk of art, and certainly never to bring up vision. That is, to be clear, visions.

To explain: For years off and on, at that point maybe always, this woman had been having visions. Or, more precisely, visionettes. Better yet, she decided, dioramas — infrequent brief flickers of startling scenes, three-dimensional, full color, stockstill. As though at some ominous surprise celebration, the hall dark, filled with invisible guests, some trickster among them lights a flare. And suddenly there they all stand, frozen in light, heads back and mouths open mid cry, before everything goes to black again.

They were dioramas all right. Twisted glass boxes of moments in time. In their silent, still way they stood out. A man with great feathered wings at his back, his forehead against a stone wall. A woman in pink diaphanous tulle, wild boars where her legs should be. Bloated bodies in rivers. Eyeless white heads. Severed hearts wet and still beating. Alarming scenes, pained and askew.

The young woman, this artist, had no idea where they came from. Were they guideposts, warnings, predictions? Or just wayward nerve axons firing, signifying nothing at all? She had not a clue, she knew only she must somehow lay hold of them. So she drew and she painted each, one by one, recasting as best she knew how.

And although they turned out abstract and off course, nowhere close to what she had seen, soon her paintings attracted attention. It was the light, people said. Or no, the shadows—something, well, something strange. How did she do it, they wondered. But the woman did not disclose. She did not admit to the visions she saw, there was really no way to explain them. And soon they made her a School of Art star.

It was not what the woman intended. It was not why she'd come to art school. But there were missteps, miscalculations. When you are young you cannot always know. And sooner or later, despite herself, she bought into the others' misguided praise and began hanging with fellow art stars.

They invited her to the Hogshead, the artists' dive bar in this town. She joined them most nights at their table, learned to drink beer and play pool. Learned all the names of the others who drank there, learned to say things that amused.

And then over time at the Hogshead, the woman got to know a few faculty too. They had heard of her work, its vogue disaffection, its dark pitch-perfect aberrance. It behooved them to know the town comers. So they asked her to seminars and coffees off campus, to dinners at their homes as well, small casually pretentious affairs. They wanted to know this rising star better. They wanted to talk painting with her, they wanted to talk music, film, books. Then they wanted to talk of food, of wine, then of their crystal wine goblets, the correct shapely stem of each imported glass that cost more than two monthly phone bills. Oh they longed to stay up talking till dawn.

At first, despite how these evenings seemed to her, the artist wanted to believe them a boon. She had hope that in one way or another they would eventually lead somewhere new. So whenever she was invited to party or dine, always she gratefully accepted. And always she thought then this might be the night, that at last the evening would rise. That sensing it, people would gather around. That someone would say something essential, there would be some small act of wonder. Or that, short of these things, her inevitable silence partway into dessert would not dampen anyone's spirit.

But the nights never worked out any better, while the invitations accrued. And in time, the artist began to fear she would not be able to keep pace. She didn't know there would not always be more. She didn't know she was only just this year's art star. She knew only that she wanted both art and life. It seemed to her that couldn't be wrong. And not realizing then that indeed it could, that the life she was choosing was all wrong, she continued to paint and to party, and let others continue to marvel. Such *élan vital*, those in her circle would say. Such eerie fecundity.

Until when, halfway into her second year of school, she felt a shift, then a shudder. And without knowing just why or even how, she watched the light in her visions start to dim. The drop-off continued, the decline grew steep, she tried to rekindle, illumine. But at last all that flickered were just some old stills, returned to loop for a while.

So she tried then to paint without them, without any vision at all. She painted and then she painted. But she found that the mysterious light in her art, like her visions, had disappeared. There was nothing beyond the fine colored surface, the strong technique she had learned. And after a few more last attempts, she knew it had to be true. All her art now amounted only to sketches, disjointed series of things, incomplete, weak, of no interest.

At which point she understood her School of Art work was through. She was not, it turned out, an artist after all and no longer had reason for painting. In fact had no business painting or for that matter acting the genial star. It was time the young woman stopped trying.

Which was also when I myself just stopped trying and settled onto Mott.

The point here being this: It is a strange thing all right to come to one's end. That is, to come to the end before it is over. To meet one's destiny early in life. To find at the age of twenty-eight, it has all come down to Mott, that Mott Street was one's fate all along.

Of course, viewed in a certain light, there is, you might think, a kind of bravery in this, in living your life already knowing your precise lot in it. Living it through, all the while sensing how poorly it will actually turn out. A bravery, yes, you would like to think. Or possibly let others think. But here is the truth as I've found it: There is also a deep, profound comfort. A divine confirmation life is just what it is and indeed you're not all that you thought. That so it will go, day after day, with no surprise or for that matter striving.

Because so it has been for me for five years, a settled, lengthy life lull. A plateau in effect, a high arid place with horizons wherever one looks. Not the new sort of horizons optimists wake up to, oh look a new horizon. Rather the comfortable same old horizons, boundaries on every side. From a plateau they are easy to see.

Although here is the thing I have found out as well. They are deceptive, these plateau's hard edges. They can make you believe, if you're not careful, your flatland is all that there is. And that if you just simply stay where you are you can calmly go on forever.

Which is why it was such a surprise when it happened. Ben's disappearance, I mean.

Geese

He bought the geese, a goose and a gander, from a neighbor. He does not intend to eat them. He wants them for company, and also because there is the stand of pines by the back door. Under the trees it is cool and feels always a little like rain. It is a place he thought geese would like. So he built a big pen out under the pines and put the two geese inside it.

And now every day, he climbs over the fence and into the pen along with them. It is an idea he had. For an hour each late afternoon he squats low to the ground, holds out a hand, and talks quietly to his geese. Tells them about how it is these days. How he is getting to know his students, how he likes the studio where they paint. Likes the house and farm as well. Likes it in general here.

These are the things he says under the pines to his geese. You have to do this with geese, he believes. And if you go every day and sit in their pen and talk calmly to them, after a while they get used to you. They trust you and like you and then you can take down the pen. They won't fly away.

Geese will stay loyal for life, he'd heard, once they get the chance to know you.

Opportunity

Ben's disappearance? Well now, there is the real matter at hand. Enough of paste-up, plateaus. Enough of the editors all back in their suites, finishing their morning's hard work. Enough, for that matter, of work at all and also of the sanatorium. Time here instead for Ben Adams.

I sit at my light table twirling my ink pen, considering. Ben Adams, I think. Ben and his curious vanishing. They are topics I keep returning to. Although, to be clear, I should add that Ben is not in fact my first boyfriend, or the first one that I've lost. When I was a graduate School of Art star, I had an excess of them, many just passing through. I've grown accustomed to boyfriends' habits. Still, the sudden, silent way Ben Adams took off has me, I must say, thrown. Despite that it's now been over three months, still I am figuring it out. Wondering, that is. Worrying too. Or sometimes, well mostly, just remembering.

The fact is, I suppose, it was easy for Ben just to slip out of sight. With the exception of Mrs. Eberline, who was onto us I would guess from the start, no one in town much knew about Ben or that he and I were a couple. It was a tacit decision we came to, for reasons that will become clear. A kind of silent oath, in fact, to tell no one about each other. And so Ben Adams and I just kept to ourselves. We were what you could call secret lovers, although it's important to note we ourselves never saw it that way. Nor did we agree on what it was then we were, which was an issue between us, admittedly. Still, definitions apart, we were happy.

He is, as I've said, a good man, Ben Adams, though even before vanishing, elusive. A surprising man, not always the same. Strong but loose-limbed in a comfortable sort of way, generous but iron-willed. Now curious, now subdued, now here, now away. Young and old all at one time.

In years, the fact is Ben is older. Well, older than I by sixteen years. It does give him a natural advantage, this extra time he has had in the world. It's allowed him to do some figuring out. How politics works, for example, why it is that people care. How life itself works, or some of it, how it has an odd way of turning on you, that it is usually neither all nor only. Ben will say things like that sometimes. And while I do not understand always just what he means, I know I have something to learn from him.

But then there is yet another Ben. The one that without any warning can turn inexplicably sad. Which may not be actual unhappiness at all, perhaps more just something like age. Or reflection. Or some natural list toward longing. But whatever the cause, the fact remains, Ben Adams is a man who yearns. The issue here being that a man who yearns, compared with someone more jolly, more festive and generally chipper—a wistful man is an obligation, one you cannot easily walk out on.

Which is an interesting point now, I think, considering Ben is the one who's walked out.

I put down my pen and give this some thought. Unless of course, I think, he has not. Walked out, I mean. By choice. I take a deep breath, sit straighter. And I remember again Mrs. E's vision of Ben and against my will, start to wonder. What if Mrs. Eberline had it right? That there's been some sort of foul play. Is that why Ben hasn't called?

So I sit at my light table and I consider this too. That Ben is somehow in trouble. It's a reach, I know, but still. And after more thought, here is what finally occurs to me. Whether or not Ben really is missing—that is, now with the possibility raised—the fact remains that he is no longer here. So then, shouldn't someone try to find out where he's gone? Ask: Ben, are you all right? Check in as she might not have before.

And well, yes, shouldn't that someone be me?

For a moment I feel very clear. And I know for once I could be on the right track. It would seem that way, anyway, wouldn't it? I need to find Ben. Mrs. E says she's seen him in trouble. How could I now not check up on him?

It is a good thought, all right, I think. Albeit one that doesn't last long. Because I remember then of course about Mrs. E, that she and her visions are crazy, to believe them would be crazy as well. And I pick up my pen and start twirling again, momentarily back to the beginning.

Until, despite my remarkably good intention just now, a new thought begins to form. In fact two thoughts come at once. And I know then it's no longer my better self thinking, because what occurs to me is this: Maybe it does not in fact matter so much if Mrs. Eberline is mad or her vision of Ben is true. Maybe something else is at play. Maybe looked at now in a different light, what Mrs. E saw is an opportunity. My opportunity. An excuse to see Ben again.

I consider this new possibility. And although I know it is not my finest hour, I feel something inside me leap. Yes, of course, I should be the one now to go and find Ben. To make sure that he isn't in danger, to rescue him on the off chance he is.

And giving up then on pure altruism, I opt straight for brazen self-interest. Yes, I think, yes. A rescue here is in order. I will go save Ben, and once I know he's all right—since it would be rude just to turn and leave—I'll stay for a while, have a talk. Explain what I've been thinking since winter. Ben will say whatever he's been thinking too. We'll concede our disagreement from before. We'll see where we both had it wrong and both feel the better for it. And with luck then, there you will have it, our chance at a second chance.

What do you know, a rescue could just work out for us. Maybe it's not too late. Maybe we'll end up all right. Isn't that how rescue goes?

And well, I think, this changes everything, doesn't it? All previous bets now are off.

Although a clarification here, before anyone goes any further or gets the wrong impression. By second chance I do not actually mean the kind that the lovesick, well mostly the discarded, dwell on. I do not mean I am hoping to get back together with Ben. I don't know if I'd want to return to all that. There were problems with Ben, as I've said, and the fact is I just do not know about him. I have never really known about Ben.

Which is a funny thing about boyfriends, I've noticed. They too often don't know about you and jump to unwarranted conclusions. That for instance it was love, a mate you were after, when you really just needed someone to talk to.

No, I think by second chance, I mean I just want to know things with Ben and me are all right. That Ben is all right. There's been no real harm done here.

Back

Again he climbs into the pen. There is more he wants to say.

Hoping for grain, the geese move in.

He takes a seat. So it's like this, he tells them. After all these years, he's come back. Here, where he had once been a student. Back to this town, the university. Back to where it began, where all of it once was possible. The painting, the light, that miraculous light, the fevered and urgent days. He has come back for them, yes, those days.

The geese stand nearby, watching.

Right, he tells them, smiles. That's right—and for the nights too. He's come back for those nights at the Hogshead. The cold beer, the pool, the old green shade. And the others like him at the bar, reeking of linseed, high.

All of them friends, he tells the geese. We were all of us friends then, good friends. Artists as well, graduate-student artists and friends. Michael, who built things, boxes within boxes, working from outside in. Jean, who filled canvas with tangled red roots and signed them "jean, jean the beet queen." Charley, who etched tortuous faces in stone, then backed over the plates with his truck. Artists, yes artists. They were all of them artists then.

The geese drop their heads, peck the ground.

And some of them lovers, that too, he says. Ones he cannot now name, though he still sometimes thinks of the nights with them, their fine long-limbed bodies, the musk of their skin. Maybe he's come back for them.

He falls silent.

The geese look up.

Or Ellen. Or maybe for Ellen.

Turning their heads, the geese study him.

Right, he says. Right. Truth is, maybe he's come back just for Ellen. For where they first met, for the house they first shared that winter.

The geese stand waiting.

He shakes his head, smiles. He has no more to tell. "You would have liked Ellen," he says.

He stands. Turns to leave. Turns back.

Truth is—

And shrugging, turning again for the fence— Truth is he has just come back, that's all. He had nowhere else to go.

Ford

But first, before rescue, a little more still about Ben and me. It's important before rushing to save, I believe, to understand just what is at stake. In this case, for instance, Ben and me. That is to say our coupling.

Which I should explain was indeed a strange thing and also against several odds. You could say it was unlikely our even meeting at all, given Ben's ways and mine. That is, ever since finding my house here on Mott, I've been inclined just to sit home alone a lot, while Ben himself is in town just this one year, staying mostly out in the country. We could have easily lived within miles of each other never knowing the other was there. Which is exactly what would have happened, I believe, if it weren't for my best gay friend, Ford.

So actually, rethinking it more, first a moment now about Ford, Ford and me. Then on to Ben and me.

When I first knew Ford at the university here, Ford was not his whole name. He was in fact known as Robert Bob Ford, named after both of his grandfathers. But just Ford is how he signed all his work, and once he began selling his paintings we all began calling him the same.

I have known Ford for over six years. We were in graduate school together, the same entering class, School of Art. For a while we were both of us School of Art stars.

But here was the difference between Ford and me. Ford is a player and he believed in the school, he believed in hard work, in ambition. He believed in success, in talent. He believed, specifically, he'd been chosen and took his star station to heart. I, as I've said, took a different route. I just painted and painted and painted. Until the day that I didn't. And haven't, in fact, since.

Ford thinks it a shame I gave up on art. It is not something we can discuss. Although after moving to Mott Street, I did once give it a try. Ford had come for a visit, he wanted to know why it was I'd quit school, and I decided to level with him. The truth is, I told Ford, the art that once made us School of Art stars is just an odd knack, that's all. A trick we both happen to know how to do. The surprise is that others don't know the trick too.

Ford rolled his eyes, said Margaret, I do not buy this. And we have ended up differently, he and I. Ford now teaches full-time at the school, he regularly exhibits and sells. And I—well, I work at the Project in paste-up.

Still, regardless of paths, Ford and I have stayed close. He is my oldest friend in this town. We are comfortable with each other, we have history. Ford is nothing if not loyal, he likes to say. He has my best interests at heart. Which in turn gives him license, he also believes, to point out all that is wrong with me.

There is reason, Ford thinks, for concern—apart, that is, from my want of dedication and generally deficient spirit. Lately, Ford says, my poor social skills in particular have begun to worry him. He believes that since leaving both school and art, I have developed attachment issues. I have simply, personally detached. And here Ford points to the fact that, though single, I have bought a story-and-a-half stone house and settled into it most evenings alone.

"You are becoming an old maid, Margaret," Ford told me last year on another one of his visits. "Just look at you, there in your sweatpants." It was after I'd just bought a color TV, and actually, it was not the TV at issue. Ford approved of this purchase, he did in fact seem to encourage it. He took me out shopping, explained chromacolor, demonstrated remote control. But then, once I plugged in the set at home, and began watching it single-mindedly, Ford, like a shot, turned on me. Well, it's all over now, Margaret. You'll only be leaving your house now for milk. Grocery shopping will become your one social event. Then you'll be back with your color TV, night after cold winter night, your feet on some raggedy hassock.

"It is what all you spinsters come to, Margaret. Sooner or later. You'll see."

In my defense, I must say that this is my first television. Or the first TV that I've owned. I was, to be honest, for a time once in possession of Ford's old black-and-white, a loan during a brief charitable period. But I was not at that point a true television fan. Ford's set tuned to only one station, local and educational, so I just watched old movies mostly, ones starring William Holden when possible. I'm not sure that even counts as TV.

But now I am the owner of a new color set, seventeen inches on the diagonal. And I began viewing, indiscriminately most nights—*M*A*S*H*, of course, *Monty Python*, *The Brady Bunch*, *Fat Albert*, *Maude*. It seemed inordinately to bother poor Ford. Although there were other things too that concerned him, he said, take my electric blanket, for instance.

I should explain that Ford only knows of my blanket because I once mistakenly mentioned it to him. How I had turned the heat down to fifty-five and purchased an electric blanket.

Ford was beside himself once again. "An electric blanket, Margaret? An EB?"

I did not at first understand. "Yes, so?" I said, and tried not to sound defensive.

Ford explained. "It's another of the signs here, Margaret. Spinsters sleep with electric blankets. Old maids. Don't you see? It's all those empty beds they crawl into. My god, Margaret, next you'll be telling me you're taking up flannel."

I gave him my best steely stare. "No, Ford," I said. "I will not be telling you this." Which I said because I had just then decided not to talk to Ford at all.

But yes, the truth is sometime in November two years ago, I indeed started sleeping in flannel. It grows cold here in winters, and when I began waking with sore throats, swollen glands, well yes, I turned to flannel nightgowns. Lanz. White eyelet ruffles at neck, wrist, and hem.

It is no particular sign, Ford, I said, when once again we were speaking. There are, I'm quite sure, married women in this town, sated single women as well, who don flannel for bed winter nights. What one wears to one's bed is no sign of sleeping alone.

Although it is true those long nights I did sleep alone. That in fact I was growing lonely.

Which brings me, if loosely, back to Ben. How it was that I met Ben Adams.

We Meet, Ben and I

It is Ford who talks me into the gallery opening where I first meet Ben this fall. He tells me I really do need to get out more, and as luck would have it, some graduate art students are throwing a little gala in town, an opening for their group graduate art show. It will do me good, Ford says, to get out and see some new people. "Look," he says, "you can be my date." Which means his boyfriend of the evening has just fallen through and Ford himself is in need of a date.

"All right, Ford," I say. I am, as I've said, his oldest friend. I cannot let him go to a gala alone.

So then, Ford picks me up at eight and we are off to the gallery opening. The gallery, it turns out, is not really a gallery. It's a storefront, abandoned in the wake of this town's recent scourge, the country's thrall with urban renewal. We are not happy here with urban renewal. The wide arc of its great iron wrecking ball wiped from the face of our town a good number of fine old buildings, and in their place left us temporary structures. That is the government's term for them, temporary commercial structures. They are actually just low-slung tin trailers, in which local merchants make do while we wait for a grand new multi-tier mall to throw us into its grim urban shadow. We thought it could not get worse. But then in place of our lovely old downtown alleys, with all the intrigue and refuse and back entrance they allowed, we were given a bricked-over promenade, where now the homeless camp out, and lost tourists convene, and teenagers roam free range.

No, we are not fans of urban renewal, mere thought of it knocks us off topic and leaves us speechless or sputtering. I have only mentioned it here to explain why we have empty storefronts, still awaiting their own demolition, right in the middle of town. And why Ford's graduate art students are now holding an opening in one of them.

It is an oddly cheery place for an opening, this store, considering that it's condemned. From far down the block, we see bright-colored lights shining hopefully from its plate-glass window. And as we draw near, we hear music and people laughing. It sounds like a very big turnout.

At the door we stop, look in through the glass at the backs of them, men and women, standing fashionably, artfully dressed in drapey dark clothes, plastic cups of beer in their hands. A young crowd, I can tell, younger than I. Well of course. Ford's graduate students, undergraduates too, maybe a few junior faculty. Budding artists all of them as well. I can only imagine how little we'll have in common.

"After you," Ford says, opening the door and bending in a gallant low bow. I blink at the spotlights behind him, and take a quick look around. Not for the art, which, as I'd guessed, is large, predictable, and cartoonish, also hung from the walls by fish wire. Not for some face I might recognize since, with the exception of Ford, I know no one in town still in art, no one in school, no one, that is, who would think to come to a graduate student art opening. And not even for the refreshments that I know must be near. The keg of beer from the corner grocery downtown, Blue Jim's, whose owners rarely check IDs. Or the long folding table set to one side, filled with homemade hors d'oeuvres on paper plates.

No, one foot in the room, what I am looking for now is the possibility of a side door, with luck by the restroom down a long hall. And beyond that, the hope of a remaining back alley. It is never too early at large parties, I have learned, to plan one's nearest escape route.

"Ford!" a young man calls from center room right. "Ford! Oh look, Ford is here!" he calls, now to the room in general. Heads turn our direction, Ford grins and waves, his arm held high. He is known here, of course. Ford is a perpetual attender of galas, aspiring tenured faculty as he is. Not to mention real working artist among this sea of grad student poseurs. He has tonight, I have only just noticed, dressed himself well for the part, retaining his workday paint-spattered boots and artfully oil-smudged jeans. Only his shirt is clean, although it is old, a blue chambray with frayed sleeves rolled. Working-artist, painter-in-oils, too-passionate-to-change-just-for-this is written all over him. It must be consoling to the others to see one so clearly defined.

Dropping his arm, remembering me again, Ford turns and asks would I like a drink? He can go find me a beer. "Why yes," I tell him. "Yes, Ford, a beer." And I know then I won't see him for the rest of the night, or for as long as I plan to stay. It will work out well for us both.

So I turn to look for that side door, there must be one some-where, all these old buildings have a second way out. I ease past tight circles of students, I am heading for the back wall. But the room is crowded and after I have squeezed by the first of the young artists and a second group of mere hangers-on, judging by their styleless black sweaters, I find there is no clear path forward.

I stand facing the backs of several young men, heads turned in toward each other the better to hear, telling rank stories from life-drawing class and periodically loudly guffawing. I wonder how I can make myself heard.

"Excuse me," I say. "Sorry, coming through." I tap at the near-est shoulder. And turning, mistaking me no doubt for his date, someone he must have only just met and has clearly already for-gotten, the man hands me a cup of beer.

"Here," he says, "I got this for you," and turns back to his fellow storytellers.

The cup is cold in my hand, the beer fresh and still foaming, and I realize just how thirsty this party has made me. I spot a small folding chair to the side, next to an empty wall, and think better of abandoning ship. At least not so soon or directly. First refresh-ments, I think. Refreshments before escape, to be sociable.

I sit down and take a drink of my beer. While it's indeed one of Blue Jim's, it is also tastier than I'd remembered, and for a while I just sit and look at my cup, happy to have found a seat.

But then, gradually, it begins to dawn on me. The floor, what's with this floor? Looking down as I am, I notice that something is off at my feet. With so many people crowded into the store, I could not in fact earlier see much of it. But now, with this space opened up here around me, I see that each of the floor's large checkerboard tiles has been painted with some sort of symbol. Black paint on white, white paint on black. Angular, sticklike symbols. The floor vibrates with their bold strokes. And I see then the reason there's no art on this wall is that it has moved instead to my feet. The tiles of this floor are the point here, a kind of graduate student installation, an art stealth attack from below.

I study the primitive markings. One vertical line, two branches rising off it, a skeleton grasping at the sky. A capital A with a circle above it, a mountain balancing the sun. A small frail cross made out of sticks, dazed and skewed to one side. A capital P drawn in three straight lines. A thunderbolt. An M. A backwards R. Now foreground, now background, now black white, white black. All pulsing the store's linoleum. It is a dizzying dance below. Patterns emerge, a sequence, repetitions, and I find I cannot stop staring.

"Runes," he says.

He Watches

She sits, head down. "Runes," he says again. "What you're looking at, they're runes. Or somebody's idea of them."

He surprises himself. He has spoken to no one tonight. He knows no one here. He does not know what made him go to her and speak. It was not like him. But so much now is not like him.

He has been watching her since she entered. A tall woman. People notice tall women, but that isn't it. Something, maybe the way she is smiling, but not smiling. Attractive, in her way, and smiling. Standing next to the tall man, also smiling, then laughing and waving to the others. People know the man, he is happy to be here. But the woman is not. She smiles again and doesn't, looks past the man. She is not really here.

Attractive woman, yes. He would say that. Unusual, wild sort of hair, rust color, gold. The room's spotlights catch in it, gleam. A tall woman, leaning now toward the man, her head to one side to hear him. He likes that she doesn't look at him, keeps her eyes on the room. Nice eyes, dark, open. Frank. And that smile. He thinks he sees something there. As though maybe. Maybe.

It quickens his heart. Something like hope. You know, he wants to say to her. Don't you?

He watches the man leave her side, watches as she stands for a moment, then starts working across the room. He likes how she moves. Gracefully dipping, easing around the others. Stopping near one side. There, she's found a chair. She sits. No longer the smile.

Out of habit he takes the small notebook from his coat, begins to sketch. She stares at the floor and does not move. He studies her profile. Strong definition, good bones. And she's a bit older, he sees that now too, a little older than the others in this room.

She does not belong here. She sits alone. It makes him want to go to her.

Runes

Runes?

I keep my head down, look at the floor. I do not know this man now standing here. I do not know where he has come from. But I know this. He has been watching me, I have felt it. He has been watching for some time now.

It is in most women, I think, this signal that a man is staring. It's an alertness, a cellular response, chromosomes pointing like a pack of trained hounds at some treed and hyperventilating quarry. Some kind of mating sixth sense. Women do not need to see the man staring to know. Although I can indeed see this new one before me, that is, the hems of his pants. I can see where they meet the tops of his shoes. And I can see he is not wearing socks.

I am interested all right, but I do not yet lift my head, I do not stare this new man in the eye. The fact is, it just now feels nice to be watched. It is not often lately I am ogled, and for the moment I am enjoying it.

"Runes," he says again. "Ancient alphabet. Norse, Anglo-Saxon. Inscriptions mostly. Charms. Curses, maybe."

I study the floor more closely. Lines vibrating on linoleum. That's what I see.

"Supposed to bring back the dead," he offers. "If you do it just right. Find just the right runes."

I look up. And I am surprised. He is older, not like the others here, like Ford's student friends. Older but not old, a big man with unruly gray hair cut short to his head. A handsome man, strong. Now backing up, unsure.

"Bring back the dead?" I say. "Some alphabet."

He smiles. He looks at me, just looks. I do not miss the kind smile, the good green eyes.

Coffee

"Bring back the dead?" she says.

She looks wary. He has frightened her. He has offered too much, too soon.

Doesn't matter, he says to her, shrugging. And then he wants to say more. He has questions. He wants them to talk.

But the room is too crowded, too loud. He can't think. "Look," he says. "Want to leave?"

She studies him. What does he mean?

The words came out wrong. All his words are coming out wrong. A moment more and it will be over. One of them will say well, enjoy the show and then she will stand, find the tall man she came in with, disappear.

All he knows is he wants it not to be over.

"Want a beer?" he asks, forgetting she already holds one. "There's the Hogshead. We could go have a beer."

It is all he can think of, the Hogshead. He thinks it's still here. Dark, knotty-pine. She might like it.

She frowns. "No, not the Hogshead."

She says it quickly. Sets her jaw, looks back at the floor. Again he has said something wrong. He shouldn't have asked. Why did he ask?

She sits, she is quiet. It is over.

"Sure OK," he says. He tries not to make it sound like retreat.

She looks up. "Coffee," she says. "How about coffee?"

Joe Trout

But now "Margaret? Margaret?" I hear. And I realize it's editor Celeste, demanding and dire, at my door. Celeste now with something important. More immediate than daydreams of Ben.

Blinking, head down, I do not right away answer. Instead I reach for the flat before me, eye there the middle column, lift and adjust it a pica to the right, as though I need just to finish this one last thing before I can be interrupted. Another nudge to the column back left. Then at last looking up, "Oh, Celeste," I say, surprised. "It's you." And smiling, as though happy to see her, albeit a little dazed, engrossed in my work as I have been, "Come in, come in," I tell her.

"I'm here about Joe," Celeste says.

Again I look surprised. And this time I actually am. Celeste does not often stop by about work. Certainly not about Joe or his eponymous and gifted series. And I wonder then if she's concerned about him or his trouble with the Trout Route. If she knows he's been acting strangely. One could venture even a bit fishy. Which, put that way and also to be fair, would not normally be an issue.

That is to say, Joe Trout is just that, a trout. Of the rainbow variety, *Oncorhynchus mykiss*, native to the American Northwest. He spends his days swimming small freshwater streams and is an uncommonly handsome fish fellow, silvery and spotted and magnificently finned with a soft pink tinge to his belly.

A creation of Celeste's, Joe heads up our gifted and talented texts. His series are the Project's most prodigious, also—due to

Celeste—its most florid. Each week she turns out a new install-ment or two; it's hard keeping up with her layouts.

Celeste calls her series the Joe Trout Adventures in Science and, in a stroke of basal innovation, along with a string of the usual phonemes she has introduced actual content. Joe's stories aren't just tales of vowel phonic patterns; he also takes on natural science.

We at the Project are agog. We'd no idea Celeste had it in her. Celeste is a dreamer, a devotee of New Age, of meditation, levita-tion, crop circles. A follower of Ram Dass, Tim Leary. An attender of Esalen and Findhorn. Who knew she knew scientific method?

And here a professional confession of sorts. Although I am hired just to paste up Joe's flats, to wax and lay out and rub down, for months now I've also been reading his text, word by every overwrought word. In this spring alone, I've seen him through numerous exploits in science—cell fission, migration, an entire Krebs Cycle—as well as diphthongs, sibilants, and hard g's.

But it is not Joe's subjects per se that engage me. My interest comes down to just this: Joe Trout. Despite Celeste's own in-authenticity, Joe is good, even heroic company, well worth my morning reads. Joe's heart is pure. He is hardworking, coura-geous, a good sport, and a tireless champion of nature. Moreover, or at least normally, he's a seeker of beauty and truth along with, at times, paired vowels. Master of strategic "ou," "ee," and "ea," he cleaves his streams on a quest—coming in, going out, turning about, seeking the unseekable Trout Route.

But just this morning, as I sat at my light table finishing Joe's latest boards, a particularly hazy lesson on weather, I could see things were slipping with Joe. He was not his old driven self. His stroke had turned flaccid, his smile bemused, and his paired vowels had dropped off considerably, softened to "moon" and "croon." Most alarming, as I have mentioned, Joe somehow had lost the Trout Route. Or given up seeking it entirely. Instead, his direction was decidedly leisurely, it was this morning a desultory float.

Then, as I burnished the lesson's last galley, a short unit on storms, and a large dark cloud passed over, a strange thing happened indeed. Joe rolled dorsal, took a breath, and floating in this position, started to move his lips. It was a kind of fishy low hum, you could tell, which he seemed to want to keep to himself. But as thunder and lightning began moving in, Joe's hum escaped his control. Growing continually now louder and bolder, it began to look something like song. Until, as the sky grew darker and the downpour let loose, Joe Trout appeared to as well. With his head thrown back and mouth open wide, he began belting out musical numbers. Show tunes, specifically. "Singin' in the Rain." Also "Come Rain or Come Shine." It was as if he'd completely forgotten himself, not to mention his station.

It is not at all like Joe Trout. And I wonder again if Celeste sees it too. If she realizes this wrong turn Joe is taking.

"Margaret," Celeste says, "about Joe."

I return to my board. I keep working. It is not my place to turn in Joe. Celeste is the series editor here. Still something, I know, must be said. So reaching again for my burnisher, "Yes, Celeste," I say. "I've been meaning to speak with you too."

Drifting past me, Celeste fails to acknowledge. She heads for my desk where I have stacked a few boards and takes a long, close look. "The thing is," she says, "I would like to know what you think of Joe Trout. I'm afraid he is getting away from me."

"You are?" I say. I turn toward her. Once again I'm surprised. Normally Celeste keeps Joe close to her peasant-stitched vest. She is not one to solicit comments. But here is my chance. I have to speak up. Who else here will level with her?

I take a breath. "Celeste," I begin.

"Hmm," Celeste says, not listening. She fingers a board, tilts her head, considers a line drawing of Joe.

She studies the art, then suddenly blanches. "Oh Margaret!" she says, gasping. "Look here! Just look what she has done now."

Celeste stabs a long finger at Joe's large trout head, mouth open in his new list toward song. "It's Emmaline again." She is sure of it.

I stare as though I do not know what she means.

Celeste holds up the board. "See what she's done to his lips, Margaret?" she says. "She's redrawn his lips, the lips are all wrong."

I get up from my table, take a look. And I am going to bring up another point then, that in the flat that she holds Joe is singing. That's the reason his mouth looks like it does. He is opening it wide in song. Although, I will add, as tactfully as I can, the text is not all that clear why. I'm pretty sure trout aren't known for their voices.

But I look at Celeste and realize she has somehow not caught all this, at least not the part about singing. Which does of course raise the question of just who is writing this series.

Celeste taps at the board again. "Just look, will you, Margaret," she says. "Joe's mouth reaches all the way back to his eyes. It's frightening, really, I tell you. What will the children make of it?"

She sighs. "Whatever will we do with our Emmaline?" Apparently now the issue with this flat is all our Emmaline's fault. Although I still think Celeste is missing the point here.

She stares at the board a moment more. Then, "Say, Margaret," she says, and she brightens.

She looks up to see I am watching her. "Do you think, Margaret," she says, "you could fix him? Maybe re-ink his lines just a little?" She points to the mouth. "It just wouldn't be right to send Joe away to the printer like this." She leans forward, lowers her voice. "And let little Emmaline win."

She smiles sweetly. She does not wait for an answer, she only stands up straight and gives me a pat. "Thank you ever so, Margaret," she says. "It is so fortunate to have paste-up in-house." Then with a wave and a swish of her gauzy full skirt, she turns, headed early, no doubt, for her tub.

I wait until I hear her office door close, then take out my Rapidograph and blade. I scratch at the clay coat of the paper and put Joe's lips back where they belong.

Still, this little patch does not change the drift Joe has taken. Joe Trout is floundering, it's clear. He has abandoned his phonics, his science—indeed his quest for the crucial Trout Route. As signs go, none of this bodes any good.

Right

He stands in his landlord's plowed furrows. Breathes in, smells the earth. Knows it's good. Good he's come back, good he is here.

He picks up a small stone, throws it far. Watches it arc, fall to ground. And knows now he longs to start over. To put his thoughts straight again. Find what was lost, the hunger once felt, the sureness he'd felt as well. Wake before light, feel hope. Know again what the next step will be. Know it will turn out right.

He looks to the end of the landlord's wide field and thinks yes, maybe here he'll begin.

Ghosts

With Celeste out the door and Joe's mouth back in place, I check the clock. There is still time before lunch for a little more of Ben. I would like now to get back to Ben. About how we first met and the happy parts. About where that first coffee of ours led.

But before I can take that particular bent, I hear a crash from Celeste's suite next door. And from my table see her run into the hall, waving a galley overhead.

"Look here, oh my god, come look here," she shrieks. And at that the other editors appear at their doors. "Just look at what's happened now." Then gathering all of us to her, "See there," she says. "There in the next to last line." She holds up the end of the galley "A typo!"

At which point we all start to relax. We know about Celeste and her typos. She can be prickly about transpositions.

But "No!" Celeste's voice rises higher. "There was no typo when I came in today. I checked that galley just this morning. But now at noon—look there," she says, giving the galley a slap. "You see what has happened, don't you? Whoever, whatever it was changed that 'r' in the last line to 'd.'"

Celeste stops, breathes in, collects herself. Then lowering her voice and offering an instructional shiver, "The word is supposed to be 'room,'" she says. "At the end of the story, Joe Trout is supposed to go off to his room."

Celeste holds the galley back up for us. She takes a second look herself. Then shrieking again, "But now that 'r' has turned into a 'd'!"

The editors recoil. But Celeste just goes on shrieking. "It's Emmaline, again. Don't you see?"

And then she stops, takes another long breath, and adds, "Or maybe one of the others."

Which is to say, we are haunted here at the Project. Some days Celeste cannot get it out of her mind. Really, we think, she should have adjusted by now, she has known of the hauntings since we all first moved in. Still, "Shh," she'll whisper and sit up very straight, interrupting whoever is speaking. "Footsteps in the hall— Who's there?" Or then suddenly pointing to a window and turning shockingly pale, "Good god," she will cry. "That face just now at the glass. We're four stories up. My god!"

Nor does she leave it at that. Frequently, to remind us all of the seriousness of our situation, she'll point to other signs. The mysterious cold spots in the hallways and suites. The rushes of wind over desktops, the sometimes sulphurous smell to the air. Or the strange noises at dusk, the loud gargling, then the unexplained banging, the moaning.

The series editors pay attention to Celeste. She is someone who knows about ghosts, they believe, a true student of the afterlife. If Celeste saw a face at the window—well, most likely there really was one. Celeste's just more attuned than the rest. More here/now, as she would say.

It's unsettling indeed, this ghost or possible ghosts that Celeste insists upon sighting. Still she thrills, I have noticed, to the thought of them. The editors thrill just a little, too. They never know what new mayhem awaits, even when it's not footsteps or floating faces at glass. Not all sightings are so dramatic. Some days they amount to mere office pranks. "Look, Joe's mouth moved!" That sort of thing. Editorial outtakes, that's all.

But Celeste bears none of it lightly. The typo just now, for instance. "You know," Celeste whispers before we disband, not leaving us to our own conclusions, "ancient Greeks said the dead know the future. They can tell you your fate."

And then nodding again at the typo of doom and clamping her hand to her cheek, "My god, think what those ghosts are saying."

The editors listen to Celeste wide-eyed. But I myself am of another mind. Celeste needs to rethink things, I think. It is only ghost stories, not ghosts, here at play. Celeste's signs are just things she believes that ghosts do. My guess is Celeste's typo was in fact always there. She's just looking for an excuse to have missed it.

And besides, I say to the editors, it's old news, this haunting of Elmwood. All sanatoriums are haunted, there is some sort of rule. And if we were more of a profitable mind here, we'd be charging for midnight flashlight tours.

The fact is, people like to be frightened, I say. It just makes life a little bigger. We here, for instance, like to think we have ghosts, as without them we'd just be text editors. Without ghosts there'd be only the ordinary.

Still there is one ghost, this ghost Celeste calls Emmaline, who is starting to try all of our patience. In the last few months, she seems to keep coming up on our floor, these past days more than ever. Or so Celeste believes. I, however, have my doubts. "But Celeste," I tell her, "it cannot all just be Emmaline."

Celeste says well yes, it can. It is Emmaline who's at fault here, yes of course. And she says then Earnest, the janitor, has seen her. "You don't have to believe me, just ask Earnest."

I nod. I say I'll look into it, as though maybe I just might. But what Celeste doesn't know is I've already heard all about our young Emmaline. Earnest filled me in several weeks ago now, soon after he'd come back from retirement. It was on a night I got caught in overtime—something I don't make a practice of—but we were behind on our annual report. Steinem had dragged with the executive letter, so I had to stay late doing paste-up in hope of making our deadline by dawn.

I was in fact just burnishing the last of the letter and beginning to size Steinem's photo when a shadow moved over my light table.

"Earnest?" I say. "Is that you, Earnest?"

"The girl in the nightie who jumped," he says. "She was one of the screamers here."

I look up. "Thought you would want to know," he says.

And I realize then I am caught. So I put down my burnisher and "Jumped?" I say. "She jumped?"

Earnest leans on his mop. "Jumped. Yes," he says. Then halting in places as though to recall, he continues. "Young girl, very pale. I remember her now. Small, quiet, kept to herself. You wouldn't take her for a screamer. But one day she came back from the treatment wing wrapped up in a bloody sheet, and it was never the same with her after."

Earnest sighs loudly. "Jumped," he says. Then he walks to my balcony to show me.

He points to the ground below. "Right there," he says. "There, where they've paved over for parking. She landed right there with her neck twisted around and they took her away in a basket."

Earnest turns from the balcony, he looks old. I nod and return to my paste-up. The night is late, and I think Earnest has finished his story.

"But there's something else you should know," he says. And I can hear him shambling his way back to my table. He leans in then over my shoulder and his voice drops to a raspy whisper. What he has to tell me, he says, is something for only my ears. He never knows when it might be close and it is better it doesn't hear.

"'It,' Earnest?" I say, still burnishing.

"The ghost. That girl in the nightgown. She's still here, you know."

I lift my head and find Earnest has taken a step back. He stands now, staring, waiting.

"There are no such things as ghosts, Earnest," I say. Which I feel obliged to point out, although something about Earnest lurking there in the dark makes me less confident of the fact than by day. "You are now just making things up."

"Believe what you like," Earnest tells me, shrugs, and continues. "Me, I seen her. Little thing, drifty, long silvery hair. She stays mostly just on the fourth floor, there by that balcony where she jumped. I tell you I don't much like mopping up here alone."

And then he pulls up a chair, sits down, and tells me more of the story.

The night that it happened, he says, they had made up her bed on the balcony. Back then, they thought air was the answer, fresh air, so everyone, even screamers, slept out of doors. In winter with furs on their beds and their feet stuffed in boxes of straw.

Earnest continues. The nurse attending that night said the girl just wasn't right. Her fever was back, she didn't know where she was. She lay restless and writhing for hours. Then well past midnight, without any warning, she got up out of her bed like she was sleepwalking. The night nurse stood too, but before she could stop her, the girl was up on the balcony ledge, holding her arms out wide.

Just like an angel, the nurse later said, dressed as the girl was in her nightclothes. And then just like an angel, the girl lifted up to her toes and smiling, tipped out into the night. The nurse couldn't reach her in time. The girl fell face first all those four floors and landed with a sickening sound.

I wince here a little. I do not like to think of that sound. But I believe this time Earnest is finished, so "It is a sad story, all right," I tell him. And I start to go back to my board.

Earnest holds up his hand to stop me. "But it wasn't the way the nurse told it. The girl wasn't sleepwalking that night."

And here Earnest gives me a look. "Something else made her jump. Something out in the night was calling her."

He stands.

"That little one in the nightie, you watch out for her," he says. "She'll be calling to you now too."

Earnest nods once toward the balcony. Then he picks up his mop and is gone.

Three

Editors' Lunch

But now it is noon, and Frances is in the hallway calling us out for lunch. It is something the editors and I do, we take lunch here together in the cafeteria. We most of us would go elsewhere if we could. The sanatorium's food service is resolutely uninspired and, what is worse, they insist on feeding us in the basement.

This last part is not all the food service's fault. When our building was still a sanatorium, it housed a large dining hall on the first floor, an elegant, sunlit place next to the building's little theater. But now Continuing Nursing has taken over the hall and divided it into meeting rooms. The continuing nurses are fond of assembling, they have annexed the theater for it as well. And as a result, the sanatorium's cafeteria has withdrawn to the basement floor.

It is a dark and moist space to dine. To get there from where the elevator lets off, we must walk through long halls with low ceilings and giant, exposed metal pipes. Where it is not just the visuals that affront. Although the food service tries to disguise it, the place has the smell of a laundry room, an odd mix of mildew and bleach. I am sure it is where in the old days they washed blood from tubercular sheets.

Or blood from the gurneys they ran through the steam tunnel below. Back in the day, Earnest says, they called that tunnel the death chute. Or so Earnest says. It is another one of his stories.

Since the sanatorium was built, that tunnel has served a purpose. Steam flows through big pipes there and heats the sanatorium all winter. But the tunnel is large, a tall man can stand up in most places, five people can fit across, and soon enough the sanatorium figured out steam is not all the tunnel is good for.

For instance, the cafeteria these days uses it as a kind of back door. The tunnel leads a long way underground and at the train tracks behind our building, there's an entrance like two large cellar doors. It's where trucks stop every week with deliveries, crates of eggs, sacks of flour for our meals, which kitchen workers haul back in through the tunnel on the sanatorium's old hospital gurneys.

But then again, years ago, when people came to the sanatorium mostly just to die, "Wasn't all eggs they wheeled through that tunnel," Earnest says. "Used to be bodies, going the other way."

Earnest explains: The directors who ran the sanatorium then didn't much want all the dying to be known. Bad for business they said, bad for morale. They didn't want other guests feeling downbeat, what with the hearse always out in the drive. So aides laid the dead bodies on gurneys instead and rolled them out through the tunnel, loaded them onto Pullmans, and sent them all home by rail.

Earnest's stories, as I've said, run to the macabre, and as usual the editors and I ignore him. When we lunch together in the cafeteria here, we try not to think of our provenance. Rather, we make a point of being informative. That is to say, the series editors take every opportunity they can to talk at length about themselves. Or about their latest romance. The editors all are single, they are forever coming up with new men.

"So much the better for romance," Lola says today as we take our places at table.

Lola, who has a generous heart but the underbite of a sea bass, could not actually be called good-looking. She is instead mostly large—over six feet of strong healthy bones, great aquiline nose, tree-trunk ankles and legs. Even Lola's voice is ample, a booming West Texas drawl that stops conversations in crowds and seems to turn in particular the heads of short men. "Them li'l cowboys jes take to me," Lola says. "Flies to manure," she adds, throws back her head, and guffaws.

Frances studies Lola from across the table. She lights a cigarette, stares. Frances is a hard woman, we all think. Celeste says it's because she is fat, well pretty much going on obese, there is no other way to put it. It's what makes Frances generally ill-tempered, we believe, although oddly, ominously serene. When trolling our halls, she does not walk so much as she glides—well, a cross really between glide and lumber—a menacing half smile about her.

Her stillness is unsettling to us here. In meetings, for instance, she sits back from the rest, holding that cryptic smile, lights her cigarette, and waits. Then if someone on staff makes a mistake, says well, it just seemed like precipitous behavior to her, always Frances strikes. She sits forward, leans toward the speaker. "You mean precipitate, don't you now, dear? Precipitate behavior," she will say. "Precipitous is for cliffs, don't you see?"

But now Frances considers Lola's comment on romance. About the necessity always of new men. "Agreed," she says, and leaves it at that.

We at the table are surprised. It is not like Frances to concede. But after she stands then to go back for seconds, Lola asks us so, did we know? Lately Frances has herself been collecting men. "She has taken up tennis," Lola says, "for the exercise, she claims, for all that runnin' around at the net." But mostly, Lola thinks, it's because of the lawyers. "So many lawyers, you know, like their tennis," she says. "And some none too well hitched, neither."

Lola stops here and gives us a look. "Married lawyers in this town play singles," she says, and nods like she's sure Frances knows one or two.

"I see," Celeste says, looking uncomfortable.

Celeste likes to keep things positive. At forty-eight, she's our oldest by a decade and also our most pampered and frothy. Of the editors, you might say she's the pretty one. That is, if you had to choose one, it would probably be Celeste, she does at least try the hardest. She wears her hair down in long flaxen waves, she smells always of musk and patchouli, and thanks to a color consultant who said, "You, Celeste, are pre-Raphaelite," she dresses in long flowing silks and gauze. It's as though she were wearing drapes, Frances says.

Celeste generally ignores Frances. She thinks now a moment on what she can add to this topic of finding men. And steering away from the adultery option, Celeste offers a new example. "Or then there is Sally Ann," she says. "I happen to know Sally Ann writes long letters to men she has never met, whose names she finds through community outreach. It must be how our Sally finds her new ones."

As usual, Sally Ann has not joined us, Celeste is speaking for her in her absence. Sally Ann does not often come down to lunch and it happens we sometimes forget her. She is a small, slight young woman with one lazy eye and olive, acne-prone skin. She is also achingly, clinically shy. She keeps all day to her hospital suite, or, when it is absolutely necessary, scurries the halls, head down.

Sally Ann, like me, is not one of us, and when we are honest, we admit it's a relief she does not come down to lunch. Although we hasten to add it is not only because of her appearance. Sally Ann has one habit particularly distracting, unnerving even to those who know her. That is, in the last year now going on two, Sally Ann has taken up with a puppet. She calls him Bones or Mr. T. Bones, and it's as though they are going steady. Never mind that Bones is just an old sock with two cereal bowls sewn in for a mouth.

"Sally Ann," Celeste says, still on the topic of men, "primarily writes to convicts. She has been pen pals with prisoners for years." No doubt, she says, Sally Ann by now has won whole cell blocks of dark convict hearts.

Lola looks thoughtful and agrees that yes, it seems to work out for Sally Ann. And then, considering, she grins and says someday she may just try it herself. Lola has tried many things in her life, she is willing to try almost anything. She has for instance just signed up with a group called Match International, Inc. They put you in touch with immigrants, she tells us, all doctors and lawyers, professional men. Match Inc. is very particular.

In fact now, Lola says, she's seeing a Zairian statesman. An elegant man but shorter even than her others, he stands only up to her sternum. But then alluding to new possibilities there, "Lordy, lordy," she says laughing and slaps her thigh. "Ain't nothin' like a brand spankin' new lover."

Celeste looks at Lola, eyes big. She pretends to be taken aback. "Lola, how can you say such a thing?" As though she herself does not know about romance. How it necessitates always new lovers. But then giving it thought, "Or rather, I mean, Lola, how could you resort to a service?" Celeste herself has her standards.

And when we most of us look down at the table then and begin fooling with what's left of our lunches, Celeste turns and addresses us all. "So very well then—tell. How really do you find your new loves?" Truly, Celeste wants to know.

Class

His students wait in the studio at their worktables. It is their first day, they are excited, unsure. They look young to him, they grow younger each year. He counts. Only twelve. Good.

He has come to teach them painting. He is a teacher of painting, still life, life drawing. We are all artists here, he tells them. We are all, all of us, beginners. He looks into their faces. He knows they do not understand him.

He is visiting, on loan from a Western state. He is part of a university there too, Drawing and Painting, School of Art. He is faculty, tenured, he teaches. It is not enough. It has never been enough, he knows.

He has come for a year to teach color and line. To show students about light, about seeing. To help them work valiantly, honestly. To help them want to work more. And then he must leave end of spring.

He hasn't much time. He starts class.

He sets his students before easels. Explains about canvas, how to mix paint, the correct way to hold their brush.

The students look at him, ready to begin.

No, he tells them. Not yet.

He asks them to wait. Be still, he says. Now watch for it.

What? they ask. Watch for what? They do not understand.

He cannot tell them. He says only they must learn first to look, truly see. They must know before they begin.

Truck Stop

How do we find our new loves? I look down at the table with the others. I will not offer well here's how it was with Ben. Because, as I've said, he and I have an understanding, we have our oath of silence. Besides which, considering that Ben is gone, there's no point now in bringing him up, let alone explaining how I found him.

Still, head down as I am, I give it some thought, that night Ben and I first met. And then I am back to my daydreams.

I look up at him. "Coffee," I say, "how about coffee?"

He looks surprised. I myself am surprised, I do not know why I offer that, "Coffee." I do not actually feel like coffee. Nor should I be proposing it to this new man. Someone after all I have only just met and who could be, for all anyone knows, some well-mannered hatchet murderer drawn in by the lights and free food.

"Good," he says. "Coffee." Then "Ben Adams," he adds, and extends me his hand.

"Margaret," I say. And we shake on it.

He smiles very big, relieved. It is a wonderful smile, broad and true, and I think well we are going to be all right here. He cannot have a murderous heart, this Ben Adams. He is only as uncomfortable in this gallery as I, and it would do us both good now to leave. This loud room and its swarm of faux student artists are wearing on both of our nerves. We have had our fill of faux artists, I will say to Ben Adams over coffee.

We end up at the truck stop in town. Well actually outside of town, just off the highway that skirts our town limits. It's the only place I know that serves coffee this late, although it will not be good coffee, I warn Ben. They leave the pot sitting on some warmer all night, probably since the truckers first stop for their dinners. Truckers are notorious for their early dinners.

The place is empty when we arrive, and we take the big corner booth. The waitress doesn't mind, she tells us. It's not like she's expecting a big party to walk in and need to sit here or anything. She says she is not even sure why they put in a booth that sits eight if you squeeze in a little, considering most people, well truckers, usually come here alone. Unless maybe they've brought a buddy along to sit in the cab beside them. Or a wife, she has seen that too. But it's not like they come here to socialize, those truckers, mostly no one sits in this booth.

"Except young couples like you two," she says. Then she tells us now don't mind her, she'll just be in the back. We can help ourselves to a refill, it's free. And she gives us a wink, like she has seen us before, she knows we want to be alone.

Ben thanks the waitress, he makes it sound like he means about the refills. And when she is gone he says, "Sorry," as though it is somehow his fault the waitress thinks we're together. Then he takes a big drink from the mug she has left him and smiles and tells me, "Good place," as though I have chosen it especially for its coffee.

He is a kind man, this Ben Adams. He does not mock waitresses, there is that. I lift my mug in a little salute and give him a big smile back.

Ben sits, takes a look around. "Funny about truck stops," he says. "You only go to one when everything else is closed. Which means you don't normally go at all. But they're OK, truck stops. Quiet."

"Big improvement," I say. What I mean is over that storefront. "What were those art students thinking?" Renting a one-room store for a show? And then inviting all of their friends. There was not even enough space for the paintings, let alone all their guests and dates. "Those artists need to be more selective," I say. And then I tell Ben how before urban renewal, a man used to sell magazines in that shop. There was just enough room for a few newspaper racks, some postcards, and a back counter for wind-up toy dildos.

"The Dead Eye," Ben says. "I remember the place."

"You do?" I look at him. "Funny, I don't think I have seen you around."

"No, I mean I remember from before. When I was a student here." Ben gives his coffee a stir. "A long time ago."

"Oh," I say. "Student." And I look at him and try to think would I have known him then. But Ben is older than I am, I can see that. We could not have been here the same time.

"In art," Ben says, and gives me a little smile. "When I was a graduate art student."

"Oh," I say again. And try to think what I have just said about graduate art students. How much I have already offended.

"You're right, by the way, about too many paintings. We did it too, we all painted like madmen then too. Like somehow it mattered. Like people needed to see what we saw."

"Well," I say, just to make it clear, "that's all right. Painting is OK." I do not say how I once painted too. "I just do not care much for the shows," I say. "Too hot, too crowded." And without meaning to I give a grim little scowl.

He smiles again. "Your friend's idea?" Like that's why I came, like I have a boyfriend in the art department so I had to come too.

"His idea," I agree. And then "Ford," I say. "His name is Ford. He asked me to come because his date didn't show."

Again Ben looks surprised. I did not need to go into detail.

"So, what brought you out?" I say, adroitly changing the subject.

Ben smiles and says oh just a whim. He was downtown, he saw the poster, he thought he'd drop by. Maybe see someone from the old days. "But I didn't know anyone. No one at all."

He reaches for one of the packets of sugar the waitress has left for us. Spins it once on the table.

"No, I mean what brings you to town?" I say. I am now just making conversation. The sugar-packet spinning I have seen before and it is making me nervous. Men do this I've noticed on first dates. Not that this is a date. It is just something I have noticed.

Ben goes on spinning the sugar. Then he looks up and says well, that's kind of a long story. "I'm teaching some art classes here. Painting, oil and acrylic. Normally, I teach somewhere else, but I swapped with a painter from here. It's a program they have, lets you try out a new place for a year." And then he tells me he's renting a farmhouse a few miles out of town. That this summer he started a garden.

"OK," I say. Like I agree with him.

OK? I am not making sense. But I have just now noticed something new, a major point I had previously missed. And I sit now staring, off balance.

The Personality

The editors, I notice, have gone silent. They sit at the table all waiting for me. I look up, Lola gives me a quick nod to the side, and I snap back to attention. Frances has returned. She has something new now to discuss, it seems, something important and unrelated to romance. She is ready to get down to business.

Shifting forward, she catches us in her reptilian bead and clears her throat for our attention. "You know," she says, striking a casual tone, "I heard from the Personality today."

The Personality? We at the table give a collective gasp. Hearing from the Personality can never be good. We all of us lean in.

Frances, gratified, continues. "She called to say she had heard from Steinem that our catalog was out—that our new readers would soon be available. And she wondered if she could get a review copy or two."

Lola, jaw jutting, looks concerned. "No," she says. "She didn't."

"She did," Frances says. "Calm as a cadaver, she asked for one of our books. That's what she said, 'Oh just something from your catalog.' Steinem told her I'd help her out."

"But—" Lola begins.

I shoot Lola a glance and nod in the direction of Celeste. And to distract us from going any further down this path of catalogs and upcoming readers, I join in and divert back to romance.

"The Personality," I say. "Now there's someone we haven't heard from for a while. Isn't she overdue for a visit?" Then I lower my voice and, although I know it's not likely, say, "Oh my gosh, do you suppose she and Steinem are through?"

I whisper the Steinem part. He would not like us talking about him. Dr. Steinem is a private person, also annoyingly good-natured—a short, slight, bald man in his fifties, who, except for an overly large head that in some light makes him look extraterrestrial, appears to be entirely of no interest. He is not one, that is, to suspect of true romance. Which is why it's not known at the sanatorium proper about Steinem and the Personality. Specifically, about their affair.

Or so we suppose that is what it is, given we have no real proof. Still, almost everyone at the Project believes it's an affair that they're up to, going on now for almost a year, ever since Steinem first contracted the Personality to make audio tapes for our series.

I should explain that we call her the Personality, or sometimes the TV Personality, only as our little code, in case Dr. Steinem is near. Actually the woman is Miss MaryBeth Malone. She's a well-known figure in children's TV and hosts a national show in L.A. She is also well-known for marrying a famous old crooner revered for his hits and a few feature films made during the Second World War. Most people would recognize the crooner and the name Miss MaryBeth Malone.

We have had visits at the Project from the Personality before, when she's flown in for one of the tapings. First she records at a university studio in town, then arrives by midday at the Project. The Personality is a small, handsome woman, probably pushing forty-five. Steinem himself, as mentioned, is small, and there's the matter of that large bald head. It is not clear what the Personality sees in him. But when he comes out to greet her in the fourth-floor foyer, and they stand there together, short and beaming, we all have to admit how much they appear the perfect little, if aging, wedding-cake couple.

Not that we then see much of them. Always they spend the rest of the day off in Steinem's office, always with the door firmly closed. The editors and I cannot say, therefore, we have in any way got to know MaryBeth. This does not in the least, however, keep us from disliking the woman.

Lola in particular seems to hold a grudge. It is, we all think, because of the crooner, that the Personality is cuckolding him. Lola has a thing for the crooner, possibly even a crush. She is, and points it out often, probably the man's number one fan. She has seen all his movies. She has each of his records, even the early hard-to-find Christmas ones. Long before the Personality came on the scene, Lola has been on the old crooner's side.

"You can tell about a man by his work," she says. "You watch a few of his films, you listen to any of his albums, you hear him sing 'O Come All Ye Faithful'—it just breaks your heart," she says. She cannot forgive the Personality for what she is doing to him.

Actually, Lola takes an interest in the crooner not just from his movies and albums. She tunes in as well every early December for his television Christmas special, with the crooner and Mary-Beth and their grandchildren. Well, actually, Lola says, MaryBeth and his grandchildren by a previous marriage. He wed MaryBeth later in life, she is twenty years younger than he and also happens to look great on camera. Together, they put on a fine show every year. The crooner always dons a red wool knit sweater and sings a few songs by the fire, with cutaways to MaryBeth listening sweetly nearby, fulfilled in the season of joy. MaryBeth is good at looking fulfilled, and when the camera moves in for a close-up, she has a way of tilting her head and contentedly closing her eyes that makes you think she might really love the old crooner.

The show moves on then, Lola says, and when her husband has finished another carol or two, there's usually one more cut to MaryBeth, this time with a book in her lap. The camera pulls back to show this, to show how she sits by the family's tree, her full-length taffeta red-plaid skirt spread out strategically around her. And then smiling and dropping her eyes to the page, she begins reading a Christmas story, something short and generally moving. She looks at the camera, Lola says, and pauses after most of the sentences.

Frances interrupts. "Yes, of course," she says. "We know all about that show, Lola. It was the Christmas show that sold Steinem on her." And then Frances quickly runs through the rest. How Steinem liked the way MaryBeth read by that tree. "Good pacing," he said. "The woman can certainly enunciate. Just the ticket for our new tapes." And then he gave her a call at her studio, offered her grant money the next day. And within the week, MaryBeth arrived here at the Project to negotiate her contract with Steinem.

"Negotiate, right," Lola says. And then says what all of us think, that most likely the affair began right then, MaryBeth's first day at the office. "It does throw a new light on the Christmas special," she adds, sadly shaking her head.

Frances coolly watches Lola. "Well, that may be," she says. Then straightening herself and getting back to the point, "But now the Personality wants to read our readers, don't you see?"

She turns, looks sharply at me. "Margaret, we must talk." And when I stare back at her like I have no idea why and try for a bemused sort of smile, she adds, "About that little secret of ours."

Secret? Good lord. I can't believe Frances brought up our secret. And in front of Celeste at that. It is something we don't speak of in public. Frances has got to know better. And I look at her now and I hold my smile dead hard on her.

To Paint Light

The students grow restless. They rush to paint, they do not first try to see. He knows he must stop them, slow them down.

He points them to paintings he was taught to teach. He brings in museum slides, throws images large and grainy on the walls. Stand back here, he tells them. Soften your gaze. Do you see?

This one, he says. Cathedral in morning light. The cathedral, its great doors, yes, but it is the light that you see. It is that one early morning. Look, he says. Do you see? Even now it is there, rising from that wall, the ghost light of that one day just beginning.

Imagine, he says. To paint light.

They stare. They do not understand.

He walks to a window, opens it wide. Then here, he says. Look. Look here. He points to the line of oaks just outside, the great oaks that circle their building, shielding it from the river.

Look. What do you see?

Trees, they tell him. Oak trees. Branches. And leaves. Black branches, black-green leaves.

Look harder, he says. What more?

Sky? someone says. There's sky.

He nods. And?

They stand, looking.

And light, he says. Do you see the light? There through the branches, through all the leaves, there. The trees are on fire with that light. It is the light that's to see, not the trees.

They look. They do not see a fire. They do not even know what they are looking for.

One day, he tells them, you will. When you are thinking of nothing at all, you will look up and you will see the light in the trees.

But how? they say. How will they know when they see it?

He smiles, says only that they will know. It will possess them, it will make them want to begin. So that then they must paint with all that is in them. It will pretty much be their one chance.

They do not understand.

You must paint what you saw, as you saw it. Not a copy, but

rather a moment, just that one instant you saw. And then you will understand painting.

He looks again at their faces.

The way in is the way out, he tells them.

They do not understand.

He closes the window. Turns up the lights. Asks them to return to their places.

Janice!

I hold my hard smile for Frances. I'm still angry, it's true, she has so casually brought up our secret, something on which our work lives depend. We do not any of us just go spilling the beans here. We're a team, after all: Steinem Associates, Unified. The point here is unification. If one of us slips and our secret gets out, most likely the whole Project is through.

That's how it is at the Project, Frances. Surely I don't need to remind her.

But I look now again at Frances and realize it is not easy smiling so hard for so long. My mouth is beginning to ache. And I realize besides that Frances is taking no notice. It is fruitless with Frances, I should of course know. She understands only what she chooses. And so while she and the others move on with their talk, I feel my thoughts move on as well, or rather, I should say, back again. Back to that packet of sugar, that is, and the crucial point I noticed as Ben spun it.

Which I should have caught right away of course, first thing earlier in the evening. It is an unfortunate lack of awareness on my part when encountering a new man socially—a disability of sorts, actually—and I have been trying for keener perception.

So now that night with Ben it occurs to me at last to stop and take a look. And there on his hand, the one with the sugar packet, there on the left fourth finger, there, after all, it is—a gleaming and gold wedding band. Gold, fat, and rubbed smooth as a river. He is married, this Ben Adams. Long married. I am having late night coffee with a long-married man.

Which need not change anything at all, of course. That is what occurs to me next. We are only just having coffee. We have only just met. Still, it is a new point, this wedding band, and something I will have to think over.

"I have two geese," Ben Adams says then. "A goose and a gander. On the farm where I rent."

I look at him, nod. But I'm still not fully attending. I am wondering instead so do I mention the ring, or maybe Ben Adams's wife? "Well now," I could say. "Doesn't your wife mind? About the geese, I mean. I would think they're a responsibility." It is the kind of thing women say, I believe, although I'm not really sure of the point. It may be only to acknowledge you've seen the ring, you know that this man is married. And that it's all right with you, all right. You yourself are just having coffee. It makes no difference at all if the man you are with just now all alone and getting to know and possibly like is in fact actually married. It is not that you have designs. You are only just having coffee.

I nod at Ben. "Geese," I say. "Yes. I've heard they are friendly birds."

We both of us just look down at our mugs. Ben gives his another swirl, I take a sip from mine. The coffee is cold. Well, we are probably both thinking about leaving.

But just then, the truck stop front door opens wide and "Janice!" a large man calls. He makes a wild-eyed scan of the room. "Janice, I know you're in here. Come back out to the car now, Janice."

Ben shoots me a look. We are the only ones here in the truck stop, the man at the door must see this. "Oh-oh," Ben says to me, low.

Our waitress appears from her back room. "Larry," she says. "Now calm down there, Larry."

"I've lost Janice," the man says to our waitress. He lowers heavily onto the counter's end stool, bows his head, and with no further notice, starts to sob.

"Larry, Larry," the waitress says. She goes to him, rubs the top of his head.

The man's back and shoulders are heaving. "Janice," the man cries, "Janice. Where is Janice?"

"There, Larry," the waitress says. "Shh. It's all right."

The large man lifts his head to look at her. From our booth we can see his face is swollen and red, soaked wet from the tears. And we can smell the alcohol on him.

Ben stands, walks over. "Need help?" he says. It's not clear if he's asking the waitress or Larry.

"It's OK," the waitress says. "It's just Larry. He comes in a lot. When it gets bad, I just call the cops."

Larry places both arms on the counter, leans forward, drops his head. He lies then, chest and face on the counter

"It's his wife," the waitress says. "He just misses his wife, that's all."

The waitress turns to check Larry, who has now gone into a moan. She turns back to Ben. "She left him. Gone almost a year now. Larry just can't seem to get used to it."

Ben nods, watches Larry. Then moving in, he stands and places a hand on his shoulder. The large man still moans. Ben does not move, he says nothing, he holds on. And after a while Larry quiets down. Leaning closer, Ben says something into his ear. And you can see then from the man's back he relaxes.

Ben stands over him watching. The waitress watches too. And then, "Thanks," she says, smiling, like she can take it from here. "I'll let him stay. He'll just sleep now, we'll be fine."

Ben comes back to our table. He offers to drive me home.

On the way I think to ask him, "So what did you say to that man just now?"

Ben keeps his eyes on the road. He gives a little shrug. "Nothing much."

I watch Ben drive. He can feel it, I guess, because in a little while more, "I just told him I know."

I look at Ben's profile. You do? I am going to ask. But Ben is still watching the road and I can tell from the way he seems now, faraway, alone, that probably Ben does, he knows.

We drive on pretty much silent the rest of the way. The evening is definitely over here. And once in town, I just direct us to Mott Street and then quickly point out my house. Although it is not all that late, I will of course not be asking Ben in.

But at the curb, when I am out of his truck and thanking him for the ride, "Margaret," Ben says, like he's just had an idea. He leans over and looks up to where I'm standing. "Have dinner with me tomorrow? I cook."

I am surprised. I hold the door open, I consider. The thought of Ben Adams's smooth wedding band does naturally cross my mind. A fact we have not yet discussed. But then "Yes," I say. "Yes, I would like that."

Which is true. I have decided I like this Ben Adams. He is someone I would like to know better. So "Yes," I say. "OK. I mean, thanks." And I write down and hand him my number.

The Plan

I sit thinking about this last part. How good and kind a man our Ben is. And I think again how Mrs. E is right. He has been missing for far too long. I really should find where he's gone. Which is to say, I must be off. I must go now and save Ben Adams. It could, after all, be just the thing that will end up saving us both.

But I know first I need a plan. For any good search and rescue, always there is a plan. Nothing happens without a plan.

And I make a few notes in my head:

1. To begin, I will need to find Ben.
2. Which naturally implies a search.
3. Which begins with probabilities, of course, searching first where probably Ben is.
4. Which occurs to me now is his farm.
5. His farm, well of course, that's where Ben is.
6. I will drive to Ben's farm now and search.
7. Well, no, not now exactly.

8. But just as soon as I am able. Right after work, for instance. Right after I get home today.

9. A new thought: I may have to use stealth.

10. If Ben had wanted to be found, he would not have gone missing in the first place.

11. Unless of course it was not his choice and he actually is in trouble.

12. In which case I will still need to use stealth.

13. So then, I will drive to Ben's farm unannounced.

14. I will look for him first at his house.

15. Then in all the outbuildings, the geese pen, the fields.

16. And should I at last discover him out in some furrow checking on crops, I will say oh Ben, oh Ben, so there you are.

17. So that's where you have been keeping yourself.

18. Well, how lucky of me to have found you.

19. Or something along those lines.

20. I will sound jaunty, as though I've not noticed we've been out of touch now for months.

21. I will act as though it is neither here nor there, all that time.

22. Now that he clearly is here.

23. Or rather, that I am there.

I think over my notes. Yes, it is a good start to my plan. The part about searching for Ben. I will indeed find the missing Ben Adams.

And once then I do, I will go into the rescue part. Which, frankly, I have yet to work out. Rescue is hard and will take more thought, maybe an additional plan. Or then again, I may just have to wing it. Because, to the point, just now I am anxious to start.

The reason being, there is need to hurry. First, of course, in case Ben is really in trouble. But also because time in general for us is running out. Ben's second semester is almost up. His year here is at a close, and I know Ben has plans not to stay. I must catch him now, before he leaves town. If for no other reason, I will tell him, so at least we can say good-bye.

Chaise du Jour

Luckily enough now, before Frances can go any further, Lola holds up her watch. "Well lookee here," she says. "Time we all light a shuck back to fourth floor." Somehow we've talked ourselves well past one.

We all rise and near the elevator doors, while Celeste is off pressing for up, Frances mercifully moves on from the Personality. Instead, watching Celeste as she saunters ahead, gauzy skirt freshly laundered and billowing, Frances cannot resist. "Celeste is certainly well cared for," she says to Lola, in a voice loud enough for all of us.

Celeste pretends not to hear, because now the elevator doors are opening. We all fit ourselves in and begin our slow ascent to fourth floor. We stand facing the front and we are all of us suddenly quiet. We remain like that for almost a floor, until from the back, when she can take the silence no longer, Celeste speaks up.

"So, Margaret," she says. "We haven't heard much from you today. Anything new with you?" It is of course just the quiet that's making her ask, Celeste has no actual interest. The editors in general have no interest in me, rarely do they ask anything personal. They do not, for instance, want to know over lunch about any of my new boyfriends, the assumption being that I have none. Still, to fill this little void the elevator has brought on, Celeste is asking me something now. It's a kind of last resort of the extroverts present when faced with communal silence.

I do not immediately answer, and as we near the next floor, "Well, so, Margaret," Frances says at my shoulder. I can feel her looking at me. And to encourage me then, I suppose, "Margaret, dear, Celeste asked you a question. Anything new? Any big date for the weekend?"

I try to think quickly. There is so much to say and really so little I can. I cannot of course bring up Ben here. The terrible fact he is gone.

We continue in silence. Still I can't think what to say. "Margaret?" Frances says. "Are you listening?"

From behind, I feel Lola give Frances a nudge. "Margaret don't like to talk much, honey." Then "Haven't y'all noticed?" she says to the group and pats me helpfully between the scapulas. Which only makes me think harder. Surely there is something I can offer. Surely I won't let myself need to.

I clear my throat. "Surely," I start to say. But I am spared then as the doors jolt open at fourth. And "Oh my," the editors all chime in at once. "Look! Chaise du Jour."

I study the foyer. It is Chaise du Jour, all right. Again. The editors are correct about that one. Right there as usual in our foyer.

Which, before we move on, calls for a note here of interest, not about chaises but foyers: This sanatorium is full of foyers. On each of the floors, in every wing, the elevators all let out at them. Yawning, rib-vaulted foyers. Though, to be clear, there were foyers before there were elevators. In the beginning, when the sanatorium was first built, it had only stairs. Everyone used what we now call the back flight, the staircase with brass rails that Earnest complains of polishing. To reach our wing in those days, people climbed up four floors and were ready enough when arriving here to sit for a while, catch their breath. Foyers were, for the times, a good idea.

But there was more to these Gothic old foyers. They were also where visitors were kept when calling on the tubercular. Outsiders were not allowed down the halls, they could not chat with patients in their beds. Though no one knew then the source of white plague, the smart money did not sit in small rooms with it. The foyers with their high ceilings and open wide floors made for safer and more sociable reunions.

Frances says well that was true for back then but it's now space that's just basically wasted. Frances would have redecorated a good bit around here. But Dr. Steinem had his own plans for our foyer. He made it into our receptionist's post, moved in a large desk, and stationed poor Marcie at it. Then, to make us look more important, we think, he brought in a dozen high straight-back chairs. As though we were expecting long lines of people, and they needed somewhere to sit down. But of course no one much ever comes up to fourth floor, our foyer is a waiting room in waiting. Or so it was until the first of last month.

Which brings me to Chaise du Jour. What the editors and I stand now facing.

Chaise du Jour started, I am pretty sure, by accident, it was not at first anyone's fault. Unless possibly the weekend janitors are to blame, the weekend janitors who are students at the university and strong enough to lift a few chairs. Certainly it was not our Tuesday-night Earnest, who is too old for the labor involved. No, it was probably some work-study student.

I imagine this is how it began. One Sunday night while vacuuming the foyer on our floor, this janitor, probably somebody new, a serious boy, bent on vacuuming all the way under things, moved a few chairs out of his way. And then, called off to a crisis on some floor below, to some louvered shade or drain suddenly jammed, he forgot what he'd been doing on fourth and left the chairs where he had moved them. Five foyer chairs all in a straight row, directly across from the elevator.

After that there was no going back, not after those chairs aligned. The next morning they got our attention right off, when the elevator doors first opened. Well, now. Look at that. Something was up at the Project. Normally those chairs sat demure, indistinct, in a conversational U near the back wall. It made us all laugh, those prim straight-backed chairs advancing like that in brigade, holding the line at the elevator. We all talked about it then over lunch. Those five chairs looked so odd, so out of their place, so rigid and alert in that single straight row. They were like some column of high-back sentries on lookout for attack by hoist. And they became our main topic of conversation all lunch, eclipsing even Lola's new squeeze who had us going the day before.

The chairs were still on our minds when we returned to fourth floor at one. Where to universal surprise we found the chairs had changed place once again. Though still in a row, now they were facing away from us, as if they had turned on their heels in one great group chair snit. Someone had moved them when no one else saw, it was even a better joke now. And each time then that day and the next, when one of us had reason to pass by them, the chairs had again rearranged. Marcie, who worked in clear sight of the chairs, hadn't herself a clue how. She is, truth be told, a great taker of breaks and often not at her desk. Meanwhile, someone was toying with our foyer.

It was Emmaline again. Celeste said it first. But by the end of the day, the others were all certain too. It was Emmaline, all right. Although, as Celeste pointed out, Emmaline would never herself let on. Still the editors all knew about poor Emmaline, that she sometimes grew restless and bored with our floor, that she sometimes just needed a change. We were happy she had found a small outlet. We were happy about the foyer chairs.

Because they have become, it turns out, our running office joke. They are something for us to look forward to. And even now, a month on, Emmaline still comes through. She has long since moved on from chair rows. Some mornings we come in to six chairs stacked straight up. Some days four lie on their sides. And once ten chairs formed a pyramid in the middle of the room like trick elephants coaxed up onto each other's shoulders.

"Chaise du Jour," Frances named the chair sculptures. After which an easel appeared, with large placards written in red, in what suspiciously looked like blood. Someone, Emmaline again naturally, we assumed, began captioning our Chaise du Jour. On Monday, two chairs set down facing each other, mirror-image; the placard: "Chair and Chair Alike." Replaced the next day by a single chair, a heart-shaped box of chocolates on its seat: "Mon Chair Amour." Followed on Thursday by two chairs again, one propped up against the other: "Sonny and Chair," which has remained pretty much our favorite.

But now today when the elevator doors open, we see Emmaline has taken a new, darker tack. The chairs line up grimly, all facing forward, and we give a collective little gasp. "Really," Celeste whispers, "she's outdone herself." Before us are not one, but three Chaises du Jour.

On the left, two chairs placed side by side, the back of each painted with a large red D; in the center two more chairs, the first painted 2, the second a capital B; on the right, one lone chair, another large red 2. Then in front of each display, an easel with placard.

For our benefit, Celeste reads them aloud, left to right:

D-Seats

Seats 2-B

B No More

"Oh no!" we all say and pull back. And I think well, of course, more bad omens. The editors catch them as well. And we just stay in the elevator where we are.

Except for Celeste, who, feeling responsible, feeling in charge, launches herself into the foyer. She gives a quick angry look once around. Then staring straight up at the ceiling, "Emmaline," she calls loudly. "That's not funny."

Studio by Night

He closes the door to the studio and leans back against it, listening to the silence. He loves it here evenings alone.

He breathes in, smells the linseed and solvent. Looks up. High ceilinged and limestone, the cavernous old room is perfect. In this room you step back, it is centuries ago within these stone walls. By day, its old skylights let in ancient sun, and at night galaxies revolve at the panes.

He brings his own canvas, his paints. Sets up alone. He has come for the painting. He tells no one. But at night, alone, he paints. The way in is the way out, he murmurs.

He works by starlight, or by the full moon. He finds his way in the painting.

Finding Ben

It's been a long day at the Project. All these visits from Emmaline and her ilk take a toll. As do the series editors. Too much talk of ghosts for one day, I think. And besides I have now more pressing business. I have Ben Adams to find. So on this afternoon's bus ride back into town, I'm anxious only to be off again to Ben.

And as soon as I'm home then, I climb into my car and head to his farm to find him. To find him and possibly save him. Or barring the need for the latter, at least have the chance to talk.

Ben rents a farmhouse ten miles out of town. You have to take back roads to get there, and if you do not have a good map your first trip, you will most certainly lose your way. But I myself know the route well, I have made many trips out to Ben's. And always I am happy to make the drive. Ben's farm is a splendid place once you're there, peaceful and quiet, with low rolling fields and a sky as wide as it's high.

Still, because it's a long drive and there is time now to think, and because after all I'm going to see Ben, I find once again I am thinking about him—once more about him and me.

The simple fact is, after our coffee early last fall, Ben and I began seeing each other. There was, first of all, our first dinner, something that I will get to. Followed by still other dinners, the beginning of our seeing one another. After which we decided it would do no harm, just now and then, seeing each other otherwise. It was a lovely time really, just seeing each other this fall.

We began dividing the visits between country and town, spending time at first at my house where Ben stopped sometimes after class. Although soon he began stopping on weekends as well. He would ask if maybe I had something he could fix, or repaint, or possibly just move. Maybe an old carburetor he could clean. Ben is handy, he liked having something to do with his hands. And when he was done with whatever small task I came up with, if the day was still warm I would fix us iced tea and we would drink it out in my backyard. Or if it was cold and raining, or, later, snowing, I would make a pot of fresh coffee while Ben stoked the fireplace in the front room. Then we would sit in our woolly socks on the floor and drink our coffee from big china mugs.

That is mostly how it went on Ben's trips into town. But the fact is I preferred visiting Ben at his farm. And not just for dinner, I liked seeing the farm in the day. I liked the long drive, I liked the back roads, the trees turning color, the heartening change of scenery. On the way, I'd open the car windows and sing.

And once arrived, I would spend a good part of my time just sitting out in his farmyard. The grass there this fall was spectacular, lush, and for a farmyard the air was clean. I would take little naps in that grass. I would lie back and sometimes, if there were breezes, if I happened just then to be lying in sun, things occurred to me that normally would not. Reveries, of sorts. I would think, for instance, how there should be great loads of laundry just now blowing in these magnificent breezes, the clothesline stretched from Ben's door to his flag. Overalls and work shirts, large white boxers, all on the line out drying. Everywhere chambray should be flapping.

And sometimes I would say, "Oh Ben, this is perfect. This place is where you belong."

Ben thought I romanticized things. "It's just an old farm, an old farmhouse," he said.

But I think there is more. Ben's farm is solid and it suits him. And although I knew in the spring he'd be leaving, although I did not tell him this next part, I would sometimes sit in the grass of Ben's farm and wish somehow he could stay.

So yes, you could say we were seeing each other, Ben and I. And the complication of course was that Ben is a married man. Something I've already touched on and something most people would not approve. But it was also not what most people would think. Ben and I at that point were just friends. I was seeing Ben Adams but we were just friends.

Well no, that isn't it either. Ben and I were not only friends. We were more, or maybe just else. Well, I do not think there's a term for what Ben and I were, especially in the beginning. The closest I came to were words just for Ben and even then I thought of him as hybrid. Part mentor, part swain, part ward.

It remains, however, that this man I was seeing, Ben Adams, was indeed a married man. A husband, a spouse, though thankfully nobody's father. It is a fact I had to remember. His wife's name, I learned, is Ellen, and until this past June, Ben lived with her in his Western state. That is all I learned about Ellen. She was the one topic that mattered that Ben and I did not discuss.

Which, I should add, did not stop me, at least in the beginning, from sometimes trying to see things from her point of view. I tried to think, for example, how I would feel if I were a wife in a Western state with a husband off mentoring and swaining. But I did not get far in my line of thought, as I had no idea who this Ellen was or if she had a point of view. Or even if she knew what was up. Then again, I was still not myself sure what exactly was up. Nor, I think, was Ben. So there you have it. We were all of us this fall confused.

Nevertheless, all this fall, Ben and I were happy to go on seeing each other, just stopping by now and then. To leave it at that. What could be wrong? What could possibly go wrong with that?

Well of course the answer is a great deal. And it could still all end terribly wrong. Although by wrong, to be clear, I do not mean wrong as in immoral. Not wrong as in sin. I am not much a holder with sin, which I realize does complicate a stance on wrongdoing, and what leads to irreparable harm.

No, what I mean here about wrong, about seeing a married man as wrong, is that it can be incredibly wrongheaded. Misguided, delusional, a bad idea. And it can indeed lead to harm, no matter the initial intention.

In the beginning, however, I did not think this applied to Ben and me. When I tried very hard to be honest, I did not think what we were doing was wrong. I was not out to take Ben away from his Ellen. Or make him change his old life for me. And except on the occasional breezy day on his farm, I did not particularly wish he would stay.

In fact, Ben's marital state was an advantage, I thought. How safe, really, married men were, how unlikely to become hangers-on. How awfully convenient, really. With Ben, I believed, life could just carry on. By summer there was somewhere else he should be, he had a Western wife to return to. And because I was already where I should be, I could stay just as I was.

Which is right where the wrong part came in.

But just now, in record time, here I am already at Ben's farm. And I drive up his long driveway to the front of his house and stop where I usually park.

"Ben, Ben," I call from the car window. I am excited to see Ben at last. But I look at his house then and notice the shades at his windows are down and his truck is not there on the side. His truck is in fact not here at all, and I know then neither is Ben.

A low cloud moves in, leaving the farmyard in shadow, and I feel a shiver pass through me. Ben should be here. Something is wrong. Something—and I try hard to think. But then the breeze picks up, the light returns, and because I cannot just now put my finger on it, I give a little shake and snap to. Well but it is only that Ben is not home. It is only my own bad timing. I have driven all this way to tell Ben the news—that possibly he is in danger and for this reason I have come to save him—but now what do you know, Ben is not here.

I sit for a minute considering. Still, what does it mean, Ben's not here? Could in fact this be what Mrs. E had in mind, that Ben is off now somewhere in danger? That someone or something has taken him away? It's possible, as I've said, Mrs. E has it right.

Possible, that is, but not likely.

So I give it more thought, I stare at the dark house, I consider the time of day, and what is likely, I think, is that Ben Adams is still at school teaching. Or painting somewhere by himself. Or then again out running errands. Danger? Errands? Just now there is no way to tell. There is only the fact that Ben is not here. And I have come all this way for nothing.

I shift back into gear and turn around. And as I make my way down the drive, I think how my plan for Ben still needs work. Specifically, it needs a timeline.

Well then, tomorrow, I think. Tomorrow I will try again. I will find Ben Adams tomorrow.

Four

Clown Dance

Thursday morning. Again I awake from the dream. Again I do not know what to make of it. Just now in the dream when I checked my side mirror for the angry large man in the van, I could see him as though he were facing me, standing not two feet in front, inclined at a threatening angle. I could see then his face swell and grow flushed, his teeth clench, his mouth stretch into a wide, mean sneer. And I knew he would scream anew at me, thrust a fist, offer something profane.

But as I watched, things took an unexpected turn. I could not at first tell what was happening. But when I looked again, I saw that his face had begun inexplicably to soften, to melt and then to run. His dark eyes dissolved into dagger-shaped stars, his mouth into a large flaccid oval. And his nose, which I had not noticed before, ballooned up to a great bloodred ball.

He began then to dance before me, spinning and waving his hands in my face, kicking a leg in the air. I stood blocked by his goofy, macabre clown dance with no room to go around, while beyond I could see the truck from the dream beginning its climb to the bridge.

The clown spun on. "Stop," I screamed, and tried to push past. But then laughing high-pitched and wild, he threw out both arms and grabbed me.

Far ahead on the bridge the truck started to skid. "Stop," I screamed. "Stop." But the clown held me tight, I could not break his grip. And as the truck began then to dive, he only held tighter, closer. "Saved," he whispered. "You are saved."

I watched the truck falling, again could not breathe. And knew the clown got it wrong.

Mrs. E's Pail

But now something new from outside, a great sloshing sound, some ocean wave breaking. Now, first thing this early day. It is Mrs. Eberline again, I am sure of it. Up to her old senseless tricks even before I have got out of bed.

I rise, go to the window, look down for the telltale red hood. But I am too late, Mrs. E has already beat her crablike retreat and is just closing her front door behind her. I keep watch at that door, I have a feeling it is not the last of Mrs. E yet this morning. And in a minute or two the door opens again, and Mrs. Eberline scurries out carrying a large metal pail.

From my view one story above, I see the pail's nearly full, the liquid there foul and suspicious. I barely have time to wonder what now Mrs. Eberline has in mind when I see her break and make a run for my yard. Then arcing the pail in a short backswing, she hurls its dark contents with all her coiled heart directly at my silver maple. Whatever it is makes a tsunami-like crash directly at center trunk, wildly splashing the grass below and leaving immediate black, parched craters.

Mrs. Eberline does not wait to watch this last part. She only snatches the pail back in close to her, turns, and runs for her side of the lawn. She is quick for a woman her age, for a hunched woman her age. She is back inside her front door before I can think to run down my stairs and stand outside in my nightgown, shrieking. Something I did early on living here, but that I have since reconsidered. There is no point in yelling, I've found. The damage is done and Mrs. E, it is clear, does not hold with remorse or restitution.

Still, as I've said, her forays of late have taken a more ominous turn. Always there has been some new attack. Just last week through my window, for instance, I watched her rush out of her house again, this time clenching a large glass jar. She held one hand clamped over the top and when she was clearly well past the property line onto my side of the walk, she turned the jar upside down. Then removing her hand from the opening, she shook the jar once, hard. Even from the distance of my second floor I could see what fell onto the cement. It was huge and black and multi-legged and had evidently been living in Mrs. Eberline's house. Looking up at my window to make her point, she stomped one foot down hard on the thing and turned, toe in, toe out. Then, wiping the sole of her shoe on my grass, she was off again running fast for her door.

Mrs. E is relentless, all right. Mean-spirited and confrontational. Moreover, I have recently figured out, she is for the most part seasonal. The trick today with the pail, for example, is just some of her spring offensive, the dank liquid no doubt related to what she considers to be spring cleaning.

In fact even before her current blitzkrieg, in every season I have spent with her living next door there has been some new aggravation. I do not know how she thinks them all up. Late this past winter, for instance, I watched her carry an old cottage cheese carton out to her walk, just at the point where it meets mine. Then studiously ignoring my face at the window, she knelt by a small-lake-sized puddle and for the rest of the afternoon, scooping her carton and tossing, she fervently bailed the winter's last snowmelt from her side of the sidewalk onto mine.

Earlier, throughout the long months of snow here, she shoveled her whole front yard into a huge drift at my garage. She was the only one on our block this year with a grass lawn the entire winter.

And then earlier yet, in the fall, Mrs. Eberline struck again as I raked.

I should explain here that every autumn I do a great deal of hand raking. It is the silver maple again, it looms large in Mrs. E's life and mine. In autumn the tree sheds its flame-colored leaves in great abandon all over my grass, so every fall I am out cleaning up. And on one late afternoon as I was raking near dusk, as it was growing too dark to see, I heard a small scuffling noise close behind and knew again it was Mrs. E. Once more she had crossed the property line, no doubt up to something unnerving.

I turned, and saw that Mrs. Eberline was right behind me,

bent at the waist, digging with both hands deep into the leaves. She was searching the pile I had just raked together, throwing its leaves back out onto the grass until in fact there was no longer a pile. She had been following me as I raked, she had been following me it seemed for some time, judging by the now former piles.

"Mrs. Eberline!" I said. "What are you doing?" Which I should have known better than to ask. It is never a productive question. Mrs. Eberline usually does not answer, and regardless, it is generally quite clear, if not plausible, exactly what she is up to.

What I meant to ask was "Mrs. Eberline, why are you doing this thing?" Which is of course even less productive, since if Mrs. Eberline has reasons for her behavior at all, most likely they are perverse, and nothing she plans to divulge.

So normally what I would have done at this juncture is move on from questions to commands. Size up the situation and say, "Mrs. Eberline, stop that. Now." Which is exactly what I said then on that afternoon I found her digging in my leaves. But as Mrs. E continued to dig, "Stop it, stop it, stop it," I ordered, my voice rapidly rising.

Mrs. Eberline looked up, then pulled something green and egg-shaped out of the leaves. "For the squirrels," she said, and held out the thing for me to see. A walnut, still in its bright chartreuse wrapping. It is how walnuts look in the autumn, I knew, as I had a tree full of them in my backyard. They had begun to fall along with the tree's leaves, which evidently had Mrs. Eberline concerned.

She stood up. "For the squirrels," she said again. She stuffed the nut deep into her trouser pocket and glared at me. I did not miss her point, that I could be so thoughtless as to rake up these walnuts along with my fallen leaves, to then throw them all indiscriminately into plastic lawn bags while the squirrels of our block went hungry.

It would do no good, I knew, to explain to Mrs. E that it was probably the squirrels themselves who buried the nuts in these leaves. The walnut tree is a hundred feet back, it is not likely the walnuts could have found their way here other than via squirrel.

That day on the lawn, Mrs. Eberline stared up at me. "Think of the squirrels," she said and shook her head in disgust. Then she turned back to the pile of leaves I'd begun, stooped, and without having to look, retrieved yet another walnut. Rising, shaking the nut up at my face, "We'll git you fer this," she shouted, furious for her starving little friends. By which, I supposed at the time, Mrs. E had some fauna-like karma in mind. That the day would come when I myself would go hungry and the squirrels would have left not one walnut.

So then, these are the sorts of things that can happen if you live next door to Mrs. Eberline. She will have the thought to rush out of her house and hurl something toxic at your maple. Or in a frenzy she'll dash again to your yard and thrash through your piles of downed leaves. She may do this because she thinks you won't catch her. Or because she thinks that you will. I myself have no patience for either.

Besides which, just now I am late to work. I have the morning bus to catch. But as I hurry out my door and head for the steps, I am stopped by what lies there spread-eagle. A young squirrel, roadkill no doubt from Mott Street, lying face up, mouth agape.

A note scribbled in crayon lies to one side, "SAVE BEN!" blasted across in block letters. Then at the bottom, in a small crabbed hand: "Before it's too late, missy."

Widow's Walk

Sometimes now at night he cannot sleep. He wanders his farmhouse, looking into all the rooms. Stands, tries to remember what he is after. Tries to remember his heart beating, the sound of the floor at his shoes.

This farm, the house, his class and night studio, they will not be forever, he knows. Soon they will end, and then—

He climbs to the cupola, looks, steps out onto its narrow wood platform. Its widow's walk, that's what they call it. A name from New England where a century ago houses on ports had roof walks. Early morning, whalers' wives stood up on their walks watching the ships disappear, knowing they'd be gone a full year. And when it was time, they climbed back to their rooftops to wait for the white sails returning. Waited then days, sometimes forever, those young wives on their widow's walks.

Standing there on his own narrow walk, looking out at the dark sky, he imagines himself onto one of those ships, a large clipper with three sails billowing. The thought makes him long to set off. And high up then on his roof, he closes his eyes, feels the journey begin. Feels himself climbing great waves of the night, slipping silently down the other side.

Slippers and Zippers

While I do not much take Mrs. E.'s note to heart, on the bus into work this morning I renew my resolve to again go find Ben today. Right after I take the bus home at four. Even sooner if I can manage it.

But when I arrive at the Project, I can see it's going to be another full day. The series editors are all milling about in the hallway, excited and talking loudly. "Margaret," they say as I pass through them. "Just look. You'll never guess." They hold their breath while I ask, "Yes, what?" Then they all watch as Lola, waving a note, fills me in.

That is, first thing this morning in our Project mailboxes was a small card in Sally Ann's hand. It is how she and Bones like to communicate. When possible they prefer just to write. This note today said only that Sally Ann thought we might like to know: Today the first-grade early readers have moved on to words of two syllables.

The editors watch me take in the news. They want to make sure I understand. After months of preliminary outlines and notes, Sally Ann is at last multisyllabic. Her first story—"On Slippers and Zippers."

It is a momentous day for first grade. And as I open my door and put down my purse, Mr. Bones calls me to Sally Ann's suite. Sally Ann and he want to hurry their new story to production, they'd like to start right away, they want to consult on the layout. Primarily, they say, they're concerned for the art, that it rise to the two-syllable challenge.

Bones and I are at odds on how to proceed. I tell Sally Ann the illustrators will have trouble with this story. That is, I am not concerned about the slippers, I tell her. There are a lot of different slippers to draw in the world, the illustrators will have a good time with those slippers. It is the zippers that concern me, I say. It is not easy to draw riveting zippers.

Bones nods his cereal bowls, says yes, he understands. He is himself concerned the story could turn out dull. But then consider the alternatives, he says. If we take out zippers, what are we left with? Really there are only clippers and flippers or possibly dippers. We cannot very well include strippers, he says.

And here he bangs his head into Sally Ann's shoulder and the two have a little laugh. Actually, Bones laughs and laughs, he is beside himself now over strippers. He says how maybe they could do a whole unit on slippers and strippers. Or better yet keep the zippers, they could call the unit strippers and zippers. Now there was an idea for the illustrators.

Bones laughs until he is snorting.

Which is only a small example of all that is wrong at the Project. And why we keep a secret. The secret I mentioned, the thing here the editors and I have to hide. Well at least, that is, the first half of it.

For this is the truth: We are just not any good at what we do here. In terms of both temperament and talent, we are all ill-suited to our jobs. To an editor, the editors cannot edit. Nor do they know how to write. I myself have no interest in paste-up. I am a bumbler at page imposition. Even Marcie is not much of an administrative assistant or wild about assisting in general.

Still, while we're inept, it is true, we are most of us not unaware.

Frankly, we say, we have no idea why Steinem hired us. Unless of course it's because we all interview well, which personally I believe is the reason. The editors especially are good talkers, they would easily have made a good first impression with a few flashy pedagogical phrases, an arcane reference to morphemes here and there. They would have only had to bone up the night before. And I in my interview just had to tell a few lively stories from art school, vaguely related to ink and type, which I could see Steinem wasn't much following but seemed nevertheless to enjoy.

Well who knows really why Steinem took us all on? But hire us he did and we are thankful. It is why we all come in to work every weekday and do whatever we can. Which unfortunately, it turns out, is not much.

This is not, of course, how we began. At the start we all meant to succeed, and our entire first year at the Project remained more or less on track. We wrote up our outlines, projections. We researched, took notes, set goals, then met daily to plan. And in all these activities and meetings, as in our first interviews, our collective forte as extremely good talkers convinced Steinem that all would be well.

But then at the Project, in this, our second year, with production deadlines looming, we stopped all our meetings, closed our suite doors, and got down to what could be called work here. Each day the editors wrote and then the editors edited, all according to plan. After which, I marked up their stories for galleys, and the illustrators sketched out the art. But once then the layouts began to emerge, and a few of us got a look, it was immediately and also excessively clear just how abysmal all of us were.

I should add, however, not everyone at the Project is yet aware of this. Steinem, for one. Who, due to the Personality coming on board at about the same time as our stories, has been distracted here more than usual. Steinem is not, by nature, an organized man; he is not long on managerial skills. And so, unmoored from our daily editorial meetings and also completely and deeply smitten, Steinem just let our little staff be. The shift left the editors all at wit's end and wreaked havoc on Steinem's professionalism.

For which now he compensates with optimism. That is, Steinem, who has not actually got around to reading any, believes our stories exceptional. He is also under the impression we've finished whole series of them and they are out there, pre-release, winning acclaim. He now refers to our books in every new grant. They've built extraordinary confidence in our funders, he says, and won no end of NDEA support. He just does not know what he would do without our soon to be award-winning series.

Celeste is the other not in on the secret. We thought it better to spare her. Celeste, as I've said, is the delicate one, our sensitive wood violet, our unstable faerie queen. She does not do well with negativity, and we have been unable to tell her the truth: Her Joe Trout Adventures in Science are by far the worst of our lot.

Not Joe Trout himself, that is. Celeste does quite well with characterization, and even, on some days, plot. I know—as I've said, I have read Joe's every rambling word. But I am not an early reader. And even the gifted among these, I believe, could not possibly follow Joe's drift. Celeste in her dreamy, unfocused way makes the most simple hypotheses obscure, a fact that, were she more syntactically astute, would break her poor editor's heart. She writes each of her stories, she maintains, to spread the good science word. She's a believer, she professes, in science—an odd stance for Celeste, we all agree, considering her other beliefs. But then because we cannot come to tell her the truth, that her stories just waste a child's time, they go off as they are to be typeset.

It is the same with everyone's stories, Frances's pedantic morality tales, Lola's inappropriate limericks, Sally Ann's latest Strippers and Zippers. None of our series should be published. But then, the editors shrug. What does it matter, really, they say. It's all just grant money in the end. The funds for the series are already in place, it's not like the Project depends on its sales. By going forth with their stories, regardless of worth, the editors are just doing their duty. Steinem's grants promised readers, and so the editors write them. The actual publishing is out of their hands.

It is not the most responsible stance. And I am pretty sure the editors are wrong about publishing without serious consequence. Because, I believe, if it were not for the rest of our secret, and also specifically me, we would all, to an editor, long ago have been shown the sanatorium door.

It's a thought we do not like to dwell on.

Frances's New Date

But now "Lunch!" Frances calls from the hallway. I look up from where Bones snorts with Sally Ann and offer a small silent thank god. Thank god for lunch, even for Frances. I stand and prepare to leave. But not to be rude before I bolt for the door, I ask Sally Ann would she like to come too, knowing it's a guaranteed decline.

As I have said, Sally Ann is too shy to go down to the lunchroom en masse. Too many people, Bones explains. When you enter, they all turn in their seats to stare. And then you have to go through a long line of more people just to get yourself any food. There are all those women in hairnets wanting to serve you things. Potatoes on the side, no potatoes? Oh but they're lovely fresh mashed, you sure no potatoes today? Then how about a little dessert? It's black bottom pie, the cook's favorite. Well no dessert either? It upsets Sally Ann's stomach, Bones says, which is why she just brings her lunch in a bag and the two of them eat at her desk.

So then, the rest of the editors and I take the elevator down to the basement. And today we're in luck. We have found a place by the windows, our most preferred seating, although it is not really because of the windows, it's not like we have a view. The cafeteria windows are small and high up, we are, after all, in the basement. We only try to sit here whenever we can because it puts us at a side wall. It is quieter here than out in the middle where they usually put the sick prisoners, the ambulatory ones from the sanatorium's infirmary wing. It's easy to spot them, some are still in their robes, the others wear little green booties. We're not sure why the infirmary makes them wear booties. But they are loud talkers, those prisoners, they have axes to grind, prison breaks to plot, that sort of convict business, and we sometimes cannot hear our own conversations for all of their jailhouse clamor.

The editors and I take our seats, we spread out our cafeteria dishes. And, immediately, as it generally does, the conversation turns to boyfriends.

It is Frances who starts us off. She has news, she wants to tell us about the man she was out with last night. He is a new one, she says, someone she just met at her tennis club. And as usual, she says, she had hopes for him. The signs were all good. He first of all belonged to the club, which means he had time for tennis and could also afford the dues. In addition, she says, he was buff. And he had a magnificent tan. "A May tan," Frances says. "Imagine." This spring there are not yet many tans at the club, a fact Frances pointed out right off to him, right there in the club's private lounge.

She was bold, she says. It is the middle of the week, not normally a date night, but she just walked up to the bar and sat next to him. Then leaning over as though they had met before, "My god," she said. "Where did you get that tan?"

"Tan?" he said, and looked down at his forearm. He had on a blue dress shirt with little tucks down the front, very elegant, Frances says. He had rolled the sleeves up a couple of times and "Tan?" he said, and held his arm out and stared at it. "On the courts, I guess. In the sun." And then he turned his arm over, studied it again. "I tan easily," he said.

Frances says well probably she should have known right then, but she didn't. Instead, she stayed at the bar and had a cigarette, then another. And eventually the fellow asked would she like to come home with him, he'd make them dinner.

"So I thought what the hell and I went," Frances says. He served pinot noir and stir-fry, which was actually quite good, Frances says. Except then after dinner we just sat on his couch while he told me again how easily he tanned. He couldn't seem to believe it, what a great tan he had. I was sorry I'd mentioned it, so I said well yes, though it might be the blue in his shirt. Blue tends to makes people look darker than they are.

Which was a mistake too, Frances says. I should have just left it at the tan because "Well, yes," he said, "it could be the shirt." And then he asked would I maybe like to see his other shirts? He had over fifty, not even counting the polos.

"His tan and the fifty shirts, that's all we talked about the rest of the night."

Lola and Frances laugh and nod their heads. They find it amusing, all those shirts. And I laugh too, mostly to show I am listening.

But in fact I am not. What I am thinking instead is how really it is not so easy having dinner on a first date. And when there's a little pause, I say, "Well that is a good story, Frances." I smile, then add but maybe she should give the man one more chance.

Frances and Lola turn to look at me. "Excuse me," Frances says. "Did you not just hear the part about the shirts?"

I smile again and pretend I did.

"The man is vain, Margaret," Frances says, incredulous. "There is no future in dating a vain man. It does not matter how much money he makes or how tanned he happens to be, vanity is never a good sign. A self-involved man does not generally get over it. If you marry him, you'll never get past it too. Give it some thought, Margaret. Please."

Frances narrows her eyes and waits for my response. She really does mean to discuss this. But I know then I cannot explain. I cannot say well but just now I was not thinking of your vain tennis friend. I was actually thinking of Ben Adams. I was just now re-membering my first dinner with Ben and how it did not go all that well either. In Ben's case not because of vanity. Ben Adams is not a vain man. But he can be awkward and inexplicably sad, also not good first-date signs. Still, I did not hold them against him. Which is, to be honest, unlike me. But oh Frances, I would like now to tell her, what a lucky break indeed.

I do not of course say any of this. I only meet her look and hold my ground. "No, Frances," I tell her. If the man gives her a call, I think she should see him again. "You don't know, Frances," I say. "Even a tanned man can grow on you."

Blue Hyacinth

He sits tonight in the cupola, thinking. It is late again, he has come to like it here late. This high up, it is silent, the air is calm, he can see far into the night. In the dark and the quiet, he sometimes can see things more clearly.

He is thinking tonight of what he would like to tell her. Small things, things in the world he has seen. An old man on a cot, holding a duck and weeping; children rescued at dawn from a storm drain. One blue hyacinth in a glass by a window, snow falling on the other side. Miracles, the everyday.

Dinner at Ben's

That first dinner with Ben Adams, I thought at the time, was highly unlikely to happen. After our coffee, or whatever it was at the truck stop, despite the fact that he asked for my number, I was pretty sure he would not call. Ben was, still and all, a married man. And it was fine with me, not hearing from him, it was fortunate in fact, that it would just pass, this first glancing blow of a date. Since, as I said, Ben is married and it was not even actually a date. No one would have to call the next day or by Tuesday the next week at the latest. And if we ran into each other at some later point, no one would need say much either, certainly not make excuses. In another few weeks, I told myself then, I just might be seeing someone new. And in six months, neither Ben nor I would remember that there'd once been this accidental coffee.

But then Ben Adams called the next morning at nine. "Dinner?" he asked. "Still on for tonight?" And "Dinner," I said. "Right. Still on." Just like that. And after Ben Adams hung up, well, I thought, OK. Dinner. It's just dinner, not a date.

But all that day at work, I remember, I could not stop thinking about that call. I could not stop worrying about dinner. A second shot, and so awfully soon, I was not at all sure it was something that I was up to. So I spent the morning just worrying and then trying very hard not to, then trying not to think at all. I grew busy with charts I was supposed to be inking and with fixing fin placement on Joe. Still I knew in just a few hours, I would be seeing Ben Adams again.

So this is how it began, that first dinner at Ben's. As soon as I arrived, I could see he had gone all out. Well, I have now had a number of dinners at Ben's and always he goes all out. It is just Ben's way and I got used to it, although it sometimes still caught me off guard.

Ben dressed up for our dinners, for one thing. It left him looking so vulnerable, I did not like it at first. He would shower and when I arrived, always his hair would be wet, combed with a straight part on the side. And always he would have on his best white shirt, starched and complete with French cuffs. He would wear this shirt with blue jeans, it's true, still it was too much. Always the cuffs would get into his dinner, and Ben would end each evening largely stained. It is what happened that first dinner we had. Ben made us grilled chicken with barbecue sauce and by the time we sat down to eat, Ben's good shirt was splattered to its elbows.

I should point out here Ben Adams thinks he can cook. He cannot, as it turns out, but he can barbecue some. Chicken. Mostly he can barbecue chicken. Barbecued chicken with barbecue sauce all over it. At Ben's dinners, almost always it was the same. Ben would put two large chickens on top of his grill and then cover them in a red barbecue sauce he bought in two-quart glass jars.

"Ben," I said, that first night when I saw the chicken filling my plate. "What is this?" And when Ben explained it was dinner, it was my half, I told him well, but it is too much. It could feed families of six, this whole chicken. "You don't have to finish it," Ben said. "You can take the leftovers with you. I will give you a bag."

He said this every dinner. Ben is a generous person with an exceptionally open heart so I never said anything more about his chicken. I only put the parts I could not eat back in Ben's refrigerator after dinner. And then later when it was time to leave and I returned to his kitchen once more, always I found a brown paper bag Ben had left on the counter for me. The bags were always just chicken-sized and made of heavy paper, ones he saved for this particular occasion.

So after our first dinner, I left Ben's house with the bagged remains of my chicken. It felt strange all right, but then I thought of a woman I knew who shuttled back and forth from her lover's house with a paper bag full of spare underwear. It can be no stranger to leave Ben's farm with a bag of chicken under my arm.

That first dinner, it was not of course only whole chicken Ben served. That was only the part I could count on. Ben has a garden, he grows vegetables there, in the fall of our dinner he had mostly just broccoli left. But the problem here is that Ben cannot leave his vegetables alone. At the last minute that dinner, he brought out a few slices of Velveeta, which he melted down to a hot yellow puddle and poured all over the broccoli, on what had until then been perfect little spears of fresh green. It was what was called for, Ben's instincts told him, he knows this sort of thing without thinking. And with the broccoli and whole chickens arranged on our plates, he arrived at the table, happy and flushed from the kitchen.

Then, before we took our seats, Ben put on some music for dinner. Almost always Ben would play music at dinner, usually Tchaikovsky, melodramatic and loud. That night he lit candles as well, dozens of candles, the room swayed with their wavering light. And then, with everything ready, we sat down at his dining room table with all its five leaves in place. The table belongs to Ben's landlord, it could sit sixteen or more. I do not know why Ben leaves in all the leaves.

So then on that first night there we were, Ben and I, at that titanic old table, with the music soaring and candles for light. We sat at the head and foot of the table. It was arduous talking, but we tried.

"So, Ben," I called to his end of the table. "Tell me about your-self." Though not inspired, it is a good opener, I've found, with most of the men I have known. They are happy enough to run with that ball, often for the rest of the evening.

But Ben only looked confused. He called back he had already told me about why he was here, we did not need to go over that ground. What more did I want to know?

I gave this some thought, and well then, I called, what about hobbies, pursuits? "What interests and delights you in that life of yours, Ben?"

As it turns out, Ben told me that night, many things in life interest and delight him. Van Morrison, for example, The Band. Other music too. Gram Parsons, The Byrds. And then there's a tape someone gave him years ago of an idiot savant who sang just like Jose Feliciano.

And here Ben got up and played that tape of the savant doing "Light My Fire." Which then reminded him of another tape he had, and got up to put on, of Lowell Thomas, live, saying fart. Lowell Thomas had meant to say heart, struck by a near fatal heart attack, but it came out as fart, and then Lowell could not stop laughing. He tried to continue the broadcast, but every few words he would think of that fart and he'd snicker, then laugh out-right, then roar, and have to start over again. Eventually he just couldn't go on. Ben Adams loved hearing that tape, you could tell. He laughed and laughed just like Lowell.

Then when the tape ended, Ben waited to turn the music back on. Instead, he sat down at the table, this time taking the chair next to mine, and said well but there are other things in this world he likes too. Pizzas, he likes frozen pizzas. And wild iris and real leather slippers. And teaching and books, of course, too. Although mostly, he said, the teaching does no good and the books that he likes are old. He just hasn't much faith in the new ones.

And then for no reason I could see, Ben moved his chair closer and grew serious. "But it's painting, Margaret, that matters."

I was not ready for this change in the evening. Ben seemed to want now to talk, he was no longer just entertaining. And although art is not a topic I thrill to, "Painting, Ben?" I said. "That's right. I remember. You told me that you teach painting." As though what was needed here was verification.

I hoped then we could go back to Lowell Thomas. I did not like this new seriousness in Ben. It was after all our first dinner. And more to the point, I can no longer bear to talk art.

But I saw I had only encouraged him. He looked at me close and said, "I have this one painting, Margaret. Now, in my head. I know its edges, its shapes, the shadows. I know where the color should go."

"So, Ben?" I said. I did not understand the issue. "Why not just paint it, begin?"

Ben looked at me, kindly. It was clear he was getting to that.

"I have, Margaret, I have. Many times. But it's no good just to paint some idea that you have, some copy of some idea. What I'm waiting for is actually to see it."

"See it, Ben?" I was not sure I was following him.

Ben raised a hand toward the wall. "For that moment, Margaret. That one moment you look and know it is there, below what you see, or beyond. Exceptional, necessary, pulsing. So that you have to paint now, before it is gone. Paint and then, if you are lucky, watch it become something true."

Ben looked back at me, closer. "Those few paintings, Margaret, those are the ones you paint for. When you have a painting like that, one that's alive, that's whole, then Margaret you've done it. You've found the way in."

I looked at Ben, nodded. "OK," I said. "Good." I was not sure I wanted him to go on.

Which did make Ben stop. He seemed to just hear what he was saying. He smiled, remembered himself, remembered us both. Then looking at me, he asked, really meaning it, "Well but what about you, Margaret? What about you?"

I gave Ben a smile in return. But the truth was I had started to tire. And I said what I say when people I do not know well ask so what about me. "Oh Ben. Really there is not much to tell."

Ben sat back, looked surprised. Which surprised me as well, as whatever spell he might have thought we were under seemed to have just come undone. And because Ben now looked so bewildered, then sad, I could not just leave things like that. I had not meant to sound rude or cut short the evening Ben had planned. So I rallied.

I brought up the Project, the editors and Steinem, a little about Mott Street as well. I explained Mrs. E, how people are right when they say you can't choose your neighbors.

Then I told Ben about paste-up, that that's what I did for a living. I tried to be helpful, I offered some tricks I thought he might use. "Here Ben," I said, thinking fast. "Here's something I have learned that might come in handy." And I explained how when inking lines into tables, I stick tape to the back of my ruler. It lifts it so when you run a pen by, the ink won't seep under and smudge.

"So Ben," I said, "if you need a straight line in a painting sometime, I recommend you add tape to your ruler."

Ben smiled and rallied too. He thanked me for the tip, he said he certainly would keep that in mind. And we talked then and laughed and Ben turned up the music. Nobody brought up art again. And when at ten o'clock I told him I should probably leave, we both had work in the morning, Ben just nodded and brought out my leftovers. "Come back again, Margaret," he said, handing me the bag. "Come back again soon. Will you?"

I have. Or I did. For a while there were regular dinners. Ben would call me at work, say please come at six, and always the dinners were the same—the long leaved table, the music, the sauced and carefully arranged chickens. They were odd, formal evenings for a man on a farm. Odd, out-of-place evenings all right, dining by candles, Tchaikovsky, with the farmer's spotted pigs in their pen just outside making noises like flushing toilets.

But, as I've said, I got used to Ben's dinners. I came to see the sweet grace of them. We were like two children making believe, dressing to dine like grown-ups, talking of things that mattered. Always those nights then Ben opened his heart, always I tried listening with mine.

I have missed those lovely, strange dinners with Ben.

Time

He shifts in the cupola, smiles. So much he would still like to tell her. About time, about them. How, given time, it could have worked out for them.

He shakes his head. But it is what they do not have now, time.

Standing, he turns for the door. Funny thing about time, he thinks. A trickster, shape shifter. A mobius, no beginning, no end. See how it twists there, bows, holds trembling, contracts, then disappears. How in an eye blink it's over.

How can something with no beginning or end be over?

He cannot answer the question.

What Ghosts Want

Celeste, strangely for Celeste, has not said a word all this lunch hour. But now, in the pause that results when I say what I say about the man with the shirts, Celeste at last makes her move.

But it's not men she would like to discuss. Celeste for the time being has tired of men, she has a more pressing topic. It is Emmaline she would like now for us to consider, it is Emmaline who is most on her mind.

"I must say," Celeste says for an opening, "I have simply had it with Emmaline." She does not think she can take one more day of that girl's shady tricks.

She summarizes for us the behaviors. All those bloody little notes from yesterday, that doomed typo, the chair shenanigans. And then last night—well, young Emmaline had been at it again. "You cannot imagine," Celeste tells us, "how mentally trying it's become for me." And here Celeste gives a faint sigh and sits back. And details the latest infraction.

This morning when Celeste came into work, there on her chair—a new bloodied note from the night before. "Miss Rogers, mum," it began in Emmaline's shaky ghost hand. "If it would not be too much trouble, we here would like you to close the window when you leave your suite for the day. Consumptives are given to colds, you must know, and with these evenings still so nippy, we all fear we could catch our deaths."

"It was alarming, finding that note," Celeste says, "first thing like that in the morning. Also, I must add, annoying." Clearly Emmaline does not have enough to do. Certainly she seems to be restless. Bored, maybe that too. Why else would she play all these tricks?

Lola agrees. "And they're not even that good anymore. Honestly, darlins', I ask you—'catch our deaths'? Please."

Celeste ignores Lola. She straightens in her chair, lets out a breath, and looks as though she's come to a difficult decision. "Ghost or no," Celeste tells us, "Emmaline has been hanging on here for too long." And for Emmaline's own diaphanous sake, she feels it's time the girl took her leave.

"Get on with her life, you mean?" Frances asks.

Celeste ignores Frances as well. "There are cedar smudge sticks, I suppose," she offers. "Or simply pure sage. We could try something along those lines. Hang up some garlic, sprinkle some holy water, see if that discourages her any."

Celeste stops, she is thoughtful a moment. She does not mean to sound harsh. "I believe we could think of it not as ghost riddance so much as a kind of ghost rescue. Really, we would be doing Emmaline a favor."

We all sit at our table and nod our heads, thoughtful as well. But no one has anything to add here. We are not up on our exorcisms or the feelings of ghosts in the way that clearly Celeste is. Frances, impatient as always to move on, says well we will just leave it to Celeste's discretion. Frances herself no longer wishes to discuss the topic of ghosts, she'd like it known.

But Celeste has still more to say. "The dead have their reasons for sticking around," she tells us, now taking the long view. "There are reasons ghosts are here," she says, "and not there," vaguely waving one hand toward the window. "Research tells us in fact that over ninety percent are here for the exact same reason."

Frances interrupts. "To terrorize and torment?"

Celeste keeps her eyes steady on Lola and me. She leans in. "To tie up loose ends."

She relaxes and gives us a happy look at how simple really it is. "Unfinished business," she says. "That is most ghosts' concern. And if we can figure out what Emmaline needs done, we might be able to help."

Lola and Frances sit at the table and stare.

Celeste continues. We would not have to worry about smudge sticks, she says, if we could help Emmaline find a little closure. "It is not easy for the dead, you must know," she says. And adds it would probably do us all good to try a little harder to understand them.

Lola and Frances give each other and then me a quick look. We all of us now know where the conversation is headed. We have been here with Celeste before. It is one of her more irritating sides, in fact, that she has appointed herself spokeswoman for the dead. That she generally sits around thinking about them. That she reads up on death and dying before bed.

Because what is disturbing really, I think, is that all her research never seems to lead anywhere much, just to more of her already vague reflections. On impermanence, for instance, and facing uncertainty together. How extinction makes life more spacious. This is how people who think too much about death start to think, I think, and worse yet talk. And if we give her time enough today, Celeste will tell us again about awakening the spiritual warrior within. Or how death can teach us to cherish the other as we learn to cherish ourselves.

I do not now think I can take another lecture. I am myself of the opinion there are already too many who cherish themselves, we do not need death as a job aid. I look at Lola and Frances and they nod. It is as I suspected, we're agreed. Mostly we here at this table try not to think about death much at all or what it might mean for the living.

We all give Celeste a blank stare.

Celeste returns to the topic at hand. What then to do with our ghost Emmaline.

"I just think we need to find out what she wants. What really she's after. What loose end is keeping her here."

Lola lets out a laugh. "Celeste, honey," she says, "I don't know our Emmaline is all that much into reasons. Seems to me she just does what she wants. Could be we're wasting our time tryin' to understand her."

Celeste gives Lola a quick angry glance. She turns to Frances and me, addresses our table, speaks slowly. "If we are going to get Emmaline ever to leave, we'll all need to help show her the door."

I look over at Lola. She herself has gone back to her lunch. She launches now into her salad.

Celeste perseveres. "What I mean is we have to give Emmaline a way out. Finish her story for her."

Now Frances looks down at her plate. Considers the roast beef that remains there.

Offended, Celeste picks up her napkin. Her voice edging up, she addresses us all. "Well, Earnest at least agrees with me."

Earnest, we see, is becoming Celeste's fallback position.

She folds her napkin in two, places it carefully on the table. "Earnest understands about ghosts," she says. "He knows there's a reason they're here."

Celeste stands then. Checks her watch. Well really, she must get back. She left out a flat of Joe Trout she'd just proofed and now she'll have to go check it again. It's been a whole lunch hour. Who can guess what Emmaline's been up to?

Earnest Knows

The fact is, I happen to know Earnest's take on why ghosts are here. Just what it is they are after. He explained it that night I worked late, the night he told me about Emmaline. And despite what Celeste believes to be true, his view is different from hers.

"She's only half right about ghosts," he says. Or only right about half. They're not all here trying to make up for their lives, for the messes they left behind. They're dead and they know it. Most are happy enough to move on and leave what they started undone. They don't mind letting the living clean up.

"And the living don't mind?" I say.

"Well that's just it," Earnest says. "That's the other half of the ghosts, I mean. For some ghosts, it's the living that keep them around. It's the living that want something, not the dead."

"Want what?" I ask Earnest. What could the living want from a ghost? Most people I know are afraid of them.

Earnest gives this some thought. "Mostly they just want time to forgive," he says, "or sometimes to be forgiven. There is a lot of that sort of thing." And then he says how with Emmaline, for instance, there was her family of five, all of them needing to forgive her, all of them cursed when she jumped from the balcony that night.

"Cursed?" I say. And I realize I have stepped into one of Earnest's little well-laid traps. There is still more about Emmaline he's been saving. Because then, "Cursed," he says. "Yes indeed." And he tells me the rest of the story.

People thought it was some kind of curse, he says. Because after that girl did herself in, after they buried what was left of her, her family, the mother, father, a sister, brother, they all fell sick just like the girl, all took to bed pasty and wheezing. And then coughing up blood, and then later still raving, one by one they all of them died.

"Not likely they ever forgave her," Earnest says. "That little Emmaline will be here forever."

Earnest stops, he is thinking. "But there are others here at night. Not the bad ones who need forgiving. I mean the ones who are here out of love. The living won't let them leave out of love. Or the dead are themselves unwilling. Either way, the dead or the living, they can't seem to let each other go. So the spirit one stays, watching out, watching over, until one or the other of them figures it's time. They're going to have to go it alone."

Earnest lets out a long sigh. "Sad situation," he tells me. "Can't be easy for any of them here."

Five

Marcie and I Take Tea

But now lunch is over and I am back at my light table, once again trying to work. Or trying at least to look like I'm working. It is as I've mentioned increasingly difficult to pretend, I have not got a thing done in the past hour. So it is a welcome diversion when the phone on my desk starts to buzz. It is Marcie putting me through to a call, with luck something non–work related.

Marcie monitors all our calls here, it is part of her acting-receptionist job. She answers our lines, then buzzes our desks to tell us we have a call. It is a great waste of manpower of course but Steinem prefers to do it this way. He does not want us accessible, he says. We have our ivory turret to defend.

I pick up the receiver. "Margaret," Marcie says on the line, not buzzing me through at all. "Margaret, have you forgot about tea? It's three-thirty, Margaret. Time for tea."

I look at my watch. I have been daydreaming longer than I thought. And so, "Tea, Marcie. Right," I say. "Meet you out in the solarium."

It is something we sometimes do, Marcie and I, we take afternoon tea in the solarium. I am happy enough for our breaks. I learn things from Marcie, I do in some ways even like her. Although it is true I also do not always trust her.

And Marcie for her part seems to want to take breaks with me. As receptionist and administrative assistant to Steinem, she is lonely for company, she says. She must sit by herself at a desk all day out in the fourth-floor foyer. And all day long, she says, she has no one to talk to and just elevator doors for a view. She is grateful for the solarium, she says.

Marcie is not really supposed to be the receptionist here. She was hired strictly as Steinem's assistant. We had a real receptionist at the time, and don't you worry, Steinem told Marcie. We'll have more than enough work for both of you. Which is true. Dr. Steinem, given to lapses as he invariably is, requires a great deal of assisting, and with that work alone Marcie would have her hands full. But only four days into Marcie's new job, the first Monday of her second week, our receptionist just didn't show up. Instead she dialed in to say she had tired of all of the phone calls, of all the answering required in a day—just when to expect our catalog, for instance, and when our new readers would ship. So ever since, Marcie has been taking our calls, in addition to filing and typing.

We are all wondering when Steinem will hire someone new. When he asked Marcie to fill in as receptionist part-time, he said it would be only for a little while, only until he could get the ad for a replacement into the paper. But it has been four weeks now since the old receptionist took off, and Marcie says she just can't keep filling in. She cannot get her own work done, reaching for the phone every time that it rings. Marcie says she has talked to

Steinem about it, that then he promises to call an agency tomorrow. He has told her this four times in a row. "It is odd," she says. "Don't you think?"

I say well yes, although maybe Steinem really is trying to hire, he just isn't having any luck. Then I tell her come to think of it we do go through a lot of receptionists here. And I add I am not certain why. We are nice to them, it is not that the Project mistreats them. Still, it could be Steinem's needs are just too great, our phone calls just too many. Maybe that's why our receptionists don't stay long. Maybe we're just asking too much of them.

Marcie believes she is meant for something far better than acting receptionist. Better even than administrative assistant. She is here by mistake, she tells me. "Marcie," I say, "we are all here by mistake." But she says no, really, she had another job offer. Well almost. She was one of three they were considering, she'd had a second interview. "I was going to be an office manager," Marcie says, "For the university's School of Pharmacy." They publish a lot of research, those pharmacists, they have a quarterly journal. She would have had her name on their masthead.

As I have said, Marcie and I are assistants here. We both could be doing more. But as Marcie points out, entry-level positions are hard to find in this town. There are too many old students who stay put here, they all try for the same open jobs, and many have advanced, if useless, degrees. She supposes, she says, she should be happy to have any work at all.

I tell Marcie well, I am happy. Compared to the other work I have had since leaving the School of Art—grinder of raw meat at a hamburger hut, potter of plants at a nursery—my position as the Project's assistant editor of design is really something of a marvel.

Although of course, I am lying here. I am too old to be someone's assistant.

Marcie, however, is not. This is her first job out of college, she has time to become something else. I am blunt with her on this point. She has nothing, I tell her, to complain about.

Still, Marcie and I are friends of sorts. And so today we take our tea in the solarium. It is where all of us take our breaks when we can, this great vaulted tunnel of lead-paned glass. It is now just the passage to the crippled children's wing, but when the sanatorium was truly a sanatorium, this was known only as the solarium. Consumptives sat here in sunlight for hours; we now recline in their same wood deck chairs. It is beautiful out here and airy and my favorite place on this floor, on good days all thick wavy glass and warm sun.

Today is one of those days. And surprisingly we are the only ones here. So I decide to give Marcie some idea of the view. "Oh look," I say. I stand and walk to the glass. From our solarium, you can see all the sanatorium's meadows, all our phlox, our blue-eyed Marys, and of course our sturdy old oaks. Staring out, I gesture Marcie to come closer. I intend to show her each one.

But just now my eye goes not to our meadows, fine as they are this spring, but beyond, to the farmer's rich fields to the north. We none of us know this farmer, his land is too distant for sanatorium strolls. But through the solarium glass up here on fourth floor, the rolling contour of his land is clear. It is this that catches my eye—the dazzling green of young corn now sprawling the farmer's black earth in concentric lopsided whorls. Stunning geometry from where Marcie and I stand.

And I know then I cannot point out anything new. Because my

Elizabeth Collison

mind has gone back to Ben, these fields remind me of Ben. How the corn is up in his fields now as well, tender and verdant and hopeful.

Oh, how good it would be to see Ben again.

Picnic

How good to see Ben again? Did I just say that? Oh I really must go now and find him. Ask "Ben, what is wrong?" Are you all right? Do you think we could both be all right again?

Soon enough, I think. Right after work, I will go right after work. But just now I need more to focus, as there is not much time left for my plan. What I need to do is not reminisce but understand about Ben and me, specifically how it went wrong. It is important to think through that part, what led to this winter's discord and Ben's subsequent, hasty retreat. So that when I find Ben, I will know what exactly to look out for. I will know how to keep him safe, how to keep him closer to home. I won't make the same bad choices.

So then, a little more still about Ben and me. About that night we went to the movies, that is, when it all began to unravel.

As I've mentioned, normally Ben and I did not go out together in public. We kept it to his house or mine. And it is how we would have continued, we would have stayed home drinking our coffee and tea or sitting around in the grass. But then, more or less by accident, I invited Ben out to a movie. It was a lapse in judgment on my part. We would probably not have had the problems we've had, specifically Ben's disappearance, if we had not gone to that movie.

This is what I am getting to.

One day late last fall I read in the paper that the Bijou was showing *Picnic*, starring, as luck would have it, my most favorite actor, William Holden. He is a specialty of mine, I have an unreasonable crush on him. I study his every move on screen, his lanky long stride and secret half smile, the lazy assured look to his eyes. I try to see all of his movies.

And so when I read about the Bijou showing *Picnic*, circa 1955, in which William Holden starred but with sizable reservation, a movie I had not had the chance yet to see, I dialed up Ben Adams immediately. "Oh we must go, we must go," I said into the phone, urgent and going on shrill. "Tonight, Ben, it's showing just tonight."

"Margaret," Ben said, "take it easy." But when I pointed out again it was just this one night, well OK, he agreed. We'd meet there.

But now, in the dark, it is a mistake, this movie, from almost the beginning I know. It is no wonder William Holden had his doubts. William Holden is older than my father by one year, born in April 1918. Which means at the time they were shooting *Picnic* he was almost thirty-eight years old, playing Hal, a carefree young drifter, opposite Kim Novak's nineteen-year-old Madge. There's no denying William Holden feels out of place and I am reminded of *Sunset Boulevard*, another of his starring films. And I think oh now he knows how Gloria Swanson felt, with her white powdery face, sharing close-ups with the tanned, flip Joe Gillis.

Still, in *Picnic* William Holden gives it a shot. As the movie begins, he is riding a freight train into town. He jumps off, then gives the train a good kick. This is a clue, we all know. William Holden will put up a good fight in this film, or that's what the director Joshua Logan believes.

But it makes me nervous. Even now in the beginning, I am concerned. William Holden just isn't acting right, he isn't his usual self, we in the audience can see it. And then when he asks old Mrs. Potts if she has any yard work for hire and shuffles his boots at her door, we're all sure this isn't the William Holden we know. He looks foolish and embarrassed to be playing a young drifter when it's obvious he is pushing forty. But someone, Joshua Logan again we suspect, has told him to take off his shirt and shoot baskets in front of Kim Novak, flash a boyish grin now and then, and swagger when he can work it in. William Holden is overplaying it we think, trying too hard, and so are Kim Novak and Susan Strasberg and old Mrs. Potts for that matter. I am worried now how the rest of this movie will go.

It only gets worse. And as the reel spins on, we all grow increasingly uncomfortable. The movie, I think, is not showing William Holden in his best light. And so when Rosalind Russell's Rosemary begins smearing cold cream all over her face and drawling her a's like Blanche DuBois, although the movie is supposed to be in Kansas, I whisper to Ben Adams we can leave. But Ben doesn't say a word, and in the glow from a close-up of Rosalind's cold cream, I can see he is watching intently. So we just stay in our seats where we are.

It is Labor Day weekend in the movie, it turns out, and everyone's preparing for that night's celebration when Madge Owens will be crowned Queen of Neewollah. Which she is, just a few scenes later, and then floated down a river in a big paddleboat made to look like a large frightening swan. It gets Hal's attention all right. And still later that night, as the town band begins playing "Moonglow" and Madge undulates toward him to the beat, Hal cannot keep his lusty eyes off her.

I take a quick look at Ben again, to see if now he is ready to leave. But he does not move. He is completely absorbed, and well it is possible, I think, Ben Adams sees something I've missed. So I sit still in the dark and try hard myself to focus.

It isn't easy, however, as Rosalind Russell has just gone into her big scene with Howard, a man she has been dating for years. Madge and Hal's dance is over, and Rosalind, who has drunk too much and apparently lost hope for Howard, begins throwing herself at William Holden. She is giving it her all, she makes him dance with her, cheek to cheek. Which is difficult for the rest of us here at the show, as we know it is Kim Novak that William Holden is after. Kim is young and has a fine chest and Rosalind Russell, who is middle-aged and loud, has stepped entirely out of line. It is clear William Holden wants nothing at all to do with her.

I look again in the dark at Ben Adams. But Ben just keeps his eyes on the screen. And so we stay through the next several scenes, which do not go well for William Holden. Police are involved, a stolen car, also a chase through a river. And then, with the sheriff and Madge's mother closing dangerously in, it is clear Hal will have to leave town.

It is what, at the end of the movie, he meets Madge by the back shed to tell her. "I'm in a jam, baby," he says. And he says how he's hopping a freight train for Tulsa. And he asks if she's going to say good-bye.

Kim Novak demurs, turns her face to the shed. But William Holden can't leave it like that. "Madge," he says, taking her into his arms. And he says then he's never told her before, but—and here William Holden looks anguished, I do not think he likes pretending like this, I do not think he believes a word of the script—"Look, baby," he says, "I love you. Do you hear, Madge? I love you."

Now Kim Novak looks anguished. But William Holden doesn't let up. He wants to know if she loves him too. "Do you, Madge? Do you?" he says over and over, although it's clear Kim wishes he'd stop.

Then in the distance we all hear the sound of the freight train. William Holden will have to hurry. So he tells Kim, still holding her hard by both arms, to meet him there in Tulsa, at a hotel where he has plans to bellhop.

Which would be a pretty good place for the movie to end. But then even though we can hear the train coming closer, although we are all growing concerned, William Holden still has a few lines left. Things Joshua Logan still wanted said. "You're the only real thing I ever wanted, baby. You love me. You know you do." Things of that sort. And worse. Thinking obviously only of himself, "You gotta claim what's yours," Hal tells Madge, "or you'll be nothing for as long as you live."

And then running for the train, which as luck would have it skirts the Owens backyard, Hal calls back over his shoulder, grinning and arm up high waving, "You love me. You know it! You love me, you love me."

By now, I can barely stand William Holden. I do not know what Kim Novak can see in him. And when, in the last scene, against better judgment she boards the next bus for Tulsa, pausing on the step to smile once at the sky, I am wildly relieved to see the lights go up in the Bijou.

I stand immediately and begin pushing Ben toward the aisle. I act like I want to beat the rush for the door. "Hurry," I hiss. "We have to get out of here now."

Marcie Tips Us Off

"Margaret?" I hear.

I collect myself at the glass and again point to the farmer's new corn. Think how maybe now I'll bring up contour plowing, keyline irrigation, things I have learned from Ben.

But I turn and see that Marcie, still waiting at our table, isn't interested. "Margaret," she says. "Come sit."

She stares at me and at last I remember—we have something here to discuss. It is why Marcie had suggested tea in the first place, why we have come here to the solarium at all, where we can be certain no one will hear us.

"Well now," Marcie says, and we pull our two chairs close together. Our cups of tea sit on the table between us. We are only taking our tea, we will say, should anyone happen to walk in. It makes us feel safe, having our tea on our table.

Marcie picks up her cup and looks at me. She is matter-of-fact, it is Marcie's way. "So here is the thing," she says. "Dr. Steinem is having an affair."

For a moment I freeze. Not because Marcie has spilled Steinem's secret. I'm not surprised about Steinem, of course. It's the affair part of what she's just said, the word, that has startled me. Considering what I've just now been thinking about, it cuts a little too close.

But then I collect myself. Marcie cannot possibly know what I think here, I am not myself clear on the subject. And in an objective sort of way, I try for interest. "Oh," I say. "Really?"

Marcie has been waiting all morning to tell me about Steinem and MaryBeth. It would be unkind to say I already know. Marcie has only just learned, I suppose, because Marcie is new and also the administrative assistant.

That is, no one here trusts administrative assistants. "They turn on you, darlin', or this ain't my first rodeo," Lola says. She is referring here mostly to Sandra, two administrative assistants before Marcie. Sandra was fond of being in charge. It was her job, she was to make sure the office ran smoothly, but she took it too seriously, we all thought. She was forever organizing our office supplies and making group decisions for us—what loud Marimekko we would hang in the halls, what new coffee urn we would all chip in on.

No one liked Sandra. She took the administrative part of her job too far. She wanted us to fill out time sheets each day, how much time to the quarter hour, for instance, we spent on the lesson on S's. See Sam, see Sam shirk. How much time drinking coffee with a cigarette, how many trips to the ladies' room. People refused to give her their sheets, they claimed they forgot to write down their start times, they said there was no point in turning in hours when they had no idea when they'd begun. They suspected then Sandra told Steinem on them, and though they were pretty sure he didn't care what they did, still they did not like all the tattling. Which is why they never told Sandra a thing.

Marcie is not like Sandra, she has not asked anyone for hours. Still, because Marcie is new, people want to make sure before saying anything much to her. It is no wonder she has only now learned of the affair; the wonder is that she has found out at all. And it occurs to me now it could be that Marcie reads Steinem's mail. I would not in the least put it past her.

"You can never guess who it is," Marcie says.

I can, of course. I wait for it.

"It's MaryBeth Malone," Marcie announces. "Miss MaryBeth from *The Magic Garden*." And then she sits forward like a young, prissy hawk to see what my reaction will be.

I open my eyes wide for Marcie's sake. "No!" I say. "Not Miss MaryBeth." I raise my hand to my mouth in utter surprise and hope that I am convincing.

It is enough, if not all Marcie hoped for. "The same," she says and leans in further to tell me what she's found out. That Steinem is a fool for Miss MaryBeth Malone. That it has begun to affect his work. She has watched him there in his office suite. She peeks in on him when he isn't looking. "Dr. Steinem," she says, "isn't up to what I think you all think he is." Instead, every day since contracting MaryBeth—if she isn't already visiting on business—he just sits writing long love letters to her. "When Steinem closes his door and announces he's on a deadline," Marcie says, "you can bet it's more mail to that woman."

We all know this about Steinem, of course. About his general disengagement. It is why there's part two to our own secret here. But I let Marcie carry on.

"Or if not writing her," Marcie says, "Steinem's on the phone to her, long distance." MaryBeth lives on the West Coast, Marcie reminds me. Steinem is forever phoning her in the middle of the day. When the rates are highest, she points out. Marcie worries inordinately about our bottom line. "It just all adds up," she says.

And then from behind us we hear, "He couldn't wait until five like the rest of us?" It is Frances now, come out to the solarium. Frances and Lola and Sally Ann too.

Marcie jerks her head up. Frances and Lola laugh. And Marcie looks at me quickly, like I could have let her know we all know. But then without missing much of a beat, "No," Marcie says to Frances. Miss MaryBeth is home with her husband by five. Naturally Steinem can't call her there.

"Naturally," Frances replies, and helps herself to a deck chair. Lola and Sally Ann sit down as well, they all pull their seats in closer. We have turned ourselves into a tea party. The editors all seem to want to hear more, they all sit and look now at Marcie. She does not herself look displeased.

"No, no," she says again. "Dr. Steinem cannot wait until the rates go down." Instead, she tells us, he calls the Personality late mornings, right after her children's show, right after she finishes shooting. She must have to run from the set to her phone. He calls her almost every weekday.

Here Sally Ann pulls out Mr. Bones, who has something to add. "Steinem's a goner," Mr. Bones says. The crooner's going to find out about all those calls. Somebody at the studio will tell him. Probably trace the number. "The crooner's not gonna stand for no stinkin' calls."

Marcie gives Bones a knowing look. "Well, and it's not just the calls," she says. She suspects Steinem also tunes into the show. She says she has watched him, he disappears at ten-thirty every day, and she thought at first he was just on his way to the men's room. "Most people around here go to the restroom about then," Marcie says. She has noticed that about us. "But," Marcie says, "Steinem never comes back, well not for twenty-five minutes or so. It is too long a break for the restroom."

Bones nods his head once at Marcie. "I can make it in thirty seconds," he says. And Sally Ann has to contain him, or he will go into unnecessary detail. How it is that puppets urinate. She takes hold of his mouth by both his bowls and eases him down off her arm.

Marcie continues. "And then one day, I saw Steinem in the alcoholics' lounge." She had gone down to their floor for a candy bar, she says. The alcoholics have vending machines on their floor, and although generally Marcie tries not to snack before lunch, that day she'd had no breakfast. "So anyway," she says, "as I was passing the glass doors to the lounge, I looked in and there was Steinem on a couch next to a guy in a robe. They were both of them watching the alcoholics' TV."

Frances jumps in here. "Alcoholics will watch anything," she says. We all turn to look. "Don't you agree? Surely you've noticed. I can't believe what I've seen those men watching." We stare. "Well, yes, on my way for a Snickers."

Marcie ignores Frances. Goes on. "The doors to the lounge are all soundproof, so I couldn't hear what the alcoholics had on." Although, she adds, she didn't try very hard either. She couldn't very well have Steinem catch her there watching him watch the alcoholics' TV.

"But it was MaryBeth, I am sure of it," Marcie says. "It was that awful *Magic Garden* show."

We all nod our heads. Dr. Steinem is more a fool than we'd thought. "Well thank god she lives in Los Angeles," Lola says. "At least he isn't watching her in person."

Marcie has been waiting for this. She almost lunges. "But that's just it," she says to Lola, voice rising. "That's the part I was getting to." And she shifts in her chair to address us all. "Miss MaryBeth is coming for a visit. She's coming to spend the weekend. And the worst of it is," and here Marcie stops for a dramatic breath, "she arrives at the Project tomorrow."

Well now, at last Marcie has said something newsworthy. The editors and I take it in. Always before the Personality has come here only on little day trips, and always before we've had warning. But now with no word whatsoever from Steinem, the Personality descends tomorrow for a shocking whole three days.

I begin thinking of all we should really prepare. Or, for that matter, hide. Then I think too about those readers she wants to get hold of. And oh well, I think, the editors and I should probably talk.

But Lola and Frances are concerned about more. "The weekend?" Frances says. "She's coming for the entire weekend?"

And "Good god almighty," Lola says. "That gal wouldn't dare. What's she gonna tell the crooner?"

Lola is with Bones on this one. She believes the crooner is onto his wife. And in this, Lola sides with the crooner.

Frances lights up a cigarette, takes a draw. "So the weekend," she says, squinting into the smoke. "Well you of course know what that means. They'll be spending it all at Steinem's. Most likely in Steinem's bed."

Things must be worse with the old crooner, she adds. The Personality would not stay overnight as she is, here for a three-day weekend, if things were going all that well at home.

Lola nods, sadly. "That poor man home all alone," she says. The crooner is getting on now in years, and Lola says she can just see the ol' boy. He is sitting there in one of his golf sweaters right now, in some leather recliner, just sitting. Lola imagines he is playing carols, some album he made for the Christmas show. He is sitting in his recliner on a fine spring day listening to "Away in the Manger" and waiting for the Personality to return.

Once in a while, the crooner gets up and looks out to see if she has pulled in. And then when he sees she has not, probably he just hobbles back to the stereo, turns over the album, and with a great deal of effort sits down again.

Lola cannot herself bear the thought. "The weekend, Marcie?" she says. "Are you sure Steinem told you the weekend?"

Marcie shakes her head no. "He didn't tell me a thing, Lola," she says. "MaryBeth wrote it to him in a letter."

And well, I think here, so I was right. Marcie does indeed read Steinem's mail. I wonder if Steinem knows this.

Marcie gives us a little smile. "The Personality is not stupid," she says. She never writes Steinem anything much, she must guess his mail's opened by somebody else.

Yes, I think, but I still wonder if Steinem guesses.

"In her last letter," Marcie says, "she wrote she'd be arriving on Friday." For the taping, she wrote, she called it "taping" in her letter. "The Personality is always careful to make it sound like just business."

Frances looks at Marcie, disgusted. "And Steinem is paying her too," she says. "Steinem would do that, for all three days, right out of one of our grant funds. Consultant fees: one TV personality, services rendered."

Lola herself is not so concerned with financials. She is still on the topic of extramarital affairs. And "Well," she says, "I jes don't think it is right. When some ol' gal's married, she jes shouldn't be seein' somebody else. And Steinem shouldn't be seein' her neither. It ain't what you call complex."

Complex? I tune back in. We have stumbled onto familiar ground here. I know something about this matter of seeing. And oh Lola, I want to tell her, you have no idea how complex it is, when you find it is you who is seeing a married man.

But Lola is off now about a previous visit from MaryBeth. That time, she and Steinem had been in his suite working all day. Until, that is, about five when Lola, who'd stayed late, noticed the shade at Steinem's door was now all the way down. And then, Lola says, when the two of them left for dinner, they jes sorta had that look to 'em.

"Right there in his suite?" Marcie says. How bold.

Lola lets out a snort and nods. It is easy to tell she is only just started on this subject of would-be adultery. Texas outrage is Lola's particular forte, yet another reason for not bringing up Ben around here.

Ben? My mind takes a sudden sharp turn. And it's no use then to pretend I'm still listening here, that my mind is anywhere but on Ben.

Because here is the thing. Just now when Lola brought up Steinem's drawn shade, I thought once again of my trip to Ben's. How once I got to his farm, the shades at Ben's windows were all down as well. And what I couldn't place then but has come to me now is that something was wrong with that picture. Ben likes things open, he likes a view, he is not one to be pulling shades. In the time that I knew him all this fall, never once did I see them down. Not even when Ben was away.

So what does that mean, those drawn shades? What were they hiding behind them? Why wasn't Ben to be found?

And despite what I've been thinking about rescue, how there is probably no real reason for it, I'm thinking I may be wrong.

White Van

But now the editors check their watches. We have talked enough for one day. And at any rate, look at the time. It is almost four o'clock at the Project. Time we were all heading home.

And I'm relieved then at last when I am back on the bus into town. I need to be off to Ben's, I still have Ben Adams to find today, it is more pressing now than ever. But the ride home is slow, we have a new driver as I feared we would, and we arrive in town later than normal. I hurry off the bus and push on.

At the crosswalk I head north, wait as normal for the light at Summit. And once again, there, the white van. I catch it out of the corner of my eye, in the haze of late afternoon sun. A large white van moving in from behind, idling sinisterly just off to my left. I turn and take a quick look through the glass. It is never, as I've said, someone I know. But then, in a glint off the windshield, I see him, the large angry man from the dream, oddly smiling and beckoning—get in.

My heart slams into my chest. So it's true, he has found me. I try to think which way to turn. The street is quiet, no one is out, there is no one to call to for help. The man could easily jump out of the van and stuff me into the back of it. That's how it goes with vans, it is why serial killers drive them. I know I should run. I start to push off. But like in a dream, both my feet stick hard to the walk.

I turn my head to call out. Maybe someone inside a house will hear. "Help me," I call. "Help me! Oh please, for godssake help!"

And when no one comes out of his house then, waving his arms and shouting, copying license plate numbers as he runs to me, I think well what now do I call? The large man in the van has arrived? He is here now in life to do me harm as the dreams predicted he would?

"Help me!" I call again. And when still no one comes, I cannot help thinking well isn't it just like a dream though? To twist things like this and hang you to dry? Instead of driving off a bridge on a country road, I am cornered here at a crosswalk, almost dead center of town. Looks like the dreams' directions were wrong.

I turn one more time to the van. Maybe I'll offer the driver a deal, or simply plead for my life. But now the sun's gleam is gone, and as I look through the glass, I see I have made a mistake. The driver is not who I thought he was. It is just some town hippy, a man with white hair and a beard from out of Zap Comix. He is gesturing to me to cross. The light is green. I've failed to notice it's my turn.

The man smiles and waves. I hurry on, I do not know what came over me. But I know now I have no more time for white vans. The number of vans in this town is uncalled for.

Mrs. Eberline, Again

I walk fast down the rest of Church and Grant, turn onto Mott, and plunge on, head down, race-walking for home. But when I stop then a moment for bearings, there up ahead I see her. Mrs. Eberline is again at my door.

She has spotted me too, she has turned and is hailing me feverishly, her arm up and waving high. I can hope only it will be a short visit.

"Mrs. Eberline, well hello," I say from the walk. I climb the bank and up the steps to my door. Then standing, towering actually, over her, I say, "Is there something I can do for you, Mrs. Eberline?"

I am wary now of course about this new visit. There is my couch to consider. And there is also of course Ben Adams. I do not think I can take any more of Mrs. E and her threats and rants about Ben. Or her visions of Ben and the trouble he is in. Just now, I would say, I have trouble enough of my own.

"Open the door, missy," Mrs. Eberline says. "I got somethin' to say." She looks at me, determined, unmovable.

Mrs. Eberline is on one of her missions, it appears. And I know from experience there's no stopping her. So I check first for any lighted cigarillo, then reluctantly I unlock the door. Well all right, I am going to tell her, come in. But just for a minute, please. Really, I have just a minute.

Before I can say this, however, Mrs. E pushes past, I assume headed for the front room. But she stops then, looks up, and suddenly breaks into a grin. "That Ben feller, he come back!" she announces. She points toward the window. "I seen his truck right there out front."

My whole body jerks back like it's just hit a wall. "Ben was here?"

Mrs. Eberline nods and smiles widely, showing all of her gums.

I look at her hard. Ben? Could it be true? She's not just imagining things?

"When, Mrs. Eberline?" I say. "When did you see Ben's truck?" I think Mrs. E is mixed up here. She's only remembering how it used to be.

"Just now, missy," she says. "Just a hour ago, while you was out at work."

I study Mrs. Eberline closely. I do not know if she knows what she's saying, it could be some other truck on this street. I do not know if Mrs. E knows her trucks.

And besides, I think, why after all this time away, why now would Ben choose to stop by? And why, when he knows my schedule, would he come when I was away?

It is not making sense. "Well no, Mrs. Eberline," I say. "I do not think it was Ben that you saw." And I offer that the truck was probably just someone a neighbor on Mott Street had called. Some plumber or TV repairman.

"We need to be sure of our facts here," I say.

Mrs. E's smile fades. She considers me, stares a moment more. Then as though she's just got the picture, her eyes narrow and she gives a short, incensed "humph."

She turns away. She is now all action. As quickly as she is able, she drops to her knees, puts her cheek to the floor, and takes a look under my couch.

"Mrs. Eberline?" I say.

She pretends not to hear me. She stands. Then straightening the hood on her parka, she scuttles back toward my entry and opens the coat closet door. Peering inside, rummaging, she reaches behind the dry cleaning I've hung there and pats along the far wall.

"Mrs. Eberline," I say. "Just what is going on?"

She stops where she is and takes one last glance. Then her shoulders drop, she turns, and she trudges back slowly to me.

Mrs. Eberline does not now look herself. Her face is pale and her eyes have gone flat again. She appears less stable than ever, and I am worried something is wrong. "Here, Mrs. Eberline," I say. "Take a rest. Have a seat. Sit here." And I offer her usual end of what is now left of my couch.

Then against my better judgment, I also offer to go get her water. But on my way back to the kitchen, apparently Mrs. E revives some. Apparently she has also thought up a new tack, I can only guess to what end, because "Tea, darling," she calls in her Belva contralto. "If you don't mind, dearest, I'd much rather a cup of tea."

It takes me a while to find the tea bags. I myself drink only coffee at home, but for Mrs. Eberline's sake, or maybe for Belva's, I make a proper tea tray. Then as I am lifting the tray holding my best china cups and my mother's silver teaspoons, I hear a creaking in the floorboards above me. A sound that can only be Mrs. E. She has shown herself up to my second floor and is pacing around my bedroom.

"Mrs. Eberline!" I say. I hurry to the stairs. "Mrs. Eberline!" I call again, my voice rising as I climb.

Mrs. Eberline meets me at the top of the stairs. She cocks her head and eyes me. "So there, missy," she says, tossing tealess Belva aside. "What've you did with the man?"

"Man?"

And I realize then what she is up to. Mrs. Eberline thinks Ben is here. That indeed his truck was outside just now, and he is somewhere now here in this house. Has been maybe for some time. Because rather than continue to share Ben with her, I've decided instead to hide him.

I take Mrs. Eberline's old, crepey hand. I lead her carefully down the stairs and station her back on the couch. I bring in our tea, sit, and pour her a cup. "Sugar?" I offer, and hand her a teaspoon to stir. Then, as kindly as I can muster, I say, "You still miss our Ben Adams, I see."

Mrs. Eberline just stares at her cup.

"Oh Mrs. Eberline," I say. I sound heartfelt. I reach again for her hand. "Oh Mrs. Eberline," I say, "let us put Ben Adams behind us."

Mrs. Eberline glares and snatches her hand back to her side. She watches me warily.

I try to think what to say. I want this issue of Ben put to rest. I want Mrs. E off my back. So I lie and say something I don't myself feel but something I think she just might fall for. I tell her how I am pretty sure, given a little time, we'll both forget all about our Ben Adams. It can happen, I say, if we try. I make it sound like we are in this together.

Mrs. Eberline does not look like she believes me. The point here being, of course, we are not in this together. We have never been in anything together. Mrs. E, if anything, is behind enemy lines. Or then again, maybe I am.

That is, simply put, Mrs. E is just no fun to live next to. For years now I have had my concerns about her. She is, as I've mentioned, an incorrigible thief, also a liar and bully. She is the reason I no longer leave things in grass or linger outdoors myself, that I keep watch now pretty much always.

Which I must say, as a homeowner and former renter, is not the kind of freedom I'd hoped for. And now knowing about neighbors like Mrs. E, about owning a home nearby one, I do not think I would buy a house again. I dislike the proximity to so wanton a force, to all of the snatching and loss. It just makes me hold tighter myself. Which is no way to be a good neighbor, I know, and also not good for the soul.

Mrs. Eberline taps at my shoulder. "Missy?"

I turn to look at her. I've been neglecting my duties as host. So I thank Mrs. E for stopping by. And getting back to the reason for her visit, "Ben Adams is not here, Mrs. Eberline," I say. "Ben Adams, you'll remember, is gone."

I stand and look at her on my scorched, soggy couch. She sits, head down, more wan and wizened than ever, and for a moment I truly do feel sorry for her. And while there is nothing at all to be done about that, still I grasp for something to say, a way to end on a more pleasant note. I tell her once more how we'll forget about Ben. How we'll be happy then back alone in our houses. "Happy enough as we were before," I say, smiling brightly and bravely. Then I walk to the front door and open it. "Just you now wait and see."

Head up now, Mrs. Eberline scowls, rises, and starts for the door. But at the threshold she stops, takes one more look toward the closet. Then she steps outside, and without turning back, lets the screen bang shut loudly behind her.

I return to clear our tea tray. I must hurry if I'm still to find Ben. But in the kitchen I look up at the window and see the sky is turning to dusk. Once again, Mrs. E has outstayed her welcome and now it is too late to find Ben. In the time it would take me to drive to his farm, it will be dark and impossible to search.

Then tomorrow, I think. Tomorrow whatever else happens— tomorrow I will find Ben.

I sigh and go back to the tray. I begin placing our cups in the sink. And it is then that I find Mrs. E and I have a new issue. One of my mother's teaspoons is missing.

Fleeting

A small postscript to Mrs. Eberline's visit, although I did not say it to her of course: How coincident she should think Ben is hiding out in this house. The fact is, at times I too have had the sense he is here. Always it is fleeting, however. I do not, like Mrs. E, expect to find him behind the dust ruffle of my bed. It's just that some- times while passing an open door I think I have caught a glimpse of him. There, lying stretched out by the fire, his feet in his old woolly socks, crossed at the ankle, toe jiggling. There again, out in back on the lawn, raising his iced tea in salute. And for a moment, again there at the window upstairs, shaking his head at Mrs. E.

It is only my imagination, I know. Wishful thinking, halluci- nations of sorts, arising for an instant to stand in for Ben. Side effects of sensory deprivation.

Such things can happen to people. People with missing limbs, for example, who feel shooting pain in an absent knee. Or the deaf who hear someone calling their name, or the blind who see shooting stars. So why not also when someone disappears, someone important to you, who has somehow got caught in your being? I think it can be just the same. Some of him still remains.

Tonight then as I am falling asleep, I roll toward the far side of the bed. And there deep in the folds of the sheets, I catch the faint, clean scent of Ben Adams.

Six

Regulations

Something I didn't mention: Last night on TV on the late night news, a story from the West Coast. An update on news that had aired several weeks before—a drowning, the victim a large man in his fifties, mentally ill, they don't know.

I remember the original story. It got a lot of national play, and it was a hard one for most of us to take. In the middle of the day, the story went, a man waded far out in the ocean, announced he was ending it all, and then began thrashing and calling for help because he did not know how to swim. Desperate to help, a woman on the beach called the local police, then the fire department. But, as the story explained, tax revenue for the county was low for the year, affecting the budget for rescue, and all the policemen and firemen too had orders not to go in after swimmers. Regulations, their superiors said. No one was to be saved from the sea. Well maybe only small children. So first responders just stood on the sand that day and watched the man out in the ocean fight for his life and then drown.

Tonight's follow-up covered a hearing in the town near where the man died. People who saw him spoke. Ten firemen turned out at the beach, they said, and not one of them got his boots wet. Fuck regulations, one speaker said. Those responders were all still men. They could have saved the guy if they'd been men.

So now this morning, again the dream. This time when the truck sails out over the bridge, local farmers gather below. They see the truck somersault high in the air, hit the ice, then start to go under. No one moves, they just watch the truck sink. And I am there in the crowd beside them all, staring dim-witted and hollow.

I awake from the dream weeping, my bed pillow sodden, the sheets twisted onto the floor.

And then there is something more. I lift my head. A scent in the air, wafting, familiar, autumnal. A slight singe to the air, now biting. Smoke, something burning. Out in my yard.

Fully awake, I rise and rush to the window. Mrs. Eberline, it can only be Mrs. E. I lean over the sill and look out. And I see her there two stories below me stoking a miniature bonfire, just under my silver maple. Stoking with what now look to be the silver maple's twigs. Hurling them back at my house must no longer suffice, Mrs. E has moved on to a pyre. Open flames here this early dawn. With the morning breeze about to pick up.

"Mrs. Eberline," I cry. And then I go for a roar. "Stop!"

Bracing for the Personality

With Mrs. E now temporarily back in her house, the bonfire in my yard doused and out, I decide to deal with this new crisis later and head off to work at the Project. My plan is to check in just long enough to tell the editors I'm taking the day off. I'll say something's come up, it looks like a friend is in trouble, and I need to go to him now. Then I'll be off to Ben.

But as soon as I arrive at the Project, I know something is up there as well. The editors are all aflutter. And when I see what it is, I know then too my escape plan will have to wait. The Personality, it turns out, indeed is coming to visit. Marcie was right about that one. The Personality in fact is expected at any time, Dr. Steinem has just informed us. And with very little warning or for that matter concern, he has asked us to take her to lunch.

This is no small request on Steinem's part. As I've said, we are not fond of the Personality here. She cannot be up to anything good, and we wish Steinem had not invited her. We would just as soon he were not banging her either.

"She will break his heart," Celeste says. "It is why the woman is here, she has come to break his heart."

Poor Dr. Steinem. We are all of us worried for him. But among us, it is Celeste who is most concerned. It is Celeste who looks after his welfare, who takes a real interest in him. Which is in her own interest as well, of course. Steinem is the reason Celeste stays employed. She could hardly be working anywhere else, not with all her long tea breaks, her many errors of every day. But here at the Project, until the Personality that is, Celeste was always Steinem's favorite. He hired her first, he took her under his wing. We suspect there was even a romance, although Celeste demurs and we have no absolute proof.

Still, whatever Celeste's feelings for Steinem, or our views, it is unlikely they will change anything much. There is just too much history with the Personality here. Frances is our clearest on the subject. She is coming, Frances says, it's decided, and we are stuck with her now for lunch.

Frances likes to think she here knows the most about the Personality. How Steinem chose her, how she first came to the Project. It was after Sally Ann had turned in her early outlines, Frances says, mostly just cat-rat-bat-gnat sorts of words. And Dr. Steinem, seeing the need to supplement, also hoping to convince adopters of the good basal-reader news, decided audio tapes were in order. It was a simple idea, and like Steinem, dull. For each grade's series, the Project would record long tedious lists of vocabulary words and offer the tapes free with the readers. Because, as he explained in the grant for the program, children must hear how new words sound before they can be expected to read them.

"'Oh' sounds before 'oo,'" Dr. Steinem reminded. And then stressed the need for perfect pronunciation from just the right friendly voice. From someone with flair who also liked children. Or at least pretended she did. Which, Frances says, is why he proposed MaryBeth.

The fact is, Frances is not the only one here who knows about MaryBeth. For some time, I have had her number as well, it is not just at the Project I've run into her. A few years ago now, long before Steinem brought MaryBeth on board, I read a newspaper interview with her. I had at that point no reason to disapprove of the woman. But as I read on, I did.

I remember picking up the society-and-entertainment section of the paper that Sunday because I had read everything else and did not yet want to do the dishes. I do not often read the society-and-entertainment section. It is usually just photos of aged matrons posing on charity ball stairs. Or sometimes a feature article or two on a small-town lady entrepreneur, the latest woman to start a needlepoint birthday card shop. The article normally makes the woman out as some kind of pioneer, when really she's just indulging her hobbies, with her husband, the surgeon, backing her. It is irritating, reading such stories, when there are women in this world who are pioneers in fact. There is the woman in this town, for instance, who started a low-income women's health center. Among her other good deeds, this founder raised money for poor women's flights to obtain legal New York abortions, when our state was not yet so enlightened. This woman has more than once been imperiled by mobs at her own clinic doors. And there are other such pioneers in this town as well, it is just that the papers don't know about them. Although to be fair, it could be pioneers don't grant interviews.

At any rate, the article on the Personality caught my eye. It was a syndicated story—filler our paper sometimes pays for—an exclusive with Miss MaryBeth Malone. Miss MaryBeth from children's educational TV, specifically *The Magic Garden*.

The story was supposed to be just about the show, which was celebrating its fifteenth year. *Magic Garden* was a half hour of oddly informative hand puppets, it was one of the oldest children's programs on TV. But as it turned out, the article was more about MaryBeth. She had a way of making herself come up. And even though she was not the show's original host and was at that point relatively new, the interviewer kept asking her well how does it feel, fifteen years in children's TV? He asked because he thought that he had to, you could tell.

From the first, the interview made me nervous. It was, for one thing, overly candid, and it occurred to me that MaryBeth and the interviewer had most likely been out drinking beforehand. More than this, however, there was just something strange about a woman who consorted with puppets. MaryBeth sounded suspect from the beginning, as when, right away, she took full credit for the *Garden*'s fifteen years. She said it felt good all those years. Gratifying, actually. Her show's little made-up world had helped a lot of children grow up in that time. Young adults were forever stopping her on the street and thanking her for their fantasies.

I could not tell what the interviewer made of that comment, but it seemed to get his attention. And for the rest of the article he just let her go on. The two of them reminisced over the show's long run and then generally went into a tell-all.

"Oh yes," MaryBeth said, "and then there was the time we had to move on from Sampson, our original lion puppet. Mr. Bixler, our lead puppeteer for ten years, had retired, and the new fellow Drawley just could not get Sampson's voice down. It was a deep voice, but the new fellow made it sound too gruff."

And here MaryBeth paused the story to explain how we in television must walk a fine line between what is interesting and challenging for children and what will only frighten them out of their little minds. "In Mr. Drawley's case," she told the interviewer, "we were concerned his lion voice was just too scary. We were afraid we'd have bed wetters on our hands. So we had no choice, we had to get rid of Sampson."

It was no easy task, MaryBeth continued. "Children are very involved in our show, our little puppets are real friends to them. We could not just let Sampson disappear and expect the children to forget him."

But then MaryBeth stopped, she chuckled, the interviewer described her as chuckling, and she disclosed how she and the producers came up with the Magic Forest. It was the first time they used the forest on the show, and it was perfect, MaryBeth said, she didn't know why they hadn't thought of a forest before. They simply had Sampson run off to the Magic Forest. It was something the children could understand, how Sampson, a lion, would be happier in a forest than a garden.

"Although to be safe," she said, "we broke the idea gradually to the children. We told them at first that Sampson had gone to the forest just to visit some lion friends and had Sampson write letters to the children. I read them aloud to the other puppets, to Arnold especially, Mr. Drawley's new rabbit. The children didn't yet know Arnold was Sampson's replacement. They still thought Sampson was coming back."

But then, MaryBeth told the interviewer, we let Sampson's letters drop off, we let the children just not think about Sampson for a while. And finally one day, when we thought the children had got used to Sampson's absence, we told them how he had written one last letter to them. That in fact Sampson wasn't just visiting the forest anymore, he'd decided to move there permanently. He had written to say he had fallen in love. It was his old high school lion girlfriend, they'd been seeing a lot of each other in the forest.

And now they were getting married and planned to settle down right where they were.

Sampson closed by saying he hoped the children would be happy for him. He would certainly have nice memories of them all and when he had little lion children of his own he'd make sure they tuned into *Magic Garden* every day. The children at home should know he would be there watching the show along with them.

"The Magic Forest was a lifesaver," MaryBeth said. "The children accepted Sampson's leaving. Their mothers wrote to say how happy they were for Sampson and his new wife. So that then, when we got into trouble on the show, we knew there was always the forest. We even changed the backdrop, we had a new one painted and added a hill and just over the hill, we had them paint the tops of a few trees. We had them put in a road sign, the kind with arrows, with 'Magic Forest' on the one pointing over the hill."

"Without the Forest," MaryBeth said, "I don't know what we would have done about poor old Rufus that day in the station's parking lot."

Rufus, the interviewer explained here for readers who hadn't been following the show, poor old Rufus was the show's real-life dog, a wolfhound-Airedale mix that throughout most of the show lay at the foot of MaryBeth's chair. Rufus got an occasional close-up on screen, but he was not often written into the script. The producers did not think much of Rufus. He was not a particularly talented dog and mostly on camera he just slept.

But we kept him in the show, MaryBeth said, because a consultant, a child psychologist, once told the producers he thought it was a good idea, a real dog on a show like ours. With so many puppets around, a dog might help ground the children. And besides, the psychologist added, children like dogs. Rufus would help the ratings.

So the producers kept Rufus in the show, MaryBeth said, but they just had me pat him once in a while. There wasn't much reference to Rufus, except that sometimes the other animals were not awfully nice to him. They teased him a lot. And the new puppet Arnold complained that Rufus was really too slow for TV. He, Arnold, a rabbit without any legs, could hop whole circles around him.

I suppose Arnold was right, MaryBeth said, because when I started backing out of my parking place that day that Rufus followed me out to the lot and suddenly realized he was lying right behind me, I honked but he just couldn't get out of my way. By then, of course, I couldn't get out of his either.

It was extremely unfortunate for the show. We could not very well tell the children I had backed over Rufus in the staff lot. But luckily we had already thought up the Magic Forest. So of course, it was a simple thing to write into the next day's script that Rufus had taken up chasing squirrels, that he was last seen following one in the direction of the forest.

Naturally then, in a few days we received our first letter from Rufus. He had met up with Sampson and his wife, and as it turned out, Sampson was fond of squirrel chasing too. Every day he and Sampson went out after them. In the forest there were squirrels enough for all. Which is why, Rufus wrote, he thought he just might stay, although he sent his best to the children. He certainly would miss all the children.

And so there in an article you have it, I'd say. She is a dangerous person, all right, Miss MaryBeth Malone. We none of us at the Project like or trust her. Well, excepting of course Dr. Steinem.

Celeste Discusses New Options

The editors and I are now back in our suites, pretending to work at our readers while waiting for the Personality to arrive. But it does no good, we are all of us far too rattled, so that rather than wait for our usual break we all rush out early to the solarium. We stand in a circle at the coffee cart and pour ourselves full steaming cups. She is late, we say. We cannot imagine what has happened to the Personality.

And then as it nears ten-thirty, as we finish our second coffees and still wait for the Personality, abruptly Celeste has something to offer. In a pause in the conversation, apropos of nothing at all, again she brings up Emmaline. Last night, she says, she read once more about ghosts. It was helpful, she says. She picked up a few new ideas, specifically on how to get rid of them. Ghosts, that is, most specifically Emmaline. And Celeste would like now to tell us about it, she wants now to know what we think.

We none of us look at her or look interested. We are tiring of Celeste and her ghosts. We have other concerns, the Personality primary among them.

Frances says, "Oh well, Celeste, just do as you please. We trust you will make the right decision. I believe you were leaning toward compassion, correct?" And she adds then she's sure compassion will work well, just so long as it's not expected of her.

Celeste leans forward, glad she has finally engaged us. "Actually, the thing is," she tells Frances, "I've decided to move on from compassion." And she says she has been thinking things over and how it just seems that trying to grasp why ghosts hang on is not actually getting her anywhere—with Emmaline, or with anyone here. "As far as ridding us of her, however, there are a number of other things we can do, and I for one would like to give them a try. But I thought someone else might want to weigh in."

And Celeste offers up then what she's considering. "There is, as I mentioned, sage. Ghosts are not partial to it, you know. But the trouble with sage is you must burn it and force the smoke into each crevice and corner. It just seems like a lot of work, not to mention damaging to the lungs. So I read then a bell would do nearly as well, you just have to make sure, as with sage, that you ring it in all the right places, in closets and attics and crawl spaces. You have to be very thorough. The idea is to get the stale air, where ghosts prefer to hang out, moving again to discourage general loitering. One book even suggested vacuuming, if you did not happen to have a bell."

Which sounded again to Celeste like a lot of work. As did hanging convex mirrors on each wall or scattering rice on the floor. "Although the latter involves an interesting theory," she adds. For reasons it didn't specify, the book explained that most ghosts, when encountering grains of rice, feel compelled to stop and count them. And because ghosts, it is known, are generally not good with numbers, they frequently forget where they are in the count and have to start over and over. If you put out new rice every night for a week, ghosts, the book said, find the prospect so daunting they soon leave for a less complicated haunt.

And then, Celeste says, the book suggested laying lines of blessed salt at all doors, which ghosts are not known to cross over. Or painting the doors red (ghosts, the book said, abhor red). "But my favorite," Celeste says, "is the shoes."

Shoes?

"Yes, shoes," Celeste says. Here too, the book offered options. One approach, she explains, would be for all of us here to place a pair of our shoes, toes pointed in opposite directions, outside our suite doors every night. The conflicting directions of all those toes would confuse any ghosts who stopped by, and eventually deter them from the floor.

But the second option is even better. Which is to gather a pair of shoes worn by a ghost when still alive and place them outside the door, both toes in this case facing forward. The message would be clear to even a half-aware specter, and by morning both the ghost and the shoes would be gone.

Shoes, you say?

"Shoes," Celeste says, and smiles her knowing smile. "They give permission to leave, don't you see? They will say to Emmaline as nicely as we can that we are no longer in need of her services. She is free to take off and pass over."

Hiking

Like the others here in the solarium, I am weary of Celeste's Emmaline, I have not been particularly listening. Instead my thoughts just as yesterday have turned back to Ben, well, back to Ben and me. Although it's a relief to see they have not returned to where we left off, that is to our unfortunate undoing. The threat of lunch with the Personality, I must say, is gloom enough for one day. So then, while there's still time before she arrives, a few thoughts here of Ben in happier times, little things I happen to remember.

For instance, Ben, have I mentioned, is a hiker. He hikes, he takes exorbitant pleasure in hiking. So this past fall that is what we did a great deal, we hiked, Ben and I, together. When we were not having dinner or iced tea in the grass, we would stand up and take a short hike.

Which at first was a problem for me, as I do not much care for going on walks. Except of course for my occasional turns about the sanatorium grounds, now in the spring for example, when the land is fragrant and fecund. Other places, other seasons, however, I would just as soon drive as walk.

But Ben is a hiker, irrespective of season. It comes, I think, from living so long in a Western state. It must be their culture, to get out and hike, to take on mountains and deserts if they must. No doubt it's from all that ruggedness there, the raw terrain, the pioneer spirit that Westerners feel obliged to maintain.

But here in the Midwest, we do not have such challenging landscape. The soft curves of our loess hills and alluvial valleys do not call a man loudly to nature. Still, in the time that I knew him, given the smallest opportunity, Ben would lace on his boots and suggest we go out for a hike.

I should mention Ben's hiking boots here. Ben owns a pair of good leather boots. They are wonderful boots all in all, the leather well oiled and worked in. Soft, lovely boots, but sturdy, reliable, well, something like Ben. They are impressive, these boots, and I think now one day I will buy hiking boots of my own. They may change my perspective on hiking, for that matter on nature itself. It could be just a matter of footwear.

But because I do not yet own any boots, when Ben and I hiked this fall I would put on my old running shoes. And then sometimes we'd just poke along the river for a while or tramp through what we call here "timber," small stands of tall trees, odd outcrops of forest, planted by homesteaders a century ago to catch prairie winds in their branches.

And then, when we had run out of river and trees, mostly what we'd do for our hikes was go out and check on the crops. That's what the farmers here say. When they want to get out of the house and leave whatever they should really be doing, they say well, they had better go check on the crops.

Slackers that we were all this fall, Ben and I, we did a great deal of crop checking together. With our eyes down, our sightline on furrows, it kept us from looking too far ahead.

She Arrives

And now Marcie has joined us in the solarium. She is worried, she says, the Personality should have been here by now. Marcie booked her flight here herself, it was supposed to have landed at eight, the taping to end by nine-thirty. But then before we have time to turn hopeful, to think maybe something went wrong, maybe Steinem took back his invitation or at last the old crooner got wise, the elevator doors open and there stands the Personality, resplendent in shocking pink.

The elevator is next to the solarium, there is only the hallway between us and so there is no escaping it, the six of us are caught huddled here with our coffees, idling. And for a moment we all just look back at the Personality, we just stand where we are and stare.

We are first of all, as usual on her visits, surprised at how short she is. We cannot get past it, how short the Personality appears, shorter than on TV. It must be all those puppets, we think, compared to those puppets anyone would look bigger on TV. But then today there is something new. What has got our attention just now is all that pink she has on. We cannot take our eyes off her ensemble—that bright pink linen coat in particular, voluminous and ruffled and tied at the neck with a bow that is really, we think, too young for her.

"Why hello there," the Personality calls, which is also something new for us. Never before on her visits has the Personality actually managed to greet us. Dr. Steinem has taken up all her time. But today "Hello, hello," she calls to us, her voice pointedly musical, and waves with the fingers of both hands. It is the way a preschooler would wave, and we know right there it's a sign. The Personality has spent too much time around children, she can no longer separate them from her. Or for that matter, them from us.

She steps out of the elevator, and walks toward us. And although she is short, although she is in fact a rather squat little woman, she is also, we can see it today, really still quite beautiful. Her skin is dewy, her eyes are a startling blue, her hair a soft honey blond.

For *Magic Garden*, we know, the Personality wears her hair

down long and wavy and many days she even adds ribbons. It is not becoming, we think, for a woman in her forties, well, mid-forties, to wear ribbons on a regular basis. But today, we see, she has pulled her hair back and up, very smooth. It shows off her bones to her advantage, she cannot have missed that fact. And although it's true her hair is generally blond, now on closer inspection we can see that in front she is letting it go a little gray. It makes her look like she knows what she's doing, this gray hair. We would be wrong to underestimate her.

"Hello again, dears," she says to us warmly, although from the "dears" it is clear she has no idea who of us is who. And then getting right down to business, she lifts her chin and in a commanding voice announces she is here to see Professor Steinem. Would one of us be so good as to let him know she is here? She believes they had a ten o'clock meeting.

She says all this as though she buys it herself, that she is just here at last for their ten o'clock. She enunciates well, Dr. Steinem is right about her impressive elocution. And then when she is finished speaking, she settles herself down into a solarium chair, throws the linen coat off her shoulders, and smiles up at us calmly. As though she has all day to wait until someone brings her Professor Steinem.

We are all six of us still standing at the coffee cart staring. But then Marcie snaps to, says, "Oh yes, Miss Malone, I believe Dr. Steinem is expecting you." Then she hurries off as though she isn't sure but will certainly go check the appointment book.

The rest of us excuse ourselves too, that is, we pick up our coffee cups and nod at the Personality. We say how, well, we'd better be getting back to our desks. And MaryBeth nods and smiles up at us, still very cool, as though she thinks maybe we'd better be getting back too.

On our way to our suites, we see Dr. Steinem coming down the hall. He does not seem to be in any hurry, he even stops and says something to Lola, something about the second-grade art, how nice we're on schedule again. He is acting quite normal, I think. We are all of us extremely normal here.

And then once in my suite—I have left the door open, but then that is normal for me—from where I sit I can hear Dr. Steinem say, "Miss Malone, welcome. So good of you to come again." After which, he shows her back to his office. It is a long walk, his office is at the end of the hall and they have to pass all of us on their way. So while they walk, Dr. Steinem tells the Personality loudly how he has an interesting project planned for her. Though he warns her it is a rather big project this time, several tapes, it may mean several more trips. He understands that she may have to think about it.

We are none of us fooled here of course. Especially not Mary Beth. As they pass my office, she laughs at something Dr. Steinem has just said—something about the Project, how very well lately he thinks we've been doing, how our grant money just keeps on doubling—and I get the feeling then she is laughing at the Project itself, at Dr. Steinem too. The Personality does not care what anyone here thinks, you can tell.

As I've said, she is a dangerous person. Smart too, in her way— well, wily. And I think now she is onto us here at the Project, onto our secret as well. Something has tipped her off. And now that she's here for her visit, sooner or later she'll get around to it. To our secret, that is, about our readers. To our catalog and first fall series that she mentioned on the phone to Frances. The

Personality knows only our vocabulary lists, the ones she reads for our tapes. She has no experience with our readers. But the Personality is not one merely to assume, as do others when they hear we write readers, that what we do here is actually turn out books. And now the Personality wants to see proof. Or at the very least, proofs.

So it appears it's time to lay a few more cards on the table. About our little secret, I mean. It's not only, as I've said, that we all of us here are inept. We are, it is true, but in fact there are some of us who are worse. Who have decided that rather than let our deficiencies run the Project entirely to ground, have instead taken things into our own hands. Have guaranteed in effect that no one need know the truth, no one need see even one woeful word of our inadequate little readers, or at least for as long as possible. Who have committed, therefore, not so much an error, as an error of gaping omission.

Well one of us anyway. Me.

To explain: When it became clear to the editors, well except for Celeste, that their stories were unacceptable, but they shrugged and still they kept writing—offering in their defense that they were just doing their jobs, the actual publishing was out of their hands—I'm sorry to say I at once saw the way out for all of us. Publishing, that is to say printing, is not technically out of my hands, since as assistant editor of Project design, I am our sole contact with printers. It's a responsibility that has come in handy of late and also key to our secret, part two.

That is, I know our point here is to turn out readers, to turn out series of readers. I also know each editor at the Project needs her job and needs to write stories to keep it. But I have read the editors' stories, board by stultifying board, and I know it would now be seriously wrong to take them any further. It would be wrong, for instance, to inflict them on children. Who might get the idea, or so I have reasoned, that life itself is like all those stories, when in fact it is not nearly so drab and drawn out or devoid of so very much meaning.

So partway into this year, I made a decision, with which the editors, minus Celeste, all agreed: Although the Project had promised to publish its series in time for the looming new school year, all our imaginative little tales of make-believe would instead remain just that—make-believe. We would have no inaugural fall release.

To this end, I have not sent one thing to a printer. Rather, as I finish each of the stories' boards, I just place it on top of its predecessor, in a pile I keep hidden behind my suite door. Which goes for the catalog boards as well, which are not even yet fully inked. It is a risk, all right, but one I am willing to shoulder. For the good of the children. For the good of the Project. For our continued gainful employment. For as long as I can get away with it.

And to date, oddly enough, it's worked out. Steinem, besotted and longing for MaryBeth as he's been, has not checked our work all year. The grantors as well do not seem concerned that we have nothing to show for ourselves. We are a publisher that only pretends to publish—a big secret as far as the reading world goes and you would think a hard one to keep. But for two years now the Project has produced not one book, and so far no one seems to have noticed.

However, here is the catch. In the last month or so, I have myself felt a growing impatience, with the Project or myself I cannot yet say. I just know that some days I am tired of the pretending, the fooling, and all of the hiding.

Which in the beginning, I admit, I did not consider a problem. I have never been much of an employee. I have never, truth be told, much tried. But with so many days at loose ends, with so many work hours to fill, I find I look now only for diversion. I do less and less paste-up, I'm behind on my boards. My mind strays at every opportunity. I'm growing forgetful, I have twice left the hot wax plugged in over night, I have left the caps off my markers. The fact is, I'm beginning to lose interest in general here. There is, after all, only so long a person can hoodwink.

But then some days I think it is more. There are days now this spring, when I stare at the glow of my light table, that I find I am called away. And when I look up to see where it is I have gone to, I find a strange sad new distance to things. It is as though there on a fault line directly beneath me, life gives a tremendous jolt, wrenching apart into halves. And from where I remain then, dazed on the rim, I hardly recognize the other side. I'm left aching and rocking and holding myself with both arms. For months this is how it has gone.

In the Grass

I sit in my suite and shake my head hard once to clear it. But enough now of our little secret. The Personality, the Project, for that matter. Enough of these dreary thoughts of work and back to the sweet ones of Ben and me. With the Personality off to her meeting with Steinem, I know there's still time for a few. Thoughts of Ben and the farm and the hiking, all that. But also our starry nights. It is something I haven't yet got to. Those lovely fall nights in Ben's grass.

It did not of course begin with the nights or the grass. As I've said, for the first month that we were together, Ben Adams and I were just learning to be friends, the kind of vigilant friends you manage to be when one of you is married. But then came the day, or rather the night, when we were no longer just friends.

It began with one of my visits to Ben's to once again check on the crops. The day was warm, we lost track of the time, and stayed out in our furrows until dusk. Dinner ended up as leftover chicken, there was no time to barbecue that night. And then afterward, although we had finished late, Ben asked would I like to go look at the stars.

Now I happen to know the front room of Ben's house came with a big red telescope. I also know Ben sometimes sits behind it, staring out at the night through the window. It makes me think Ben's landlord did much the same, that he was a stargazer too, so I've no idea why he left his telescope. Maybe it was just a passing fancy of his, something to fill long farm winter nights. But I like to think it meant more. I like to picture the landlord there late at his window, searching the stars, bedazzled. That it was not all just earth he was tied to.

But tonight Ben is not thinking of his landlord or what it might be that beguiles him. He says only who needs a telescope, Margaret? The evening is clear, for October warm, and would I like just to go out and look up?

Ben is excited, he has in mind a show-and-tell, I can tell. Ben knows a lot about stars. And so I say well sure Ben, OK, although in fact what I'm thinking is how late it's become, that it will not be so easy now driving back home. The road from Ben's is rutty and dark with sharp curves hard to see even by day. Still, "Sure Ben," I say, and try to sound like I think it's a wonderful idea.

It turns out then in fact it is. Because when I follow Ben out his front door, incredibly there they all are, thousands of stars, making the whole night glimmer. Well who knew there could be so many stars? It is not like this in town, I tell Ben. We have stars there, yes, but they are only the usual few town stars, diffused and standoffish, stuffy. But here out at Ben's the country stars shine, exuberant and free and, well, startling.

Ben walks a little before me, an old army blanket under his arm. He is headed for the farmyard's front bank. "Here, Margaret," he calls. And I can tell Ben has done this before, this is where he comes nights to watch the whole sky on his own.

He sits down and leans back on both elbows, so I do the same. And then pointing up, "Look, Margaret. Cassiopeia!" Ben says, as though she is some old friend of us both and how happy we are to see her.

"Cassiopeia?" I say, and peer hard at where Ben is pointing, as though I know what it is I am looking for. And I realize right there I need to stop Ben. I do not know my stars, I am not a tracker of constellations. Ben should understand this.

He does of course. It is why he has brought me out here. But I am saved then from a lecture on Cassiopeia the Queen and the stars that make up her throne, also why she occasionally chooses to hang from it upside down, because just then a night breeze blows over Ben's farm and sends a little tremor through me.

Ben does not miss my shivering, nor the fact it is late, that the temperature has dropped considerably. "Cold, Margaret?" he says, and looks at me, then doesn't wait while I pretend I am not.

Rolling onto his side, Ben reaches on past me, and pulling the far edge of the blanket, wraps it back over us both. We lie close in now, Ben's head next to mine. The blanket feels warm and I smile. I look at Ben, he smiles as well. "Good, Ben," I am going to say. "The blanket feels good." But "Shh," Ben says, putting his hand up to stop me. And then before anyone knows it, we are kissing.

Now here is something I have learned about kissing: Scientifically speaking, it is directly proportional to proximity. I read this once in a social psychologist's report, although of course it's not really news, or the psychologist's point, considering the range of most lips. The psychologist's point was that something more causal is at play, that even without real emotion involved, proximity by itself can promote kissing. Actually, the psychologist did not say kissing exactly, what he said was intimacy, that proximity between people promotes intimacy. But really in my case it is kissing.

I have never been the same since that report. It has ruined perfectly fine moments with men I have known, or for that matter with men I did not know. Because since that psychologist's report, when I find myself physically close to some man, say when attending a crowded performance, if I make the mistake of turning to look at whoever is seated next to me, if he happens then to reach down at my side of his seat for his program that's just slipped to the floor, I am taken by an irrational, overwhelming urge to lean in and plant a kiss on him, often on the nearest ear.

But with Ben, it is more now than just that we're proximate. It is more than a passing stranger's ear. Because now we are kissing and kissing and kissing. We cannot seem to stop kissing. And then touching and holding and rolling in close, then rolling up onto each other. Followed by even more kissing. It is surprising us both, I'm pretty sure. What is going on here under this blanket?

And now look at this. Things have taken yet a new turn. Ben is sliding his kisses down onto my neck, he is saying my name at the dip of my throat, "Margaret, Margaret," over and over until it is almost a moan. And now moving his hands down the sides of my shirt, now under my shirt and onto my skin. Now down, down to my jeans.

I'm aware of only how close Ben is and how large and exciting and good. And also how surprisingly nice he smells, clean, something like rain. I lie still and feel Ben push up against me, feel the thrill of his body on mine. And my hands then reach out for him all on their own and fumble for his belt and belt buckle.

So that was our first night as more than just friends. After which, Ben and I stargazed a great deal. All fall, in fact, we could not either of us seem to wait for that time in the evening, after dessert and before one or the other of us took our leave, that one or the other of us would pause, then say well, here's an idea. Want to go look at the stars?

We Take the Elevator Down

But now it is noon and the Personality is only too pleased to have lunch with us, she says. We are all too dear to give up our lunch hour for her. She makes it sound as though that is what pleases her most, the sacrifice we have made for her.

But really, I think, what pleases her most is that so many of us have shown up, that we all seem to want to spend time with her. We do not, of course, tell her it's because Dr. Steinem asked us to. And besides, that is not the only reason. We are all curious about this woman. We would not for the world miss lunch. Although it will also be tricky, we know, spending so much time alone with her. We will need to keep her diverted, we will need to keep conversation light. We will need in particular to keep her off the topic of the Project's readers.

Because Dr. Steinem has asked that Celeste be our lead hostess today, she is the one to pick up the Personality at his office, to bring her back down the hall. The rest of us, however, are ready, we stand outside our doors waiting. And when we spot her then on the way toward us, we see she has put that shocking pink coat back on. She must think we are going out for our lunch, well she is in for a big disappointment.

But the Personality spots us then as well. She sees we are all out in the hall. And smiling and looking pleasantly surprised, she calls, "Oh, are we all going to lunch?" After which she tells us the part about how she is really, only too pleased.

Lola, who, as second lead hostess, has planned our lunch-hour itinerary, says oh no, it is our pleasure she is sure, and laughs loudly. Then she wedges in between the Personality and Celeste and taking the Personality's arm, says, "We all just wanted to get to know you, hon. We've heard so much about you."

So then, Lola and Celeste take off with the Personality for the elevator and the rest of us follow. We all fit in, although we are shoulder to shoulder. From the back, Frances grumbles that Sally Ann's purse is taking up too much room. She could for once leave Mr. Bones behind, he does not have to spend the whole lunch hour with us.

Marcie taps the Personality on the shoulder and whispers that Mr. Bones is a puppet. "He lives in Sally Ann's purse," she says. Marcie figures, I suppose, she should warn the Personality now. Sooner or later Bones will offer up something most likely unfortunate at lunch, and it is better that the Personality is prepared.

Because Frances is hungry and does not care how Bones might behave at lunch, she says to the elevator in general that this is Mexican Lasagna day. Then, for benefit of the Personality, she explains, "The cooks here rarely stick to a single cuisine. Last week they served Szechwan ribs with a side of wilted collards."

Lola starts the elevator and on the ride down, she stops briefly at the third floor. It is Lola's way of giving MaryBeth a tour of Elmwood, as Steinem requested. That is, the doors open at third, we all stand staring out, and Lola says, "Well and this is Chemical Abuse. Alcoholics and drug addicts, mostly." There is no one in the hall, we are staring at a door across from us, which is closed. So far it is not much of a tour.

But just as the elevator doors are about to shut, a man runs down the hall toward us. He is trying to catch the elevator before it leaves. "Wait," he shouts. He is a large man, strong, a workman of some kind, he has on a plaid flannel shirt. His eyes open wide as he runs. He looks like he is in trouble.

Lola pushes the button for hold. "What are you doing?" the Personality exclaims in a loud whisper. She stops smiling and grabs involuntarily for Lola's sleeve. "The man's a drug addict," she hisses, loud enough we can all hear. "He'll want to knife us for our purses."

She is going to tell Lola to start the elevator again, to quick, close the doors. But it's too late, the man has made it. He stands for a moment panting, trying to catch his breath, and then he pushes into the elevator along with us. It is a tight squeeze, he has to turn and drop one shoulder to fit, and it leaves him facing into the top of the Personality's head. She stands staring straight in front of her.

"What floor?" Lola asks the man. She sounds cheerful, like some elevator operator who is happy to have a job.

The man is still panting and doesn't yet seem to be in any shape to answer, so Lola pushes the button for ground. She must figure it's a pretty safe bet for a man like this on the run. The doors creak shut, but the elevator just stays put. We all wait, we do not ourselves move. There is only the sound of the man in flannel trying to catch his breath.

Then comes a loud clank in the shaft above us and the elevator begins to drop. It is moving very slowly, Lola looks as though she is about to say how slowly it is moving. But then the man in the shirt seems to have his wind back because he says in a low voice, "I come to turn myself in for drinkin'."

He is talking to the Personality, it is her head he is facing. She only stares at the doors. "I come to turn myself in for drinkin'," he says again, louder, as though maybe the Personality didn't hear. "They said third floor, they told me at the desk, third floor, so I go to third floor."

The man is shaking now, we can all feel it on the elevator. He is talking louder and louder and because the Personality isn't saying a word, Marcie, who is standing behind the man, tries to be of help. "Third floor," she says, and pats him once on the back. "Yes, you had the right floor."

"But no," the man says, very loud. "Nobody's there, see? I get to third floor and I look up and down and there ain't nobody there."

"Oh well," Lola says, and laughs as though that's easy enough to explain. "It's noon, they're probably all out to lunch."

Which is the wrong thing to say, all of us in the elevator know. There are drug addicts on third floor they keep always strapped to their beds, they do not all just go out to lunch.

It is not clear why the man could not find anyone on third floor. But we have reached ground, and the man is shaking quite badly now. Lola opens the doors and we are thankful when he starts to get off. But he turns then, he faces us, he looks frightened. "It will be all right," Marcie calls from the rear. "Come back at one o'clock," she says. "It will be all right at one."

The man looks at Marcie, then turns and starts to walk toward the front entrance. Lola pushes the button for basement. But then, just as the doors are closing, the man turns and starts running back toward us. The Personality gasps, she is afraid he will get on again, he will want to ride with us now all the way to the basement, maybe have lunch with us too. But the man does not try to stop the elevator this time. He only looks at us through the gap in the doors, his face pleading.

"They won't turn me away, will they?" he says. But the doors close and we do not any of us have time to answer.

We ride to the basement then and as we get off the Personality says, "Good god, do you get those people on the elevator often?"

She imagines the alcoholics and drug addicts have nothing

better to do than ride the elevators all day. But Lola sets her straight. She takes the Personality's arm and steers her under a large pipe toward lunch. "Oh no, darlin'," she says. "Addicts take the stairs. We hear them up and down, up and down all day." Then Lola offers, "It's the crippled children who ride the elevators."

The Personality looks surprised. "Crippled children?" she says. "You have cripples out here too?" And Lola says, "Oh my yes. A whole ward full, just the other side of our solarium—two floors up from the sick convicts' wing."

The others nod vigorously in accord. But then because I have not been contributing, I suppose, all the ride down and even now, because it's clear I've not even been listening, "Isn't that right, Margaret?" Frances says, and gives me a jab from behind.

Ben's Story

I have not been attending, it's true. The fact is, I'm still thinking of Ben and me, about our nights there in the grass. And how this fall in the dark at Ben's farm, it was not only all starlight and kisses. How sometimes we would stop and roll onto our backs and just lie for a while very still. Until after a while more, someone would say, "There is something I want to tell you."

It is not so unusual, I think. Lying outdoors in the dark can make people want to say things. To say something to someone that matters. And so now and then on our nights in the grass, Ben and I would just talk and tell stories. About times we were young that have stayed on our minds—swinging alone in a park at dusk, knowing the exact point where the sun dropped down. Seeing an ocean the very first time, the thrill of wet sand between toes. Small things we just happen to remember, things we've not told before.

There is one of these nights in particular I remember, and a small story that Ben had to tell. Which was a big story when he told it, I think, it's just that now I remember only parts.

That night Ben said that when he was young, there was a redwood tree in his front yard. Ben was raised in the West, his family owned a small ranch. It was not so unusual for houses to have redwoods then. But this one redwood tree was spectacular. It was the biggest one on their whole ranch, so tall you couldn't see to the top. And when Ben was little, he said, he was convinced it was his own tree of life. He took that redwood to heart. Every day he would lean in close to it, his chest pressed into the bark, and he would stretch out his arms on either side. If he tried very hard, he'd believed, he could reach all the way around.

"I just thought I should try for that tree," Ben said. "I thought at the time it could happen. I would reach blind with both arms around that big tree and one day on the other side I'd feel the tips of my fingers touch. I guess I just thought that is what it's about."

I turned and tried finding Ben's face in the dark. "What Ben?" I said. "What's what about?"

Ben looked back, I could just see his eyes, a shimmer of light caught in them.

"All of it, Margaret. All of it." He stopped. I could tell he did not much want to explain. But then, "Love, Margaret. Take love, for example. I thought maybe that's what loving was like."

Ben stopped again. Then watching me closely, his voice lower, "And if you were lucky, then dying too. Maybe something like dying too."

Lunch with the Personality

Now at last we are at the cafeteria. Celeste, who, like me, has not said a word since we left our floor, pushes the door open for the Personality. "Well here we are," she tells her. Then without saying anything more, she hands her a tray and a fork wrapped up in a napkin. It is all she can muster as hostess.

The Personality revives at the smell of hot food, she tries to look pleased to be here and thanks Celeste with a nod. Then she says brightly how she has been looking forward to lunch. She seems to have worked up an appetite on the ride down.

It is Mexican Lasagna today, Frances has called it correctly. As we start through the line we can see a woman who is serving large squares of it there halfway down, between the soups and assorted Jell-O salads. Usually the cafeteria offers a choice of entrees, today there was also fried chicken. But we are too late. The chicken, a server tells us sadly, was gone by twelve-fifteen.

We all take the Mexican Lasagna and "Over here," Lola calls and leads us to an empty table. She has found us one in the middle of the room, we have to walk only a short distance to get there.

Our table is next to one with four men who are sitting in lab coats. In a low voice the Personality asks if they are from the convicts' floor. She has not missed Lola's point that there are convicts, ill convicts, in this building, and she thinks now these men in white coats must be the convicts' physicians. "No, sugar," Lola says, "they work at the animal lab." In a building behind us, she says, where they do research on very small animals. And then Lola adds, "Vivisectionists, I reckon."

Luckily, as we are eating later this noon, we have our table to ourselves. We do not know if the vivisectionists have heard Lola. We all just sit down and spread out our trays. And "Well, isn't this interesting?" the Personality says when she has got a good look at her lasagna. The cooks have layered corn tortillas between the ricotta and sauce, we can see them jutting out in little triangles at the side. "Corn tortillas in lasagna, who would have thought?" the Personality says. And Lola replies, "Beats getting 'em cut up in yer Jell-O." You can't imagine, she tells the Personality, what they try putting in Jell-O around here.

We all take a bite. It is not as bad as it looks, we agree. And so we consider the lasagna for a while, how the chili powder the cooks have ad-libbed goes well with the lasagna's red sauce, although it does seem strange mixed in with the ricotta.

But then because there is only so much to say about Mexican Lasagna, we soon find we have exhausted the topic. And for a moment we all just sit silently and try for another bite. Which is when, to fill the void or maybe just out of meanness, the Personality directs us to Sally Ann. Apparently she's picked up on the graceless way Sally Ann slumps now over her plate and also on the oily locks in her food. She does not know this is normal for Sally Ann. She thinks only that Sally Ann could use a few pointers—etiquette, hygiene, posture— because then "My, Sally Ann," she says. "Is that how we sit at table?"

It is a rude question, it was intended as rude, and immediately

Bones is out of the purse. Glowering at the Personality from the table's edge, he barks, "What's it to you, lady?"

The Personality is taken by surprise, she jumps a little in her chair. It is only a small jerk, still we can tell, despite Marcie's earlier warning, she wasn't expecting puppetry at lunch. But then she recovers, she remembers who she is. She stares at Mr. Bones and, incredulous, asks, "What is this, a joke?"

"No, no," Marcie says. Marcie is still anxious to keep peace. She feels responsible for the Personality. As administrative assistant, Marcie often feels responsible for more than her share. "Don't you remember?" she says to the Personality. "I told you in the elevator, this is Mr. Bones. He's a puppet."

The explanation does not help the Personality, we can see. She has already figured out Bones is a puppet. She is only too familiar with puppets, in fact she is sensitive on the subject of puppets. She thinks maybe we are mocking her now with this Bones. And she plans to make clear, we are pretty sure, she did not come all the way to this rotting sanatorium to be mocked by some degenerate's puppet. The Personality is not one to be mocked.

But before she can say so, before she can stand and walk out of the lunchroom as she has undoubtedly decided to do, Bones says, "Shh, listen," and cocks his whole cereal-bowl head toward the cafeteria's south windows.

As I've mentioned, the windows in the cafeteria are small and high, at grass level with the outdoors. Still they do let in light, and because they are open, they also now let in noise. So when Bones tells us shh, we all turn our heads and listen. And yes, there is the sound, wheels screeching on gravel. One, maybe two large cars, pulling fast into Elmwood's guest parking.

We listen a moment and then "Drug addicts," the Personality says, her eyes big. She must think some of the addicts from third floor, and maybe a few convicts from second, have got loose for the noon hour and are racing cars in our lot.

But she is wrong because we see the cars then, they stop near our side of the building, and here's something new, they are the highway patrol. Two patrolmen now run past our window view headed toward Elmwood's side doors.

"The highway patrol!" the Personality says. "There, you see?" She still thinks all this stir has something to do with drug addicts. The patrolmen have come to arrest some of the addicts.

But "Shh," Mr. Bones says. He's just heard something more. So we all listen again, and we hear it too. Something beating at the air above us, a kind of slow flapping like some giant flag caught in a steady breeze. Except now it grows louder and faster. It whips up its own high wind, oak twigs and a plastic cup and sections of newspaper whirl past the cafeteria windows.

Then we see it, the pontoon feet appear first, and we all know it is AirCare, the helicopter the university hospital deploys for all outlying emergencies. It is something brand new for the hospital and apparently a wise investment. Given the large drinking-age student population, our town is prone to emergencies, and since AirCare arrived, we have all frequently spotted it overhead. But this is the first time any of us has seen it actually land. Right here, right in front of our sanatorium.

We watch the helicopter hover, looking for a place to set down. The parking lot is full, and a patrolman is now directing the pilot to the grass alongside, to two large picnic tables waiting there. The helicopter turns and swings sideways and begins to drop for the tables.

"Look, look," Mr. Bones says. He is excited. We are all excited, we had not counted on an emergency for the Personality's lunch. It does add, we think, to the visit.

Then as we watch, before the helicopter's pontoons even touch ground, a man and woman jump out of one side, each carrying leather satchels. They are quick, they bend low, heads below blades. Even in half crouch they run fast.

The patrolman runs as well to meet them. There is a great deal of wind now, it flops their trousers against their legs and whips the cap from the patrolman's head. He lets it go, and grabs the woman by the arm. Then together all three of them run to the sanatorium's side doors and disappear quickly inside.

We watch as the helicopter touches all the way down. Its blades continue to turn. It is an emergency all right, we all know. The pilot has kept the engine running.

And then everyone in the lunchroom starts to talk all at once, at all the tables around us. Everyone is asking what is it, do you know? What happened? AirCare normally flies just to the highway for crashes, it has never before landed at Elmwood. It must be something bad.

One of the vivisectionists leans across the aisle and says to the Personality he bets it's one of the convicts. "Probably slit his wrists," he says. "You get some of that type out here." Although it must be serious this time, usually the infirmary just patches them up. "The guy must have done a real good job," the vivisectionist says.

The Personality takes in this news. But she still holds with the drug addicts we can see, although we do not know why she favors them so, not with a lunchroom here full of convicts. Still, she says to our table when the vivisectionist turns away, "If it's anything I bet it's an addict." Probably shot himself full of mayonnaise when the keepers weren't there watching. And then she tells us how she once read an article about it, how some addicts, when they can't get their hands on heroin, will shoot mayonnaise or peanut butter into their veins. "It gives them some kind of rush," she says, although it cannot be good for them, is her guess. Often they die, but if they live almost always they end up in a nursing home. "No, it's a drug addict, definitely," the Personality says, and nods her chin up at AirCare.

Frances stares at the window where the Personality points and says, "Well yes, that may be. But isn't it odd they haven't taken back off yet?"

We all look through the window at the helicopter. Frances is right, it has been some time since the man and woman with the satchels jumped out, maybe ten minutes, although we're not sure. But we can see the pilot looks bored. He is still in the helicopter, the blades are still turning, but he has picked up a newspaper and opened it. He must always keep something with him to read for long emergencies like this.

The Personality turns back from the window, she wants our attention. "They are a real problem, those drug addicts," she says, tapping her plate for emphasis. If she had her way, they'd all be locked up in prisons. It is a mistake, she says, to have them running about a sanatorium like this, when people are trying to work. "It is a wonder," she says, "Professor Steinem can get anything done here at all, with drug addicts all over the place."

But then "Oh no," Mr. Bones says. He has come out of Sally Ann's purse again and is jabbing his head and the whole length of her arm at the window. "Oh no, Sally Ann, oh no!"

We look back at the helicopter and we see the pilot has cut the engine. The blades slow their speed, they turn slower and slower, then make half another turn and stop. It is not a good sign, no, oh no.

"Well there you are," Frances says. "Whoever, whatever he was, apparently he didn't make it." And without waiting for the rest of us, Frances stands to leave. There does not seem to be any point now in staying. And she herself has deadlines.

We all stand up too. We push in our chairs, we start for the cafeteria door. No one is talking now. Even Lola does not have anything to offer, and it is quiet in the elevator on the way up to fourth. We do not stop for a view of any new floors.

It is all right, the Personality tells us. She does not much feel like a tour just now. She looks, we all notice, a little peaked.

Washcloths

One more thing I've just remembered about Ben. Ben and me and the matter of washcloths, an issue on which we initially disagreed.

That is to say, Ben Adams, when I met him, did not keep one single washcloth, he did not in the least believe in them. It was a sign, or so I thought then, of something to keep an eye on, an early warning of some covert feral state or general vagabond listing.

To be fair, it's been an issue with other men I have known, they did not use washcloths either. I do not fully know why this is. It could be there is something unmasculine, or maybe just anticlimactic, about standing in the full force of a hot, sudsy shower—naked and hirsute, vigorously rubbing at armpit and chest, shaking back water into the light, enjoying it all immensely—and then stopping to dab with a small wet rag.

I do not have a feel for the gender implications of washcloths. I just know that when men are left to themselves, men who are single and live mostly alone, often in one-bedroom apartments, these men are unlikely to stock any washcloths. Which makes it difficult if you are to stay over some night and find in the morning you have nothing to bathe with but soap. You manage of course, you figure it out. But it is not the same, and it is not, I think, too much to ask of a man to keep a few washcloths. It's not like they take up room.

Ben Adams, of course, is not single, nor was I planning a sleepover and bath. This waking mornings together is a step I've not taken with boyfriends, or at least with the general majority. The prospect was always too unsettling, and then again far too settled. So it was not something I was inclined to try with Ben Adams, although the topic did one day come up. A topic related, as I was getting to, to washcloths.

That day, Ben and I were just back from a hike. I had come unprepared. I'd worn sandals, it had rained, and I stepped into his bath then to wash the mud from my feet. "Ben," I called, searching the cabinet. "Ben, where are the washcloths?"

"Washcloths?" Ben called back. "You want washcloths?'" As though this were some new vocabulary word he needed to try out in a sentence.

I should mention Ben Adams is not a man who is intent on housekeeping details. He has, for instance, not bothered with the matter of sheets. I know this because I have seen the sleeping bag that is draped the length of his bed. With a sleeping bag opened on top of a bed, you can just lie down and zip the bag up. You do not actually need sheets with a sleeping bag.

Still, there is no real substitute for a washcloth, I have found. It is not all that easy to shower while scrubbing, for instance, with a sock. And so, "Washcloths," I walked out of the bathroom and said. "We need washcloths here, bud."

"Right," Ben replied. Then he shrugged and said he would look into it. By which I knew he would not.

It was that same night then, after we'd once again gone out to see stars, that Ben Adams proposed I just spend the night at his house. It was late, why drive home? He would make up the bed.

"No, Ben," I said. Though when he kissed me and asked in a whisper was I sure, I could leave right at dawn if I wanted, and started again to slide his hand down my side, asking again was I sure, I knew that probably I wasn't. Still, "No Ben," I said, and grasping for straws, reminded him he kept no washcloths.

I consider it fate then, and yet another sign, that two days later Kresge's dime store announced a big sale. We in this town are concerned for our Kresge's, the shelves of late have looked meager, and it could be the new Woolworth's that went up out of town is stealing little Kresge's thunder. So we were happy last fall to see Kresge's step up and mark down to Woolworth's level.

I myself stopped in for a browse and it was then that fate took its turn. Kresge's stocks everything and there at the back, next to a stack of thin bath towels, there gathered into bundles of bright pastels and bathed in a golden light, rose dozens and dozens of washcloths—not at the storewide twenty percent off but all on unbelievable half-off clearance. They were a store feature that day, a sign perhaps of low regard. But a sign nevertheless, and un-deterred by the half-off stigma, I gathered up several bundles of twelve and made my way back to the cash register.

Flushed and excited, I drove to Ben's farm to show him my lucky find. By another stroke of what could only be fate, Ben was not at the time at home. So I grabbed for the clothesline he keeps on his porch and started wildly to string. Ben has his own method for clothesline, it's true. But what we needed now was something more triumphant and much higher. So with the help of Ben's twelve-foot ladder, I stretched my new line from the house to the pines, then back again, next on to the flagpole and around the two oaks beyond. Then I clipped on the washcloths, all five nubbly dozen, cheery buttercup yellows, rosy pinks, baby blues. And when a breeze rolled in high, as I knew that it would, the cloths overhead flapped merrily, no, gleefully all around Ben's half-acre yard. It looked like a happy farmyard announcement. The grand opening for some large open-air stall, a used car lot in holiday mood. Or maybe like high mountain prayer flags. Yes, like great strings of terry-cloth prayer flags, bright and healing and free.

When Ben pulled up in his truck then, he did not say a word. He just stood in the grass, looking up.

"Washcloths," I said. "We have washcloths here, bud." And pointed out we were set now for years.

I would like to say that delighted with my wit and generosity, Ben laughed, head back, full-bellied and loud. And he did. But then he did something more. Still smiling but now looking close up as he does, he took me by both my shoulders. "Thank you, dear Margaret," he said. "Thank you."

By which I knew we had just then moved on from washcloths.

The Personality Has Questions

We follow the Personality off the elevator, relieved to be back on fourth floor. It's been a stressful hour for all of us, we are happy that lunch is over. And we are looking forward now more than any of us can say to returning Miss MaryBeth to Steinem. It is Steinem's turn with her now.

While the rest of us stand with the Personality and wait, Marcie hurries down the hall to find him. Then, "Here," we say to the Personality. "Here, let us sit out in our solarium. It is a good place to wait and recover." Let us all just sit here and suffer awhile until Dr. Steinem arrives. And would the Personality care for a coffee?

Marcie comes hurrying back down the hall much too soon. She finds us out in our deck chairs and, breathless, tells us Dr. Steinem is tied up on the phone with a grantor, an extremely major grant funder. He had only enough time to tell Marcie he could not be disturbed. And that he sends his apologies to Miss MaryBeth, it is fortunate she is in our good hands. He should, he added, just be a few minutes more.

I can feel our collective hearts sink. We are stuck with each other those few minutes more that Steinem has ways of extending. And what occurs to us of course, well what is our concern, is that now the Personality will get around to our readers.

She sits back in her chair, and with a peevish little shimmy, drops her coat from her shoulders. She looks off toward the solarium glass, breathes deeply, gathers herself. And then just as we feared, she sits up a little straighter and seems now to have something to share.

But first she smiles her *Magic Garden* smile. I have seen this sort of smile before. I imagine it is the one she gave Rufus just before running him over. No, I do not like the look of that smile. It is our lunch, I would guess, what we and the drug addicts have just put her through. She is holding the lunch hour against us. And she's determined to get even.

So now the Personality leans toward us. She smiles again, this time kindly. She just wants to be friends. And she turns to Celeste. "Well now, Celeste. It's Celeste, is that right? Professor Steinem tells me you are writing about fish."

It is related to nothing we have said so far. But it is angling toward the topic of our readers, all right. It can't be the Personality is just trying for rapport, to show her interest in us.

And I am right of course because immediately then, before Celeste can answer the question, the Personality turns it back to herself, which is of course where her real interest lies. "Well yes, fish," she muses. "You know, I once thought about having a fish on the show, a puppet, I mean, maybe a carp, but it just never seemed to work out." The show's producers were split on what a fish had to offer, the show's writers couldn't think of good carp lines. So, the Personality says, she finds it interesting that Celeste, all on her own, could come up with a whole series on fish.

Celeste stands just then at the coffee cart, brewing a fresh cup of tea. She pretends to be busy straining the leaves. She pretends she's not heard this mention of fish, that she's not caught the reference to Joe Trout. But she is thinking about it, you can tell.

The Personality turns to the rest of us then and she gets at last to her point. She understands, she says, our new readers will be shipping soon. She would be interested, she says, in knowing more.

The Personality is on delicate ground here, and we do not any of us know what to say. It's bad enough, we think, that we must dodge around Steinem when he talks of our books as if extant. But now the Personality is here and she is curious. It's just like her to ask what we've been up to.

She sits and takes us all in. We do not any of us say a word. We just sit in our deck chairs and look as though, actually, we do not wish to discuss it. But the Personality is interested. She does not want just to let the subject drop. *Magic Garden*, she says, is always looking for something to read to the boys and girls there at home. And then she asks what we were all afraid she would: So then, does anyone have a book from our new offerings she could use? We could consider it a kind of field test.

For a moment we all freeze. We look at the floor, we are silent. But then finally Frances speaks up. She has an easy out here, she sees. "Well no," she says, she does not think her third-grade readers would do. "We are a little beyond *Magic Garden*," she says. Her stories are all future perfect and riddled with subjunctive mood. MaryBeth needs something more basic. And then gesturing the Personality toward Sally Ann, "Really it's the earlier readers you want. Isn't that right, Sally Ann?"

It's wrong of Frances to sacrifice one of us like this. Still, we all turn to stare at Sally Ann. Although we know she does not have a series either, we cannot help checking just in case, on the outside chance some publisher's proof has magically shown up in her suite.

Sally Ann blushes. She is not used to so many staring at once. And the Personality says then, "Yes, Sally Ann. You must let me see some of your readers. Dr. Steinem informs me the stories are all quite lively."

Which is a lie, of course. As I've said, Steinem has not read any one of our stories. And Sally Ann is far from lively. Someone is not telling the truth here, probably the Personality.

Sally Ann doesn't look like she knows what to say, and as usual reaches for her purse and Bones. We watch her fumbling and yes, we all think, maybe Bones will come up with an idea. Although the Personality did not seem much to take to him at lunch, it may be that Bones now can help us explain ourselves. But Sally Ann has run into a snag. She cannot coax Mr. Bones out of her purse, her fingers all jam in his bowls. Sally Ann is in trouble, we can tell.

It is Celeste then who speaks up for us all. Ever since the Personality brought up fish, she has been debating whether to jump in here, to go into any kind of detail. But although she is not one to flaunt, she says later, it seemed the only thing really to do.

"Perhaps you would like to see some of our new Joe Trout readers," Celeste says, as though she did not hear the Personality address her before. "They are part of our supplemental materials." Celeste is being modest. She could have easily said they are part of our gifted series, our exceptional, talented materials. It is how Dr. Steinem's proposals put it, although we all know it is really just Joe Trout.

Celeste is being modest, but she is also being a fool. She is, as I've said, not in on the secret the rest of us are. She doesn't know not to offer what doesn't exist. And I realize I have to step in here. "Well but I'm afraid that series is a little behind, it is still really just in flats. Remember, Celeste?" I say. Joe Trout is only in paste-up, I remind her, loud enough for the Personality to hear. It wouldn't be practical to read him just now. The imposition would throw off the plotlines.

The Personality raises an eyebrow. She must wonder at all our reluctance. "No really, it's fine," she says to Celeste. She can just look at a few of the boards. It will give her the general idea.

I shake my head a hard no at Celeste. And she seems at last to understand. No, it isn't wise to show things before they are ready, people will only criticize. So she says to the Personality that well, better yet, she can just tell her a little about Joe. And without waiting, she plunges in.

Joe Trout explains science to children, Celeste says. He came to her, that is the idea of a trout occurred to her in the first lesson. Which was the water, that is hydrologic, cycle, Celeste reminds us. She was at a loss at first, you can imagine. Where to begin? It was a cycle after all.

But then it just came to her one evening while waiting at a restaurant to be seated. There in the lobby were two large tanks, the kind where you could select your own seafood, trout and lobster mostly. And while watching them swim around and around, "Fish," Celeste thought. How perfect. Yes, a fish could narrate the water cycle. Not a lobster of course, but a trout, a trout would do very well. You just had to think how it would look to a trout, Celeste tells the Personality, then explains:

You could show first the pond, the trout watching the rainwater fall from a cloud to his pond. Then you could follow him swimming that pond water into streams, and from streams into rivers, and out to the sea. And then, while he lay floating there on his back, riding the ocean waves, you could watch him watching that very same water evaporate back up to a cloud.

"All I needed really was a trout," Celeste says. "And the rest was all pretty simple."

The Personality says, "Well yes, it certainly is that. Simple." And then she says it has been her impression that fish are rather stupid by nature. She cannot imagine they could teach a subject like science.

"Oh but trout," Celeste says. "Trout are different." Studies show they are exceptional for fish. Gifted, actually. They can be trained to jump, to carry things around in their mouths. "Like porpoise," Celeste says, "You'd be surprised."

"Yes," the Personality says. She would. Then she looks down the hall, checks her watch. Yes indeed, she says, her voice trailing off, she finds Joe an interesting approach.

Which she does not, of course. She is not even listening now, she is only anxious for Steinem to return from the phone and retrieve her. "Does anyone have the time?" she says. She thinks maybe her watch has stopped.

"One fifty-five," Celeste says. And then she says how, because Joe was such a hit that first lesson, she decided he should narrate the series. From water cycle naturally on to weather, then friction and how shadows happen. "And more," Celeste says. She has so much more planned for Joe Trout.

The Personality, who is still checking her watch, says well yes, certainly. She would have expected that of Celeste.

The Personality has given up on us here. And wonder of wonders, she no longer seems interested in our books. She just shifts back farther into her chair and gives her coat an impatient tug. Dr. Steinem will never get off the phone, she is thinking, you can tell. And she will remain forever in this deck chair in this sanatorium full of addicts, trapped by a gang of vacuous editors who insist on discussing fish. The Personality is wondering why she ever thought visiting Elmwood was a good idea.

But then we hear Dr. Steinem coming our way. "MaryBeth," he calls. "Oh there you are, MaryBeth." He waves to her, and at the solarium door he smiles brightly at us all. He nods in particular to Celeste. He is pleased we're entertaining the Personality so well. We have not all this time just let her sit reading magazines by herself.

"Henry," the Personality says. Her voice is flat, she does not sound particularly glad to see him. She only holds out her hand from her chair. Dr. Steinem pats the hand fondly, then helps her stand and places her coat all the way up on her shoulders.

"We're off," he calls to us over his back, as he steers the Personality toward the foyer. And "Oh Marcie," he calls from the elevator, and tells her just to take messages, he won't be back the rest of the day.

When the elevator doors close, "Well then," Celeste says, and walks back to the coffee cart for more tea. She is certainly glad to have had that little chat with the Personality. She would have hated to have her leave with no idea of what it is that we do.

And she looks then at Sally Ann. At least someone here was genuinely instructive. And turning to the rest of us, "Really," Celeste says, "we all must learn to present ourselves better."

Seven

The Editors Deconstruct Lunch

After Steinem and the Personality take off, the rest of us remain in the solarium. We cannot wait to find out what we all think, how it went with the Personality.

Celeste says well lunch was certainly more than we hoped for. Mr. Bones, who is out of the purse now, nods his cereal bowls up and down. And damn straight, Lola says. Then adds how that ol' gal won't be comin' back anytime soon.

"Still," Celeste says, "it's too bad about the helicopter."

Frances agrees. "Yes, we hadn't planned on anyone dying."

And here Marcie jumps in. "Well, at least it was no one we knew."

Marcie, although not inner circle at the Project, is quick to learn things in this building. While the Personality was grilling us just now, Marcie was back at her desk, checking with Elmwood's other administrative assistants to see if anyone knew who had died. And it turned out of course one of them did, she told Marcie it was some part-time custodian. An old guy, Marcie says. Just worked here a couple of nights a week and normally he wouldn't have been here at all but he came in to have lunch with some workmates. And they kidded around, took him to where they keep their brooms, and shoved an industrial one at him. To see what he was made of, they joked. And then right there in the hall, the guy gave the broom a good push and dropped face first to the ground. His heart gave out on the spot.

"So it wasn't a drug addict at all," Lola says. And she tries out a laugh, as though we sure had the Personality there.

Marcie waits for Lola to finish. She has more still to tell. And then because Marcie is new and doesn't know that we know him, "The guy's name was Earnest," she says.

Earnest?

For a long moment no one says a word, nobody moves, except for Frances, who lights a cigarette. We are stunned. We are all of us now thinking of poor Earnest, all those years here he slumped over his mop and his pail. And maybe then thinking of our own sorry selves, slumped over our desks and light table.

It takes us a while more to recover. Then someone says well, it was certainly a difficult lunch. Someone else says well yes. And Frances says yes too. All right, then. All agreed. And taking a drag on her cigarette, "Can we now all please just move on?"

I am for once glad for Frances's candor. Because there is something I've been wanting to say. Earnest is one thing, the Personality another. And since there is not much to be done now for Earnest, it is the latter that has me concerned. The Personality suspects us, I'm certain. All her questions just now are a worry. I think it's those questions we should be discussing, not lunch, bad as it was for Earnest.

And I guess Frances is feeling the same way, because she says to the editors, "The Personality is onto us, you know. Our secret is out."

And taking another long drag, Frances as usual goes too far. "The Personality knows we've been faking it. She knows we're never going to publish a thing."

Frances is upset and not thinking. She has forgotten not everyone here knows.

Celeste sits up straight in her deck chair. "We're not?" she says. For a moment she considers. Swallows hard. "When are we never going to publish?"

We all turn to look at Frances. She sighs. "I said never, Celeste. Never, that's when. We have never once sent a thing to press. Every flat we have ever checked over is still there right behind Margaret's door."

Celeste blinks, absorbing the news. She gives it more thought, which then we can see takes a sudden sharp turn toward alarm.

Not really wanting to know, "Joe Trout too?" she asks, her voice hushed.

"Especially Joe Trout," Frances says.

Celeste turns and gives me a long stricken look. "Margaret," she says. "How could you?"

After Picnic

I do not right away answer Celeste. First because I do not actually have any answer. But also because I'm distracted. Because, that is, with the turn things have just now taken, with the Personality closing in and the Project in general falling apart, I find I am reminded again of Ben, of that night he and I took a wrong turn as well. That night of *Picnic*, I mean. And what became of us after.

So then, to get it off my chest and move on to more pressing business, here is what happened after *Picnic*. More or less blow by blow.

Leaving the theater, first thing, I tell Ben I cannot imagine what got into William Holden. "This was not his best movie," I say. If I were William Holden, I would not be putting *Picnic* on any résumé.

Ben does not say anything, he only just watches where he walks.

I tell him well, yes, and I am offended as well by Kim Novak. That so often she begged off in that movie. "You cannot help feeling her Madge is no towering genius," I say. "'Oh Ma, what is it just to be pretty?' What kind of line is that?"

Ben looks down, says he does not know.

Well, I say. I just did not care for that busty young Madge, that's all. William Holden could certainly have done better. He could, for instance, have gone on dating Audrey Hepburn.

Ben just stares at his feet. He is thinking of something else now, it's clear. Something troubling, from the look of him. It is the movie, all right. William Holden has upset Ben Adams. He is embarrassed for William Holden, he is embarrassed for me, that William Holden is my favorite actor. Well, something has made Ben turn quiet.

Ben looks up. "Would you like to get something to eat, Margaret?"

I stop and study Ben's face. It is late, nearly ten-thirty, I had been assuming we would just say good night now. Ben would say well he had better be getting back home. But instead "We could drive to the truck stop," he says. He's pretty sure we can get our booth.

Again I consider, hesitate. The truck stop? I am thinking.

Where the waitress thinks that she knows us? And did Ben just now say "our booth"?

Ben gives me a near pleading look. And so while I am concerned at his choice of venue, "Sure, Ben," I say. And I wonder then if maybe he's just hungry. I've known men to act strange when they're hungry. And I think well to tell the truth I am myself a little hungry, the movie has been a strain on us both, we could both probably stand to eat. The truck stop is open, it will be OK. Their service is quick, we can order their late night breakfast special, and maybe Ben will perk up after a hash brown or two.

But at the truck stop, it does not get any better. Ben sits without speaking, without looking at me. He waits for his eggs and plays with his fork, walking it in an oval before him.

"Ben," I say. "I would like to apologize for William Holden. I do not know what went wrong tonight, but I do not think William Holden was acting his age. Really, you have not seen him at his finest."

Ben looks up. He seems dazed, as though he has been somewhere else.

"Margaret," Ben says, and blinks. "Margaret," he says, and grasps for the words. "Margaret, I have been thinking. That movie just now has made me think."

"Yes, Ben?" I do not like this new tone in Ben's voice.

Ben takes a deep breath. "The fact is, Margaret," he says, "I could not take my eyes off that movie. It was like watching my life just now. You don't know."

I look at Ben, I am concerned.

He takes another breath. "The thing is, Margaret," he says. "I feel sometimes like William Holden."

"William Holden?" I am surprised, I cannot say that I see it. And I worry now where Ben is headed.

"Well not William Holden," Ben says. "I mean I feel sort of like Hal, that drifter, that guy that he played. I feel sometimes like I am just jumping off trains. I do not even know at what towns."

And then Ben says he is sorry, he does not mean to burden me here. "But Margaret," he says, "I have to tell you some things."

I sit very still and nod at Ben. And I think how I am sorry I ever brought up William Holden.

"Ellen says she thinks I am lost, Margaret. She says the last few years I have been just kind of wandering."

Ellen? His wife? Ben Adams has brought up his wife. This cannot be good.

I nod again. I do not know why.

"Ellen sees things sometimes, Margaret. She does not miss much."

Ben looks down at his hands. He sits silent and sad and away. And as I watch, something happens inside me. I see for the first time how alone Ben is, and I do not think I can bear it. Ben Adams is good, he is kind, he should not be feeling so bad. And I find I am wanting to touch him, to tell him it will be all right.

I do not, because now without warning he looks up. He is suddenly urgent, he wants me to understand. "It is like this, Margaret," he says. "When I saw William Holden just now kicking the dirt and making trouble because really he didn't belong— the thing is, I knew he was onto something. The only one in the whole movie who was, well maybe except Mrs. Potts."

Ben leans forward, more urgent still. "But the point is, Margaret, William Holden was onto something. I mean the man was alive. He was on the run and alive. And he knew that he wanted Madge Owens." Ben takes a long breath. "And he knew that he had a chance."

Ben reaches for my hand. "Here is the thing, Margaret," he says. "As I watched him just now, I knew something too. I knew all that he was is in me as well. Inside, that is who I am." Ben keeps his eyes steady. "It's only outside I teach art and I'm married and I live in a four-bedroom house."

I look at Ben. I try to make sense of his words.

He slows down. "But Margaret, you must know. It's worse when you are all those things. Because you cannot just jump the next train out of town. And you know it is no good, you cannot go on staring and staring at Kim Novak, not when you are married to Rosalind Russell."

He takes another breath, speaks more slowly still. "It just isn't fair to Rosalind."

Ben lets go of my hand and looks down. He stares at the table awhile, then begins walking his fork toward its oval again.

I watch him, I consider what he has said. And leaning in closer, I catch his eye. "So, Ben," I say. "Is there something you should be telling me? Is there something I should know?"

He sits, then begins to nod. "Yes, Margaret," he says. "There is." He keeps his head down, but I can tell. How sad again Ben Adams is.

"Don't you see, Margaret?" He puts down his fork and stares mournfully at me. "I think I am falling in love with you."

Love? For a very long moment I just sit. Then, without knowing what I am saying, "Oh dear," I say. "Oh my. Love?" I try to think. When did this become love?

Ben reaches again for my hand.

I give him a little smile, and feel my jaw clench, my face grow hot. Still I cannot think.

Ben stares and looks even sadder. "So here's what it is," he says, and he tells me then he has been thinking about things a great deal, even before the movie tonight. "And I think I'm in love with you, Margaret. That's just it. I think that maybe I am."

I sit very still. Oh no, I think. Oh no, no, no, no. This wasn't the plan. "Oh Ben," I say.

I look at my hand lying moist now inside his warm grasp and think of what Ben has just said. I think then of Ellen, his wife, a woman I have never met. And I do not know what to do.

I sit, head down, watching my hand in Ben's. And after a while, "Oh Ben," I say. "There has been a big mistake." And then I tell Ben I would like to leave. I would like very much to go home.

I look back up at his dear, sad face. "It is late, Ben," I say. It's too late.

It Worked for William Holden

He drives her home from the truck stop. He opens the door for her, tries to smile, then pulls out of the parking lot fast. Things are not going well. He has just said he loved her, that is he thought maybe he might. She has not said that she might love him too. And it is important to him now to get her home fast and mercifully out of his truck.

It is quiet on the ride back. She isn't talking. He can just see her from the corner of his eye. She only just sits in the passenger seat and looks straight ahead at the windshield. And he knows now it was wrong, a mistake, saying what he did about love.

But it worked for William Holden, he thinks. In *Picnic* just now, it worked for him. William Holden had swaggered and bragged all through the movie, he called women babes, he drove honking and honking to Kim Novak's house, and when he danced, he swiveled his hips, held his arms out wide, and clicked his fingers at the dark. William Holden was letting out a lot of stops, he was pretty much letting himself go, and people in town clearly liked it. He was charming them all, you could tell.

And you could tell, he thinks, there was something more too. It was not just all charm with William Holden. There was something else on his mind. So he'd watched for it, and at the Labor Day dance, when Hal and Madge danced on the dock all alone, it happened. William Holden pulled Kim Novak close to his chest, he turned her hand in his, palm to palm, looked into her eyes, and meant every move that he made. So that, no surprise, late in the movie when it came right down to it, he told Kim he loved her, just like that.

William Holden risked it all, and then he told Kim he needed to know, did she love him too? He said you love me, baby, you know it. And then he kissed her for luck and jumped back on a freight train for Tulsa.

It worked out for William Holden, he thinks. That kiss sold Kim Novak, at the end of the movie you know it. She is going to go with him, she will join him in Tulsa, they will start a new life there in Tulsa. It will work out for Kim and William Holden.

And at Margaret's house, as he walks her up to her door, Now, he thinks. It has to be now. You have to go after it. You have to try.

He reaches for her, turns her so she is facing him, holds her hard by the shoulders. And then everything happens at once. It is like *Picnic* all over again. It is William Holden now doing all the sure talking and holding. It is that drifter in *Picnic*.

"I love you, Margaret," he says. He takes a breath, tries to think. Tries not to say more. But before anyone can stop him, William Holden is at it again, swaggering in the old bare-chested way, saying, "You could learn to love me, Margaret. We could start our lives over. Begin."

She blinks, opens her mouth to speak.

He brings one hand under her chin and tilts her head back so that he is staring now into her eyes. "I love you, Margaret," he says.

And then he cannot say he knows anything more. But you have to claim what is yours, he thinks, and he puts both arms around her, holds her close, and feeling her warmth, kisses her full on the mouth.

It stuns him and leaves him reeling. But he holds on, closes his eyes, goes for a long one the way William Holden kissed Madge. And there are no thoughts in his head at all. He wants now only to stay here at Margaret's front door, holding this strange lovely woman, holding and holding and kissing.

Our Secret Is Out

"Margaret?" A sniff. A pause. Then louder, "Oh Margaret, Margaret. How could you?"

It's Celeste again, upset and about to go into a howl. I come to at the sound. I am not sure what to say. And I think maybe now we should change the subject, return to the departed Earnest. We should all show more concern for Earnest.

But Frances is at it again. "A valid point, Celeste, dear," she says. "How could Margaret? Really we'd all like to know."

I look at Frances, surprised. As if most of them didn't know already. Really, Frances should take more responsibility here.

But Frances is not yet finished. She takes a quick drag on her cigarette. "And how could Margaret get away with it?" she says. "That is another question we've had. Personally I've suspected it was only a matter of time before somebody found us all out. Actually, I've known it all along. People never get off free with anything, you know. I believe we're all finally in trouble."

Lola says, "Well now, Frances, whoa there, girl. Maybe the Personality just thinks we're slow. You know, a little thick. Reluctant to ride our high horses. That's why we don't trot out our books. And even if the gal does think somethin's up, who says she'll say so to Steinem?"

Here Lola addresses us all. "It's just her word against ours, am I right? Maybe she'll think Steinem won't believe her."

Frances gives Lola a long look. "And maybe we're all sittin' in tall cotton here too. Isn't that how your people put it? No, we're in trouble, that's clear. We'll probably all lose our jobs. And we have Margaret mostly to thank. It was Margaret who thought up not publishing."

I should be defending myself here. "Wait a minute, Frances," I say. "This wasn't all my idea."

Slowly Frances turns her cold stare to me.

"Well, all right, yes," I say. "It was my idea. But the rest of you thought it was a good one."

Celeste still is not sure what's going on. "You mean we'll never really turn out a reader? But what about all that grant money we've had? You mean we have nothing to show for it?"

Here Bones is out of the purse and unaccountably grinning. "That's right, Celeste. You're getting warm."

Now Lola looks worried. "So what happens if Steinem figures it out? Or one of them ol' boy grantors? Do we have to give the money back?"

"Yet another good question," Frances says.

The editors as one turn to me again. In a flash, they see unemployment, and a possible lawsuit, looming. And by my hiding their flats, by my saving their jobs, it is all clearly and only my fault.

"Well so much for teamwork," I tell them. So much for Steinem Associates, Unified.

And washing my hands of the editors in return, I go back to a last thought about Ben.

Tired

That night at my door, I do not remember expecting Ben Adams would tell me again that he loved me, that then he would kiss me the way that he does. It is not how we've been—there's been kissing, yes, but not like this—and it takes me by surprise. But before I can think that, what a surprise it all is, here is how the next part of the night goes.

Ben moves in to where I am standing, takes hold of my shoulders, and turns me around to face him. Then for a very long while there is only Ben Adams, alive and holding me tight. And oh my, I think. I cannot say how all this has happened, what exactly it is happening now. Suddenly Ben is here leaning against me, declaring his love and kissing me. How did this happen, I am thinking.

"Ben," I say. "Ben." But I cannot then think what else to say, and Ben goes on kissing me still. Until—could it be?—I feel a kind of shaking begin low inside. And oh no, I think, no. This is no time for trembling arousal, much as it might be for others. There are things we need to get straight, Ben and I. What is called for is focus, not lust. But before I can fully finish that thought, now I feel I am shaking in fact. Shaking and shaking, my whole body is shaking and won't stop.

I try to breathe, to gather some wits. What exactly is going on here? It isn't normal to shake so. And after more thought, what occurs to me is this is something much more than just lust. That given our history and Ben's marital state, then these abrupt declarations of love, what we probably have here is shock. Shock can do this to a body, can't it? Make one shake uncontrollably and even writhe.

Which is possible, I think, until I think then no, wait. No. And I feel again what it is I am feeling and think my god. No, this is fear. That's it. What I'm feeling is fright. I'm afraid. At which point I feel something new rise from below, a breathtaking, blindsiding panic.

Well, there you are—lust, shock, fear, maybe panic. If I could think just now, I'm sure I could not for the life of me say which it is. So instead, as my head starts to clear, what I go back to is what a surprise this is and also that it isn't right. It's one thing to take a roll in the grass, quite another to call it love. This declaring and kissing is not any of it right.

Besides which, the kissing is now going too far. I can no longer breathe, I can no longer tell who it is who is kissing.

"Ben Adams, stop!"

Ben opens his eyes. I have got his attention, and he lets go of me. He drops his arms, stands very still, and watches my face, waiting for whatever comes next.

I stare back at Ben. I do not know what comes next, what should come next. I only know I cannot do this.

"Ben," I say. "Oh, Ben." I try for a smile. "What I mean, Ben, is wait. We need to wait here."

Ben looks at me like he does not understand, studies my face, then looks away.

I reach out for his arm now down at his side. "Ben," I say, "Ben, it will be all right."

I have no idea why I say that. It is not all right, not at all all right. Now in this one moment, everything is changed. Everything is pretty well ruined. Still I hold on to Ben's arm, because I cannot now think what else to do. I only want somehow to help.

"I think, Ben, we are just a little tired here," I say. "It has been a difficult evening."

Ben turns to me. He does not smile. "No, Margaret," he says. And he draws back from my grip. "I love you, Margaret," he says, his eyes steady, as though he needs to make us both understand. "I am not tired, I am in love."

I do not know what to say. I do not know where to look.

"Oh Ben," I say. And I think oh please, Ben, do not say anything more.

Floppy

But now back again to the solarium, as Marcie—who has been listening to the editors talk, to their wailing and conviction I've just cost them their jobs—Marcie, it turns out, has news for us. It is, in the end, not good news. It is not news that the editors want to hear. But it is news that absolves me and while I'm concerned, I cannot say I am not relieved. Because now Marcie straightens her shoulders, breathes in, and says, "You know you needn't worry you're going to be fired."

We do not any of us know how to take this. It is not really Marcie's call. And cocking his cereal bowls in a smart-alecky way, "Oh really?" Bones says right at her.

"Oh really," Marcie replies. She looks at us, takes another breath. "The fact is, on Monday we're all being laid off."

The editors and I sit immobile. For a long moment it is perfectly silent. Then "What?!" Frances explodes and speaks for us all.

"Laid off," Marcie says. "The Project is folding. On Monday Steinem plans to leave us a note. Along with each of our pink slips."

Here Marcie grins. "I read his mail," she reminds us. "I know where he keeps all his reports. And when he left last night, I let myself into his office, I decided that it was called for. It's just seemed strange, the way he's been acting, the way he's put off getting a receptionist. So I let myself in and I read everything I could find. He's leaving with the Personality on Sunday, she is helping him pack all weekend. He is leaving for good, and he is closing the Project behind him."

Celeste opens her eyes wide. "No," she says, and stares blankly. Then her eyelids flutter and backing up, she collapses into a chair. It is not turning out a good day at all for Celeste. Abandoned—by her livelihood, now by her Steinem. "No, no, no," Celeste wails from the chair.

"Well, of course he ran off with that woman," Frances says. Frances has quickly recovered and in fact she is now not the least surprised. "They're probably on their way to Mexico right now. They probably told the crooner it's business." Frances laughs.

"But it *is* business," Marcie says. "That's what I'm saying. Dr. Steinem is leaving to go work for the Personality in L.A. He starts his new job on Monday. I found the draft of the note for us, explaining."

And then Marcie fills us all in. It took her most of last night to piece it together. She read all the Personality's correspondence, well, from the last month or so. The Personality was sly, she did not come right out in one letter and propose it. Still Marcie could tell, maybe better than Steinem, what the Personality had in mind.

"The woman is worried about the *Garden*," Marcie says. "One night last month some guy from her show got arrested in a Santa Monica bar. The papers down there had a field day because the guy was on *Magic Garden*. It worried the Personality, made her think maybe the show needed to change, needed some kind of new image.

"It's what got her thinking about Steinem," Marcie says. "That a PhD might help the *Garden*."

Frances sniffs. She cannot herself imagine Steinem as anyone's image. "Oh well, possibly the Salvation Army," she says. She can imagine he might brighten up that place. "The Personality must be desperate," Frances says.

"Well yes," Marcie says, "although she plays it down in the letters of course. She wrote only that there had been a little trouble with Lawrence. That was the puppeteer's name, Lawrence. Everybody in L.A. knows Lawrence. He does Floppy, it's this kind of puppet spaniel with big droopy ears who took over for some real dog they had. And the thing is, you actually do see Lawrence, his face, on the show. Sometimes he and MaryBeth have little heart-to-hearts, they let him sit on a stool out beside her with Floppy stuck on the end of his arm.

"Like Mr. Bones," Marcie says, and smiles at Sally Ann. Bones nods his bowls once, collegially. Celeste herself, listening, sits forward. Frances lets out an exasperated sigh.

"So anyway," Marcie says, "in her letters, the Personality just says there is this little trouble with Lawrence. She doesn't go into it much. She says only they will have to let him go and it is making them rethink their format. What would little children like? If not Floppy, what? And so they want to discuss it with Steinem. Because he knows about children."

Lola laughs. "Maybe they're confused and thinkin' of Bones. Maybe it's really Bones they are after." Lola looks over at Sally Ann. But Mr. Bones is back in the purse again and Sally Ann just sits oblivious.

"But the thing of it is," Marcie says, "it's more serious, this trouble with Lawrence, than the Personality lets on. I can tell by her letters that something is up. So I call my cousin, I have a first cousin in Santa Monica, and I call her and ask does she know about it? And she says she does, everybody does, it has been all over the papers, although in her opinion those papers have gone too far. The thing in the bar must have been at a slow time, there must not have been much other news."

And then Marcie tells the story. What happened is this. Lawrence took a girlfriend to a bar that night. Lawrence was, the cousin said, something of a lush and he and the girl spent a lot of time at that bar. Everyone there knew both of them. The girl was maybe only twenty years old and Lawrence, who was fifty-five if a day, the cousin would swear by it, liked to bring the girl to show her off. The night Lawrence got arrested, the girlfriend was wearing a Floppy T-shirt. You can buy them in L.A., shops carry them for kitsch, white T-shirts with a big picture of Floppy on front. Apparently the girl wore no bra with hers, which turned heads in that bar, you can bet, and maybe why she and Lawrence just stayed to their bar stools drinking all night.

But then after a while, Lawrence began getting loud, he started talking in this loud goofy voice, his one from *Magic Garden*. It attracted attention, some people in the bar came over to where he was sitting. And then, the cousin said, Lawrence just seemed to lose it and started into a routine from the show. To everyone's surprise, he slid his hand up under his girlfriend's T-shirt and "Good morning, boys and girls," he said to the people at the bar. "Floppy is glad you could join us today." And then he wiggled Floppy's ears from underneath the shirt, he made Floppy wiggle his nose too.

The drunks in the bar thought it was funny. They laughed and called, "Do it, Floppy!" They came closer and asked Lawrence is this really Floppy? They asked him how the heck Floppy was. They asked how Floppy were.

The girlfriend, who hadn't drunk as much as Lawrence, started to get angry. Frightened too. There were a lot of drunks in the bar that night, they were moving in close and she made Lawrence stop the show. She pushed his hands away, she tucked in her shirt. But the drunks called, "More, more" and Lawrence tried to go back under the T-shirt. "Just one more show, Floppy," he said to the girl, "one more Floppy." And "Floppy, Floppy," the drunks shouted. They all thought they were having a great time.

Well, the cousin said, the girl started screaming, there was a cop just outside, and before any of the drunks knew what was up, he had them all under arrest. Lawrence too. Lawrence in particular. When the cop ran up and grabbed him, he still had his hands on the girl.

It all came out in the paper, the one the cousin reads anyway, and maybe they made some of it up, you can never be sure, but everyone was talking, just the same. You can guess, the cousin said, what it did for Floppy T-shirts.

"So that is the story," Marcie says. "Once the papers got hold of it, the Personality had to fire Lawrence, there was nothing else she could do."

"And now she wants Dr. Steinem to do Floppy?" Celeste asks. "Professor Steinem?" She looks at Marcie, bewildered. Henry S. Steinem in falsetto, pretending to be a spaniel?

Lola laughs out loud, she throws her head back and laughs Texas style. Lola at least is beginning to feel herself again. "Professor Floppy," she says. "Well I guess we coulda guessed as much."

But then she looks at Celeste and closes her mouth and tries hard not to smile. "Sorry," Lola says. "Just struck me funny."

Celeste looks dreadful. Marcie tries to help. "The Personality didn't say anything in her letters about Floppy," she tells Celeste.

"She only said she wanted Steinem to come visit, have a look around. He could be some kind of consultant, she said, an educational specialist. They needed more education on the show, that was all."

"Consultant my foot," Frances says. "The Personality just wants to fool around. I know that woman."

Celeste does not seem to have been listening. She is still back on Floppy, how Dr. Steinem will now end up on a stool with a spaniel halfway up his arm.

"She's going to make him talk like a puppet!" Celeste wails.

Across the room, Sally Ann clears her throat. Bones is again out of the purse. "And just what is so wrong about that?"

We Prepare for the Worst

There's not much more on the subject to say. The Project is closing, that's all. And I sit in the solarium now only half listening as the others begin winding down, too. Frances and Lola trade some tired remarks from deep inside their deck chairs. Celeste lies collapsed in hers. Sally Ann keeps her head down, consulting with Bones. And Marcie sits forward, halfheartedly offering "Oh and one more thing."

Their voices are low, the sounds fading. And when I look out at them all, it is as though I am watching ghosts. As though soon we will all just be specters here, like little lonely Emmaline. The end is near, we can see it. Already we are disappearing.

So I try to imagine how it will be, when we are none of us here, when there are no breaks in this solarium, no solarium then at all. And what occurs to me is just this: How much we do come to depend on the things we think we are only resigned to. Work, for instance, rushing to catch the bus every day, riding it home with the bread man. Coffee at ten, sweet rolls on Friday, Lola's whoops from the second suite. The creak of the floorboards as Frances trawls past. Knowing the others without looking up too, just from the sound of their footfall.

And knowing then too just what each one will say before they even begin. Knowing the facts of each new romance, hearing the editors retell them at lunch. And later hearing the editors again in their suites on their phones to their Arthurs and Jean-Pauls. Knowing they yearn for these calls to come in, knowing we each of us wait all day, listening for Marcie's buzz.

So then, depending on these things as we seem to do, we cannot always be on our guard. And it will happen, therefore, sooner or later we will all be taken by surprise, by when these things are no longer there. Which no doubt will be, we now suspect, the case this coming Monday.

Frances speaks up. "Well of course it will be this Monday. Why would Steinem waste any more time?" It will be this Monday that we'll know. First thing that morning when we arrive, in our mailbox in its envelope with our name on it, there—our pink slip, clipped to a short note from Steinem. "Just you wait," Frances says. "Do not say you did not see it coming."

We all know Frances is right. And I try to imagine it then. Everyone's note will read the same. The Project is finished, it will tell us. Nicely, maybe not in so many words. But finished, the end. No gentle phasing out, no final text, no closing afterword. The note does not explain why. Just that we must have our desks cleared by three. Oh, and that we'll get two weeks' severance pay. It's the least the Project can do.

As we come in that morning, we'll each stand by our mailbox and even though we have been prepared—it is generally what we expected, we are all out of a job—still it will come as a shock. We will not at first be sure we believe what we've read. And the few of us gathered there early will say well maybe it's just Lola again, one of Lola's little jokes. Lola, knowing what we all suspect, would think to write a note like this, she would pretend it had come from Steinem. She would think it was funny. The day an electrical short in the fire alarm set off the sprinklers in our ceilings, Lola thought that funny too. She was the only one of us who laughed. Lola, who sat at the time with a layout spread out on her desk, four-color separations, just watched the ink run and hooted and slapped her thigh.

So we'll all read our notes from Steinem on Monday and say oh it's just Lola again. Except that Lola will arrive and reach for her mail and look as disbelieving as the rest of us. And then there will be nothing left for any of us to do but just stand in the hall awhile more and stare at our pink slips in silence.

Until Lola again, Lola herself will rally. She will remember how much we have all of us always disliked it here. And "Well now ladies," she will say in her big Texas drawl. "Time we had us a party."

Frances will jerk her head up and stare as though she cannot have heard Lola right. "Party?" Does she really think this calls for a party? I will look too and wonder well what really to Lola does not call for a party? The other editors will stare in silence as well.

And after another minute or two, we will all just turn and go back to our suites and start clearing our desktops and drawers.

Margaret Here

But now I'm aware of a distant sound, muffled, repeating, urgent. Bones looks up sharply from his Sally Ann and calls, "Margaret! Telephone! For you." He points his bowls toward my suite. Bones is nearest the solarium door, he can hear that my desk phone is ringing. Since Marcie is slumped out here with us all, she was not able to buzz the call through.

I rise and walk slowly down the hall. I am in no hurry to answer the phone. Most likely it is only some printer on the line, wondering where are those flats I promised? Well yes, that was months ago. But still.

The phone rings again. It is irritating that Marcie could not just pick up first. I do not like taking anonymous calls. Why doesn't Marcie go back to her post?

I decide to let the phone ring. Marcie will get the idea. She will know then to hurry back to her desk and do her acting-receptionist duty. That is, properly buzz me through.

My phone rings again. Well, it's clear Marcie is not going to help out here. So I sigh and lift the receiver. And though my heart isn't in it, "Steinem Associates," I say. "Margaret here."

For a moment there is only a small scratching sound. Static, snow on the line.

Then "Margaret," I hear on the other end. "Margaret, it's Ben."

I take a quick breath. I listen. "Ben?" I say. And I feel a strange heat start low in my chest and rise up into my face. "Ben Adams?" I hold the receiver tight.

"Is that you, Ben," I try again. Ben now all of a sudden calling? Ben after all these months? Ben from out of nowhere now here on the line. "Ben," I say. "Is that really you?"

Because it occurs to me of course it cannot be. It is just my imagination again. Ben cannot just like that be back, here on the phone on a workday. Real Ben is gone, disappeared. He is someone I need to go find.

And it occurs to me next that if this voice on the phone is not now just in my mind, then it must be some kind of prank. An impostor calling on the line. Right, I think, that must be it. Some doppelganger has got my number.

But "Yes, Margaret, it's Ben," the voice says. And I know of course that it is. No one but Ben has such a lovely low hum to him. I would know that resonance anywhere. It is Ben, all right. Calling now out of the blue.

"You sound far away," I say then. Which is true. Our connection is sketchy, his voice sounds like an echo. "Are you calling long distance, Ben?" I do not know why I ask him, it is not of course the point here.

"Long distance?" Ben says. "No, Margaret." And then after a pause, "Well yes. In a way." Another pause. Ben seems to be having trouble here. "Well I mean I am calling from the farm."

"The farm, Ben! You're at the farm?" And I think well aha, I was right. All these months Ben's been gone he was out at his farm. I would have found him today in any case. He has only called now just to throw me off—

"Margaret," the voice says, "have dinner with me tomorrow. Can you?"

I do not right away answer, as though I need to check my calendar. Which is not of course it, I am actually only trying to breathe. "OK, sure, Ben," I say. And then just like the first time with Ben this fall, I cannot seem to stop. "Thanks, OK sure," I say again. "Yes that would be nice, Ben. Thanks."

"Good," Ben says. "About six." And then I hear a click.

"But wait, Ben," I am going to say. "Tell me—are you all right?" And where have you been? Why did you go? Why is it you haven't called?

It is too late. The line is dead. Ben did not even say good-bye.

My god, I think, my mind spinning. Ben Adams has called. Ben is back. He's all right. And he wants to have dinner.

I sit at my desk and I smile at the window. Ben Adams is back! And I wish then there were people to tell. Not the editors of course. But people. Don't you get it? I would say, take them by the shoulders, and give them all a good shake. Ben Adams is back and wants me to come to dinner! I stand up from my chair, kick off my shoes, and make happy little hops in a circle.

But then I stop—what am I doing here?—and stand still. The thought has just occurred to me "Why?" For what reason has Ben called and not before? Dinner, yes. But what more? To start again? Is that why Ben called? Is that what it is that Ben wants?

Then, as long as I'm on the topic, "And what is it exactly I want?"

Well that is the question, I think, isn't it? That has been the question all along.

And I sit back down and I put on my shoes.

He Calls

He has to see her one more time. He calls to invite her to dinner.

She answers before the phone rings.

Margaret, he says. It's Ben.

He does not remember the rest. But she is coming, tomorrow he will see her again. As she pulls up the drive, she will smile very big and wave to him from the car. And she will run to him then, he will hold the door open wide.

He stops, feels his heart rip in two.

Ben at the Door

Reeling from Ben Adams's call, I return to the editors in the solarium. And while they still slouch in their chairs and think their own thoughts about Monday, I find I can no longer think at all. Or rather I can think now only of Ben, of how it will be with Ben again. And the thought that occurs, well the memory really, is the one I return to most often. A difficult one, and one I've not yet explained. The last one in fact that I have of him.

I should say here that while we recovered, Ben and I, from that night and that kiss at my doorstep, while we went on seeing each other this fall, it was, as I'd guessed, not the same. Ben was careful not to bring up love again, or for that matter William Holden. And whenever he drove me back to my house, I was careful never to linger.

252   **Elizabeth Collison**

In this way we got through to Thanksgiving well enough and on up to Christmas vacation. And then for a while, I did not hear from Ben Adams at all. I assumed he'd gone home to his Ellen to spend the holidays back in the West. For three weeks there was simply no word. But in January on the year's coldest day, much to my surprise and relief, there was Ben Adams again at my door, ringing and ringing the bell.

I'm Leaving Now

By the time he awakes, she is already up and starting her bath. He opens his eyes, stares at the ceiling, hears the bathwater running.

"Ellen," he calls and walks to the bathroom door. He knocks once. "I'm leaving now, Ellen."

He knocks once more. "Ellen?"

For a moment he waits. There is only the sound of the water.

He turns and walks to the bedroom door, opens it, takes a breath. Steam from the bath has not reached the hall, the air feels cool and good in his lungs.

He is careful to close the door after him. It shuts with a small, single click.

Outside, at the stone wall that borders the Merrills' front lawn, he stops, takes a seat. The Merrills' house faces theirs, directly across Dublin Drive, the wide circular street where he lives. Now lived. He does not think the Merrills will mind his sitting awhile on their wall.

He needs to think. He has just left his wife of twenty-one years, he has said good-bye from the other side of a door. A simple act in the end, twenty-one years in the coming.

For days before, they had talked. She agreed. It was true. There was nothing left now for either of them. How strange it turned out, that it could be so close, so possible as not to end. You stayed on for years or you left in a morning and the difference was the click of a door.

Jason Plumbly, twelve years old and the street's paperboy, rides his bicycle fast down the walk. Swerving in close, reckless in his race to deliver the news, he hurls a rolled paper toward the Merrills' front steps. It misses and lands in the junipers instead, while Jason speeds on up the street.

To the left and a little behind him, he hears a door open. Willard Merrill has emerged for his paper. Willard calls, "Hey there, Benny." He does not seem surprised to see Ben sitting on his stone wall. "Great day, hey?"

His name is not Benny, no one who knows him calls him Benny. Willard is being neighborly here. It is how the people on Dublin all talk, hale and grinning as they invariably are, to keep from knowing each other.

He nods to Willard, watches as Willard, who is nodding as well, retrieves his newspaper from the shrubs. Turning back toward the steps, Willard offers a jaunty wave. "Take 'er easy, Benny," he calls, and escapes back into his house.

It is no good, he thinks, sitting here on the Merrills' stone wall. Now Willard and the rest of the Merrills too will be looking out their front window, asking each other if he is OK, if he will just go on sitting like that in their yard.

It is getting late. Soon Rick Butler across the way will be opening his garage. He will wave, wonder too what's going on there across the street. And the Randolph twins will be out on their Big Wheels making loud ratchety noises in their drive. They will stop and stare, point.

He stands and begins to walk. Up ahead, leaf blower roaring, Jim Plander stalks his lawn, head up, ready with more neighborly greetings. Marilyn Francis drives by, station wagon full of groceries, honks merrily, drives on.

He walks faster. From out of nowhere Jason Plumbly swooshes his bicycle past on the right.

He takes two steps more. And staring then only at the young birch that stands at the exit from Dublin, he begins to run.

"Margaret," he calls. The leaf blower roars, no one can hear. Margaret, Margaret.

We Need to Talk

Ben stands on the front step, stomping the snow from his boots, and tells me he needs to talk. We need to talk.

He asks if he can come in. "Please," he says, "it's important." He has no jacket, he is wearing just his old flannel shirt.

"Yes of course," I tell him. "Come in. You will freeze standing out there like that."

Once inside—before I can say here, come sit here with me, warm up, and how was your Christmas—he tells me he and Ellen are through.

"What, Ben?" I say. "What?" You've left your wife? Ellen? I am going to say.

But I do not because now without stopping Ben tells me more. There has been a change of direction, he says. He will not be going back West again. And at the end of the semester he'll be leaving town here as well.

And then Ben says he's been doing some thinking.

"Come with me, Margaret," he says. "Come. We'll leave here together."

I look at Ben. I am not sure I know what I'm hearing.

"We'll go on the run," Ben says.

Still looking, I start to smile. It's a joke, right? "'Go on the run'? That's good, Ben."

"No," he says. No. He has begun all wrong.

Ben takes a breath, starts over. He knows it may sound sudden, he says. He knows we haven't known each other long. He knows it hasn't always gone well. But he has been thinking, for a long time he's been thinking. About us. About leaving, about just taking off. About starting all over again.

Ben stands before me. He is serious. "Things are different now, Margaret. I'm free. We're free."

I look at Ben. This cannot be happening. Ben must be talking about somebody else.

"Come away with me, Margaret."

I turn my head, try to breathe.

"This is our chance, Margaret. Say something."

Air, I am thinking, we need air. But I turn back, look up. Ben is upset, he does not know what he's saying. I do not want to upset him more. "Look, Ben," I say. "Could we talk tomorrow? You are just back in town. You have been through a lot." I watch his face closely. "I think we should talk tomorrow," I tell him. "We will both feel better tomorrow."

Ben looks at me, questioning now. "No Margaret. Not tomorrow." He shakes his head. "I will not feel any different tomorrow."

And oh no, I think, oh no. Not again. Not all the declaring again. And I pray Ben will not start in.

"I love you," Ben says. He wants me to hear. "I love you and things are different now." He opens his hand, extends it.

I step back.

Ben looks at me. "I love you, Margaret. I have left my wife and I love you."

I watch Ben's face, I listen. There is something new in his voice now, I can hear it. Something shifted and plaintive. I can see it as well in his eyes. Ben has just told me again that he loves me. He loves me! And he wants me to say now I love him too. To say it was only the fact of his marriage that kept me from saying it before.

I watch Ben, he is waiting. And yes, I would like to tell him. Yes, I love you, I have loved you now for a while.

But still I cannot speak, cannot think. Cannot stop all of the thinking. Because this is the truth. I do not know what it is I am feeling. And I do not know why. But here is what I suspect. If I were to say now Ben Adams, I love you, and we were to rush into each other's arms, we would neither of us know what then. The awful, long settling in? Facing each other, confirming. Reassuring each other, ourselves. Yes, I do love you, yes. Yes, yes, yes. And then the thousand domesticities, the endurance. The day after day after dayness, both of us down in some basement rec room, stretched out in our Barcaloungers.

The thought of it is unbearable. I care for Ben Adams. I would like now to make him happy. I would like more than anything to help. But love? I just do not know about love. I have never known about love.

Ben smiles, tender and clear. He reaches again for my hand. "I am leaving and I want you to come with me," he says. "It's really just that simple." And then maybe because he sees I still have nothing to say, he tells me, "You don't have to answer right now."

I look at his lovely smile. I think how steady this man is, how good. How I would like now to say oh yes, Ben, let's both of us run away. Let's be happy someplace far away.

I take a deep breath. "No, Ben," I say. "No. I cannot go with you. There's no need to wait for an answer. I already know."

Ben blinks, then for a moment stares. "I see." His voice grows quiet. "Well yes." He nods, serious again now. "Of course." He lets my hand go.

I watch Ben turn for the door. I know now he cannot look back at me. I reach for him, touch his sleeve. And because there is nothing else to offer, "Ben?" I say. "Ben?"

Ben closes the door behind him. I listen. For a moment outside it is silent. And then, very loud, the sharp squeal of tires as he backs his truck fast from the drive.

Eight

Moonglow

I awake Saturday morning to "Moonglow." The song, I mean here the song. And for the fourth time this week, I am left with the remains of the dream.

But this time there is something new. As the van passes the truck on the bridge, as the truck spins and begins its leap from the rails, strains of "Moonglow" swell from below. And then slow motion, as it tumbles midair, the truck starts itself to rise. It comes out of its final full circle, at the place where before it would shoot for the ice, and instead lifts off and takes wing. Ascending as though weighing nothing at all. A truck, a bubble, a feather.

A voice hums the next bars of "Moonglow." And as the truck grows smaller, rising out of sight, "Theme from *Picnic*" begins to intertwine.

Lights

Early that morning he puts up the lights. He is up at dawn, stringing them tree to tree in the stand of pines outside his back door. They crisscross over the geese and over his garden below. He reaches one wire to the flagpole and back and lets it swing in high looping arcs. And when he is finished, when he has covered the sky with his cat's cradle of lights, he plugs them all in at once.

There are hundreds, all colors, blinking, and at first they confuse the geese. They look up and honk and shuffle to the back of their pen. They huddle together in the festive light, still honking and looking up.

When he sees her, he'll tell her. The geese can't seem to get over it, they keep one eye always on those bulbs. And so now he will have to plug in the lights only late in the night, after the geese are asleep.

Which is OK really, he will tell her. It is better when it is late, with all those tall old black pine trees flashing red, green, and blue like some nighttide carnival pitched camp on the farm. And it is a wonderful thing then, all right, to wake in the dark, dazed and alive, to Gypsies dancing under the pines.

I Seen You

"Theme from *Picnic*" continues to rise and swell. I lie in my bed and smile. It is early, the sky outside is still dark, I know with luck now there is still time for sleep.

But suddenly a loud popping, then crackling sound, and I am instantly on my feet. I head to the window and pull back the curtain, although I know already what it must be. Now even before dawn, Mrs. E, unnecessarily out rummaging at something. It is Mrs. Eberline again, with an unusually loud trash bag of cans. I am almost certain of it.

Although now when I look down, it is not Mrs. E and her bags that I spot. In fact, because of the dark, at first there is nothing to see. But I realize then there is something else, something I know from before. Smoke, the smell of smoke in the air. Mrs. Eberline must be back at her bonfire, back sacrificing my maple twigs.

But the smell is much stronger than before, and it is then that I begin also to see it. A small black plume rises directly below me, illuminated by an eerie glow. Which I realize now is from flames, orange-red flames, lapping from under my garage wood door.

I rush down the stairs and out to my yard. I grab for the garden hose. And there, while my neighbors on Mott sleep steeped in their dreams, I stand in my nightgown and aim. The hose is on jet, the water turned on full, I blast my garage door from up close. Well now, I think, surely the sound of it will bring out the entire block. But strangely when I turn then to spray to the side, there is only Mrs. Eberline, right next to me.

"Mrs. Eberline!" I say. I look at her up close. "Were you just now in my garage?" There is no lock, the door is old, she knows that I hide things behind it. It occurs to me she has figured this out.

Then I see a new flame crawl from under the door and I turn to keep my aim on the wood. But there are flames now escaping each side of the door, and a new plume of smoke from the garage window, and I am uncertain where to point the hose next. Mrs.

Eberline herself is no help. In the glow from the fire, I can just see her red hood retreating. It is no time to give chase I know. And I throw down the hose and search frantically for some very large kind of bucket.

Which is also when I hear the sirens, high and whining at first, then louder and close. The Krantzes' dog begins baying, and all down the block upstairs lights flicker on. So my neighbors on Mott are awake at last, and someone has called in a fire truck. I must hand it to Mott once again. And while I am sure, had I had a little more time, the garden hose and my bucket would have done, I am happy enough when I see their truck to let this town's fire department take over.

Besides which, I must find Mrs. Eberline. Who has now scuttled to the back of the crowd of concerned neighbors forming on my lawn. "Mrs. Eberline!" I call and run toward her. There is no time now to go back for a robe. I must catch Mrs. E before she escapes, there are some things we need to get straight here.

Mrs. Eberline makes a break for her yard, moving fast. I follow, my nightie flapping. I run as fast as I'm able, given bare feet, and at her side door, I overtake her. "Mrs. Eberline, stop!" I shout. Then barring the door and still panting, "This time, Mrs. E," I gasp at her, "this time you have gone too far."

She gives me a quarrelsome look. I see the skirt of the caftan below her red coat and I expect then to hear from Belva. "But dearest, whatever do you mean? 'This time'? I'm afraid I'm not following you."

From the side I hear the firemen's hose send a great blast of water at my garage. The crowd on the lawn starts to cheer.

I look at Mrs. Eberline and stand my ground. Her insanity will not save her now. "Mrs. E," I scream over the sound of the crowd. And then searching for the words, "Mrs. E, this will not do!"

She stands before me and looks up. Dropping her hood back, she gives her old hair a toss, and lets it fall forward, Veronica Lake–like. A slow insolent smile comes to her. "'Do,' darling?" she asks coolly, staring past me.

I do not know what more to say then. I do not know how to get through to her. My shoulders are aching, my arms hang like lead, my nightgown is sodden and frigid. And suddenly I no longer feel angry or afraid or deeply, deeply wronged, just simply, incredibly tired. Firefighting at dawn in a nightie has at last got the best of me.

I search for Mrs. E's face. And in a voice I know she will take for defeat, "Mrs. Eberline," I say. "What is it you want from me?" And when still she just stares out from under her hair, I put the real question to her. "Why do you hate me so?"

This last seems to get her attention. She shakes her head, takes a step back, and pulls up her hood. Then switching swiftly from Belva, she sucks in her gums, stares hard. Eyes narrowing, voice rising to a screech, "I seen you that mornin', missy," she shouts. "Dead of winter, and you send him away."

It's my turn to step back. Him? So once again this is still about Ben. This fire and the other before it, the attacks on my yard and my tree. This has all of it been about Ben.

I look down at Mrs. E. I have nothing to say. And I see a surprising thing. Mrs. Eberline turns, drops her head to her chest, and begins silently to weep. Shoulders shaking, she is truly now crying. No acting this time, real tears.

"That Ben feller's gone," she says between sobs. Then jerking her head up, glaring, "And it your fault he ain't comin' back."

I stand for a moment startled, watching Mrs. Eberline cry. Then without any warning, I feel the tears start as well. Regardless of what I know about Ben, I suspect for once Mrs. E's got it right.

I step to the side. Mrs. Eberline starts for her door, and I reach out for her as she passes. I want urgently, oddly to thank her. But as I look down for her hand, in a fumbling attempt to touch it, I see at the opening of her parka's front pocket the handles of my new garden clippers. The ones I most recently stored from her grasp in the deepest cupboard of my garage.

"Mrs. E!" I say, and at that Mrs. Eberline bolts. She is inside her house and slamming the door before I can get out anything more. So I am left then in a nightie standing alone, muttering up at her house. Mrs. Eberline, this has got to stop. Not only have you just set fire to my garage, you first pillaged it for my clippers. This is it, Mrs. E. I have had it.

Or words to that general effect.

And as I hear then the fire truck pulling away—they have doused all the flames and the garage, it turns out, is still standing—I think well yes, maybe Frances was right about Mott. There's no need to live next to a madwoman.

Breezes

From the lights, he moves on to the yard. It has been a wet spring, the grass has grown, he will need to mow one last time. The landlord has left him the mower. The farmyard is large, he looks forward to doing the work. He looks forward to his morning outdoors.

These days the farm is alive with spring breezes. They come rolling in up the front banks, all day they excite the air. They ruffle the lilacs along the road, they give the swings a good shove. They catch in the American flag overhead, flapping and clanking it at its pole.

And the air then fills up with the farm. It smells of new soil turned over, it smells of the spotted pigs. Or, like now, it smells of the fresh-cut grass on the banks that he has begun to mow.

And always this spring it makes him stop what he is doing and smile. And always he cannot remember just when he smelled air so good.

It reminds him how much he will miss all this when his work here is finally done.

Toasts

I put Mrs. Eberline and Mott Street behind me. I will worry about the garage next week. Because now it is Saturday evening, my dinner with Ben at six. I have been happy all day just thinking of it.

Although on the drive to his farm, when I turn off the radio so that I can think of it more, just how it will be, I find instead Mrs. E's words are still in my head, how I am alone at fault here. And then I do not at all know what to think or what Ben Adams himself might be thinking. Or how it will be not seeing him for so long, whether he will be happy even seeing me now. And I feel something inside me then open wide and my heart turn sideways and plunge. It is all I can do to keep driving and not turn around for home.

But once I see Ben's lovely green yard, the old square white house, when Ben opens the door to me, grinning, I know it will be all right. It will be dinner at Ben's, just as it has been before.

Except that tonight at dinner Ben lights just one candle and centers it on his long table. And when our grilled chickens are ready he turns off the lights so there is only that one candle burning. It makes dining tricky. In the candlelight now I can only just make Ben out, a small floating face at the farthest reach of his long and dark dinner table. It is a strange way to dine, it's true. And just now, sitting at my end, searching for Ben through the gloom, I do not know if I can take such distance. It is as if we've ended up on some slow-moving train, some once grand Orient Express, sitting opposite each other in separate cars, staring through a thick beveled window.

Ben turns up the music. Tchaikovsky in the background soars. He lifts his glass. He smiles, starts to speak, his lips move. But I cannot make out a single word. We are too far apart, the window between us is closed.

I do not like the strange muffled sound of Ben. And I stand up and move to the chair next to his. "Oh Ben," I say. "Please Ben, tell me how you are. It has been such a terribly long time." But then I cannot wait for his answer, I ask what is really on my mind. "Are you all right, Ben? Is it all all right then?"

Ben sits, his smile fades. He looks at me and does not answer. He only just looks at me sadly.

And oh no, I think. No. We cannot start dinner like this. Not after so long apart. And I decide on a quick change of direction, something lighter to start with than how we both are. Some jollying up, some stories. If Ben has nothing to offer of his three months away, I can at least tell him something of mine.

So while our chickens sit on their plates and grow cold, I first catch Ben up on Mott Street. I tell him about Mrs. E, I figure he'd want to know. I mention the pail, the dark water, the rustling of cans she's been up to. I leave out on purpose the fire. And then I move onto the Project, the editors there and Joe Trout. Things Ben has found interesting before.

"Celeste at work says there's a ghost in the sanatorium," I say. "Her name, she says, is Emmaline."

I decide this is a story I can throw in. Everyone likes ghost stories, Ben will like hearing about Emmaline. So I tell him how Celeste says she is at her wits' end. She believes Emmaline has been toying with us, redrawing the lines in Joe's art, leaving strange notes, moving the chairs in our foyer.

And then I tell him how just this past Thursday, Celeste came back up from the lunch hour, panting. "Emmaline, again," she wheezed, before collapsing in the solarium. And when we ran out to her, asked what had happened, she just whispered the words "steam tunnel." But because we had no idea what she meant, Celeste sat up then and collected herself.

"Emmaline was down in the steam tunnel again," she explained. "The one that runs under the cafeteria. One of the workers there told me the tunnel had been broken into last night. And when this morning the workers checked for their gurneys, they found them all upside down by the cellar doors.

"That's no ordinary steam tunnel," Celeste reminded us all. "It's the death chute, you'll remember," she said. "Emmaline knows it's the death chute. She knows what those gurneys were used for. The girl has no respect for the history here. No respect for the poor souls before her."

Then, I tell Ben, Celeste shook her head and continued. "It's Emmaline all right. She's been riding around on those gurneys, I just know it. Freewheeling it down that tunnel, legs stretched out wide. To Emmaline it's just one big party."

I think this is a pretty good story. And "My lord, Margaret," Ben would normally say here. "Celeste must be out of her mind. Tell me more." Ben is an extremely good listener. He would usually say something like that here.

But tonight Ben just sits, looking down.

To get his attention, to let him know that is it, the story has ended, I let out a sigh. I make it sound like I have had it with Celeste and her ghost. I say, "Well but of course I am not a believer. I know it was not Emmaline in that tunnel. It was not Emmaline either who fooled with those chairs." And I am going to tell him then just who it was.

But Ben looks up here and smiles just a little, to let me know he's been listening after all. "A ghost at the Project?" he says. "Is that right?" And then he says well the thing is, he's beginning to believe in ghosts more and more. "Or I would like to," he says. He just likes the idea that the dead might get to come back. Might get some kind of second chance, to hang on for a little while more. To remember and be remembered.

"Oh Ben," I say. "You can't be serious." But I give it some thought, the part about a second chance. And I decide I should probably clarify. "I mean," I say, "I'd like to believe in second chances too." That is, in the end, why I've come tonight. "But ghosts, Ben?" I give him a little pat. "Sometimes, you know, Ben, it's too late."

He stops me. "Margaret," he says, "I am leaving."

I look at Ben, surprised. As I said, he is a good listener. It is not like him to interrupt. But he looks serious now, and I know that he means it.

"Leaving?" I say.

And I realize what we are talking about here. What this dinner is for. Ben is saying good-bye. It is spring, end of semester, Ben is going away. So it's true. Well he never pretended it was otherwise.

Ben looks at me to make sure he's been clear. I meet his stare and although I try not to, I think of that cold winter day I last saw him, how he told me then too he was leaving. I know Ben must be thinking of it as well. And for a moment I cannot move, afraid it will all start again.

But Ben only just sits at the table. And when he does not say anything more, he does not tell me he loves me, he does not ask me again to leave with him, I find I myself sit silent. I have to give this some thought.

But I have no more thoughts, there is only the fact Ben is leaving. So after still a while more, I reach for my wineglass, raise it high. I have my own toast to offer. "Then this is to you, Ben. Here's to you." And I smile very big and say I am happy, so happy for him. And I think yes, I probably am.

Ben takes my hand, lowers the glass. "Margaret," he says. "Please listen. It's already been decided. I am leaving, I have my own reasons to go."

Ben lets go of my hand. He looks tired. He turns his head, sits and just stares. And when finally he speaks, he does not look like he is even talking to me.

"The time here is over," he says slowly. "This town is used up, all the spaces, all the lives here are taken."

I watch Ben. Used up? He is not making sense. Something has called him away.

Ben turns back. "It's over here, Margaret." For a moment more he stares. Then abruptly he shifts in his chair, leans forward. He is talking now only to me. "It's over here, Margaret. For you too. Don't you see it? You have to get out."

He looks at me close, takes me by both my shoulders. "It is no good what you're doing here. Dreaming your dreams. Riding around on your buses." Then sitting back, tired and quiet again, "You do not have forever."

He looks at me, for a long time he just looks. And after some time more, addressing the air, "What are you waiting for?"

I do not know what to do. I have not seen Ben like this before. I think I am losing him. "Ben?" I say, "Ben?" I reach for him.

As though stepping back into the sun again, squinting into its glare, Ben shakes his head hard. He smiles. "My god what was that?"

I smile too. And I look at his face, I touch his cheek. I want to know he's all right. And I wish then with all of my heart that we could just both be all right. This is our last time together, Ben. I wish we could have just one last good night.

And I guess Ben is feeling the same. Or maybe it is just for old times' sake, but he says then, "Well here's an idea. Would you like to go look at the stars, Margaret? Would you like to go lie in the grass?"

Do Not Forget Me

He walks out to the farmyard ahead of her. Lays out the blanket on the front bank, smooths the sleeping bag on top. Waits then for her to join him.

Leaning back, he searches the sky. The night is clear, there are more stars than he will remember. And out of the corner of his eye, he sees for the first time this spring a streak of faint light in the sky. A meteor, then below it another. And another. Splashes of stardust in the night. Margaret must see this. "Hurry," he calls.

Hurry, Margaret. Oh hurry. There is so much he would like now to tell her. How he still loves her, will love her still. That he does not want to be leaving.

But the pull is too strong, each day it grows stronger. Already he is turning from her world. Now soon he will see it, the light that before he had only just glimpsed. There—sunlight on snow, suspended, glistening, a snowbank of stars, all there. The painting he had in his mind, at last he will finally see it. The way out is the way in. He must tell her.

And oh how he longs now to hold her, say do not forget me. Do not forget about us. Do not forget the sweet time here together, our nights here in the grass.

He hears her footsteps. She calls out his name. He aches at the softness in her voice. How faraway already she sounds.

Later That Night

"Ben," I call. "Ben, where are you?"

"Hurry," he calls. "Shooting stars."

He is lying halfway back on the front bank, looking up and pointing above him.

"Margaret," Ben calls. "Quick, look at that one."

I hurry over to him. But because it's so dark in Ben's yard, it is not easy running while looking up. It is like coming in late on a movie you're watching while stepping over feet you can't see.

"Here I am," I say, feeling for the edge of Ben's blanket. I sit down and look up. For a long while I look. We both look, Ben and I. But we do not see one more shooting star. The display is already over. "Wouldn't you know, Ben?" I say.

He nods and without saying anything more stands and walks back toward the house. And then, as I watch, hundreds and hundreds of small brilliant lights flash on over our heads. Christmas lights, strings and strings of them—high up, exultant, and shimmering. They hang suspended over Ben's starry sky and through the branches of Ben's stand of pines.

"Oh my, oh my," I say. And when Ben is back on the blanket next to me, I point at the pines. "Look, Ben. Look. Lights in the trees."

Ben leans back, peers. "So you see it, too." We both smile and know what we mean.

And for a while then we just lie on our backs, side by side. And after a while more I tell Ben how all those lights just now make me think of some big high school dance, a spring prom at an old country club with paper lanterns strung out over the pool. And girls there are dancing, I say, they are all in full skirts, flowered chiffon dresses with petticoats underneath you can see whenever they twirl.

"A prom?" Ben says. "Sure. That's OK." Although it isn't what he was going for. He just thought the lights would look nice, that's all.

"The lights look nice, Ben," I say. "That's what I mean."

Then we lie for a while more and it is true, it's a fine thing, on a spring night, to be lying outside on your back in the grass and to gaze up then and see Christmas lights. It is a night now of quiet, soft breezes, the lights rock gently over our heads and as we watch, we both of us start to grow sleepy.

The lights sway and sway and I tell Ben how I was wrong about the spring prom. How it is more now like being at sea, like we are on some great ocean liner. And I say how there has been a party on board, and someone has strung up lights, but now the party is over and all the passengers have returned to their berths. Except Ben and I are still out on deck, and in fact here we are lying back in our chairs, our feet up on the rails, watching the lights swing with the waves.

"That's good," Ben says, yawning. He likes this idea better, he likes that we are out riding waves. Although lately, he says, he's preferred more to sail, but yes, an ocean liner is OK too.

Ben rolls onto his side then to face me. He puts one hand out and touches my ribs, he starts stroking along my side. And when he moves his hand up over my ribs again, I reach out to touch him as well.

It is the sort of thing we used to expect, when we had been lying in the dark in the grass. After we talked for a while like this about whatever had come along, when we had both talked enough, then it was likely we would start touching each other. One thing would lead to another.

And oh, see now how Ben works his way out of his jeans. How I reach out my hand for his hip and feel the smooth, cool skin there. It always surprises me a little, his skin, that someone as large as Ben is should have such lovely fine skin. I begin moving my hand from Ben's hip to his thigh, now toward the inside of his thigh, and Ben says out of the dark in a sleepy voice, "So, Margaret, do you feel it?"

This surprises me too, we do not generally talk at this point. Once we start touching, no one says anything much, it is not really the time for discussion. I had thought we both agreed on this. But as Ben has asked and I'm not sure just what he is asking, "Feel what?" I say.

"The scar," Ben says. "My scar. Can you feel it?" He puts his hand on mine and moves it a little lower. I can feel underneath my fingers then a ridge beginning under the skin. It is ropey and thick and before I can ask, Ben moves my hand up to his chest. A thick scar rises there as well. How strange, I think, I do not remember that scar.

And I am about to ask Ben about it. What happened? Tell me the story. But I stop because now Ben is moving his hand along the side of my neck and down under my shirt at the shoulder. Lower, below the blanket we've just pulled over us, I can feel his other hand start to stroke. And now we are neither of us much interested in stories. We just lie in the dark running our hands over our lovely smooth skins and rolling together on the blanket, sometimes whispering oh my oh my oh my.

Much later then, as the sky turns first gray and then pink, and Ben lies asleep still holding me, I turn my head and look up. Ben's lights are still on, we have not thought to get up to unplug them. They cross and loop high overhead, and as I watch them, still swaying a little, I think well yes, this is it. This must be all anyone could want. This night, on the other side, we have felt the fingertips touch.

Nine

He Awakes

It is only just dawn Monday morning. He opens his eyes and stares at the landlord's ceiling, at the gentle beige and bubbled paint above. He thinks: Something is happening here.

Slowly, he slides his foot down across the bed. He feels a cool breeze from the window. Then stretching, reaching with his hands, his feet for the corners, he lies spread-eagle, bare-chested and exposed to the day.

His eyes close. He lies still listening to the morning sounds, to birds mostly, the individual, insistent trillings.

Cool mornings in spring, sparse ones like this with no blanket—these are the best, he is thinking. When he can feel his skin so perfectly, to the cell, here in the farmer's bed. He will have to remember this morning.

And he knows then. It is time. This is the day he is leaving.

Buttonless Sweater

There are moments of being in one's life, I have read. Pivotal, numinous moments when at last it all becomes clear. You understand, you know, you just know. And then for all of your life that comes after, you are never again the same.

I have not had such moments. But this morning while boarding the bus for the Project, on this our fateful pink-slip day, I think I may have come close.

I waited as usual for the bus at town center. And as it's still spring, I had on my light blue sweater. Mornings in this town have a chill, and when I wait for the bus I am generally glad for a wrap. But my blue sweater does not have buttons, it was made just to hang open in front, so to keep out the cold I have always to clutch the front edges in a wad at my chest.

It was how I was standing when the bus pulled up. And without warning it started right then, my moment of knowing, just as the bus opened its doors. I reached out for the railing to board, which, because I used both my hands, meant I had to let go of the sweater. At that same point a strong spring breeze begun out in the country swept in over the bus and caught me dead in the sternum.

The cold air passed easily through the weave of my blouse and, although I do not normally give them much thought, brought my attention to my breasts. With the cold air contracting my skin, I could feel every bone of my rib cage, the compact paired flesh there in front, the puckered nipples, the areolar goose bumps. And I felt something happening to me. I felt suddenly, crisply defined.

My foot still on the bus bottom stair, yes, I thought, yes. This is it. This is it and here I am. Here are my breasts, here are my ribs, here is my buttonless sweater. And here is town center, here is the bus, here the wondrous bus driver. And here then the breeze, here the wide sky, here the unseeable stars. Here is every part of it all.

Which I hasten to add was not yet the numinous moment. It was what happened after.

I stepped into the bus and found a seat. I sat breathing fast, feeling flushed. And then yes, I thought, it is possible. I do not know why I hadn't thought of it before. It's possible to rouse, to arise. It is sometimes even very simple, only a matter of a cool breeze at your chest that catches you one morning braless. Yes, of course. People can awake, start again.

In fact, I thought then, taking myself as an example, I had never intended to be what I was. A homeowner who never much feels at home. A liar and a cheat in the workplace, a secret lover who cannot seem to love. And with that blast of cold air, I did at last become clear. I understood that these things could change, that what I'd become was in fact not necessary. What was happening here was a chance at escape, a denying of mistaken destiny.

Other people, I know, must have these thoughts too. Not only people like me. Married women, for instance. Some days, they must say aloud to themselves they do not have to be married women. Or hard-laboring men or the rich and complacent or wastrels and scalawags for that matter. It must sometimes occur to them as well when they are feeling out near the edge, desperate over their fetters. They must have the thought they must flee or die, die to this life and not know it. Except then the thought will frighten them. They have families, jobs, duties, addictions. They cannot run now. And they will say to themselves just be still. It will pass, all things given time always pass. And they will pull their hair back in matching red combs or lower their welding helmets or light up another Cuban cigar and grow busy or distracted or hopeless.

But just now I have got it. It is possible in this world to start over. You have only to find some other new town, just board a bus in a stiff breeze. And then I turned to the window and saw myself there and thought you are not fooling anyone here.

Still, it occurs to me now that this moment of mine was what Ben Adams was talking about. Well what do you know? Ben Adams was onto something. William Holden, that drifter, too.

Steinem's Note

And then here is the surprise when at last I arrive at the Project today. Steinem's little turn of events. There is, as we expected, a note waiting for us in our mailbox—but it is not the pink-slip sort of note we had thought. Instead, Steinem has written us all to announce "Happy Reorganization!" He is not leaving to go work for the Personality after all. In fact, the Personality is coming full-time to work here. It was decided, the note said, over the weekend. The Project is saved, we all here are saved. And we have the Personality to thank for our deliverance.

The editors are stunned. They had no idea this was coming. They cannot believe that after our lunch, the Personality would sign on for more. Whatever could the woman be thinking?

I have an idea. That is, I have just now been giving it some thought and I believe the Personality has a plan. She has indeed figured out our secret. She has probably called a printer or two. She knows we have turned out not one single book. And she has figured the cost savings there.

That is, the Personality understands it is economically more sound for the Project just not to print. Dr. Steinem's forte is the theory of reading, not, all in all, the reading. He also excels at grant money. Why would he need to publish, too? Producing a book would come at a price and necessitate all kinds of new duties—marketing, sales, distribution. And then too, if we were actually to get our books into some readers' little hands and found that they didn't help them, imagine how that would go over. Bad reviews could irreparably harm future grants. And where would that leave the Project?

No fool, or for that matter, spring chicken, the Personality has studied the Project's financials and figured the bottom line. She must know as well she's too old for children's TV. And she recognizes then a grant-subsidized gravy train when she sees one. Far better, she's told Steinem, that they stay the course, just proposing and outlining and laying out boards, then, naturally, more proposing. It makes perfect sense, really. But it will take many hands, as she knows Steinem knows. And here she would just like to reiterate that she, MaryBeth, stands ready to help in any way that she can—as, say, his new chief of staff.

Steinem's note, of course does not go into all this. But it does end with yet another surprise. All this lack of production, lack of anything at all to show for ourselves, has won me a Project promotion. I'm to become our new editor of design. Steinem's note implies the Personality herself has suggested it. No assistant about it, I'm now full-on editor of production and design. Which is a convenient move, I can't help thinking, since the Project has not had a real editor of design, just my perpetual assistant position. Steinem will not have to promote anyone above me.

So there it all is in one side of a note. We stand at our mailboxes dazed. I am being rewarded for my duplicitous ways, and the Project will go on and on.

Party

When they had read Steinem's note again once or twice and knew it was real, they would all still have jobs, the Project would indeed continue, Lola reckoned she'd try again. "So now, ladies," she said, "can we party?"

They all raised their heads from their notes and grinned. Well all, that is, except Margaret. And "Yes!" they exclaimed. "A party!" What a very, very good idea. Now really they had something to celebrate, they all needed to raise a glass. To the Project. To Margaret's promotion. To life pretty much as it had been.

It was decided. A party. At three.

And as soon as the liquor store opened, Lola went out for champagne. Meanwhile, Sally Ann, Marcie, and Bones began pushing tables together. Celeste thought she'd seen a white linen somewhere and went off to rummage in closets. "Just the thing for the punch table," she said. Frances herself dialed a caterer she knew. They make wonderful little cupcakes all set out in tiers. She was sure they could deliver yet today.

And while the others went looking then for more things to do,

Margaret herself took to the stairs and quietly slipped out the sanatorium's back door.

In Other Words

It is true. I skip out on the editors' party. It would not make any sense, my celebrating with them now. Soon enough they will understand.

I have left my letter in Steinem's box, to take the place of the note left for me. Thank you for the promotion, Dr. Steinem, I wrote. I must say I am surprised. And while I must also say I do not understand you, I appreciate your confidence in me. It is, I realize, an opportunity and it would be ungrateful and imprudent not to accept. Still, this seems as fitting a time as any to announce I am taking my leave of you. The Project and I are through. I resign, Dr. Steinem. Effective today. Warm regards and best wishes, Margaret.

The series editors will forgive me, I think. But really I must be going. I have an appointment to keep, well a mission of sorts, a matter of life or death. There is something I must tell Ben Adams. Now, before he leaves town.

I drive all the way to his farm, windows down, singing to the open fields. It is a fine spring morning, cool and bright, and "Fly Me to the Moon" is what comes to me. I sing it with all of my heart. "Fly me to the moon," I sing. And then I sing, "In other words." It is one of my favorite lines and probably the best part of the song. "In other words, in other words," I sing to the passing fields.

What I have to tell Ben is just this. At last I am certain. All the signs, all the dreams are in. And I know now I have made a terrible mistake. I was wrong, it turns out, about us.

And I will say then I am ready to run off with him. We can leave today, I will say. We won't need to pack. We can take the bus, eat cheese sandwiches in our seats on the way, and look out the window for our town. For our new town, Ben, I'll say. We will start a new life in some other town. Like Madge and Hal, only better.

And "Oh Ben," I sing loudly out the window, "fly me, oh fly me to the moon."

And then because I am not yet even halfway to Ben's farm and have a little time to kill, I think about all the rest there's to do. Clearing my desk at the Project, I cannot just forget about that. The resignation letter to Steinem, well luckily that is done. Little notes for all of the editors, maybe for Emmaline too.

So much to do, so many to inform. Ben Adams and I send our regrets. We're unable to stay, we're sorry to say, we are starting our lives anew.

And I try to imagine it then, our new life, and how it will soon begin. How we will ride on our bus and find our new town, we will know it as soon as we see it. How then we'll buy a small farm just a few miles beyond, one with breezes like Ben's other place. And there our house will be white, our yard green and rolling, we'll have a clothesline of course. And first thing, just as soon as I get off the bus, I will start up a large load of laundry.

I think of myself out there like that, I think of living with Ben. And then—it is because of the clothesline, I suppose, that I've been thinking of all that laundry—I imagine myself as some farm-wife. Ben's wife it must be, a woman likely to hang out her wash.

It takes me by surprise. Ben's farmwife? What a thought, I think. What madness! It makes me laugh out the window. But it interests me now too. And so, maybe because I have a few miles yet to drive, I consider this subject of farmwifery. It will hurt no one, I think. Ben will not have to know. And so I carry on for a while.

I think how if I were Ben's farmwife, I would spend each morning cooking. I would prepare great hot lunches for Ben, there would be potatoes and thick gravies and chicken-fried steak and when it was going on noon I would go to the back door and call, "Ben, Ben." And he would come back from the fields, leave his old muddy boots on the step, and open the door all smiles, very tan. It would make his eyes look so green. He would stand there awhile just grinning, and then in his socks he'd step in. He would give me a kiss and say how he was hungry as a bear, sure did smell good in here. And then he would scrub his hands clean in our kitchen sink before sitting down at our table.

After our noon meal, when Ben was back out in the fields, things would slow down for me. There would be more laundry to do of course, I have no idea how we would have so much wash, but I would hang it out flapping on the line.

And then maybe I'd turn to some weeding there in our handsome raised beds. I'd put on big rubber boots like Ben's, but I'd keep on my farmwife's apron, the kind with a bib and a pocket, and I'd go walk the rows of our peas and beans. I'd pull up all the creeping charlie I could see. And then later, around three, when the sun had grown too hot for it, I'd leave the weeding and go visit the geese.

It is Ben's idea, to again keep two geese on this farm. They would be large, noble birds, they would walk with their heads up high. And when I visited, I would climb over their fence the way I've watched Ben, and I'd sit down in the pen alongside them, pine needles all around us. And for an hour or so in under the boughs I'd just sit and tell the geese things.

There is more besides I have to do on our farm. There are still the pigs to feed. But look—now I have reached Ben's old farm, the real one, and the long gravelly front drive and the lilacs.

I pull up to the front by the house. And today, just as earlier this week, I see that Ben's truck is not there. What, no truck? At this hour? I get out and I check the back of the house to make sure. But there is no Ben and this time I know he is not just out running errands.

Oh no, I think, this can't be. Ben is not here. I have come all this way to tell Ben the news and now— Could it be? He's left town? How could he have left so soon?

Oh no, oh no. Ben, this can't be!

And I realize that suddenly I am crying. Which is surprising and not at all called for, crying at something like this. There are ways to find people who have left you behind. There are numbers to call for help. But here I am crying, all right. Crying and crying and then sobbing.

And well, that's enough, I think, trying to get my breath. But still it is such a big disappointment. There is so much I have to tell Ben, and on the drive here it had worked out so well, that I do not think I can just turn around and go back home now without him.

I sit down right there in the grass of Ben's farmyard, throw back my head, and bawl.

A sound. I look up. Ben's landlord is here. He steps out from around the side of the house and he stares at me now. He looks wary. The landlord is not usually around here mid-morning, usually he finishes his chores before dawn, and I have never before run into him. I do not know if he recognizes me. But it is possible he recognizes my car, or maybe he's just concerned, this strange woman crying in his yard. He walks toward me, hand extended.

I am going to ask him where Ben is. But he says first, "Say there. You all right?"

I nod up at him. I smile a little.

He bends down, looks close at me. Smiles too.

"Mornin'," he says. "That's better." He does not know my name, I see. Well Ben would probably not have mentioned my name to him, if he mentioned the fact of me at all.

He studies me. "You're that friend of Ben Adams, ain't you?" And then he stops smiling, his face changes.

"I'm sorry," he tells me.

"Sorry?" I say. I think this landlord does not have to be sorry. He did not make me cry.

"About Ben," he says. "Sorry, about Ben, ma'am."

He stands back up. He starts to turn, he is going to leave. That is all he is going to say? Sorry about Ben? How could he know about Ben and me?

"Wait," I say. I stand, reach toward him. I am going to ask what he knows.

He turns back, looks at me. "I mean, you was friends and I'm sorry." He shakes his head. "Terrible shock. The missus and me didn't know till we heard on the news. About the accident, I mean. Was all you heard on the news those first days."

He stops here. Watches me. Goes on. "I know that bridge,

you don't want to be driving it fast. Ben never had a chance of it, ma'am. Not in that river. Not on that cold a day." He shakes his head again. "Coldest day of the year. Hard to believe it's three months he's been dead."

And he looks at me again and I guess he sees something there on my face, because he touches my shoulder, gives it a stiff pat. "I'm real, real sorry, ma'am."

Then he remembers. He says wait there, disappears into the house, and brings out a cardboard box. "Here," he says, and holds it out toward me. "Ben's things. His wife didn't want them."

I hold out my arms. I do not know what I am doing.

"There's not much," he says. "Some books, a couple shirts, hiking boots."

He places the box in my arms. "Oh," he says. "Right." And goes back inside, brings out a small stretched canvas, places it on top of the box. He smiles but he does not pat me again. Then tipping his seed cap, he is gone.

Some Other Town

She drives back into town with no memory of how she gets there. She remembers nothing for days. Until early one morning, just as the peonies are opening, she awakes from a dreamless deep sleep.

Listening, she lies still. Birdsong. He had told her about it, made a point. She smiles, thinks how like him. Remembers.

In a rush then she rises. There is a great deal she has now to do. Call Mr. Abbott, put a sign on the lawn. Call Ford, say he can have her TV. Call the paper, stop service, water the plants. Leave out new clippers for Mrs. E.

And when she is done, she will head for town center, she will board the first bus she sees. Find a seat by a window, ride to the end of town.

And then? She stops. She does not know. She has not thought this part through. But it occurs to her then she can just keep on riding. It is possible, yes. She will just stay on the bus and ride. To some other place, some other town. She will look for it out all the windows. And when she sees it at last, she will know.

She is late, she must hurry. But as she is leaving, she goes back for the landlord's box, finds Ben's hiking boots there.

She places the boots outside the front door. Touches one more time the soft leather. Then turning, she rises up to her toes and makes a run for the bus.

Acknowledgments

I am grateful to so many for their help on this book: to Connie Brothers, without whose support the manuscript would not have left my computer; to my agent, Stephanie Cabot, amazing in all ways, who believed in the book and did not give up; to Anna Worrall and Ellen Goodson of The Gernert Company for their excellent comments and help; to my editor, Hannah Wood, whose outstanding insights and unflagging friendship have made this a better book; to Jan Weissmiller for her great kindness and generosity in getting the book into others' hands; to my parents, Margaret and Guilford Collison, for their encouragement and respect for writing and books; to my inestimable early readers and book friends: Anne Collison Johnson, Janet Collison, John Collison, Paul Johnson, Diane Padilla, Patricia Page, Jylian Gustlin, Jim Harris, Pamella and Bud Nesbit, Peter Henriksen, Jennifer Vine, Michael Ham, and the Madeira Club; and throughout, to Scott Alkire, my partner in all things.

About the Author

Elizabeth Collison grew up in the Midwest and now lives in the San Francisco Bay area. She received her MFA from the Iowa Writers' Workshop and has worked as an editor, graphic artist, and technical writer. This is her first novel.